A
LONDON GIRL
OF THE
1880s

A
LONDON GIRL
OF THE
1880s

M. V. HUGHES

Oxford   New York
OXFORD UNIVERSITY PRESS

Oxford University Press, Walton Street, Oxford OX2 6DP

London New York Toronto
Delhi Bombay Calcutta Madras Karachi
Kuala Lumpur Singapore Hong Kong Tokyo
Nairobi Dar es Salaam Cape Town
Melbourne Auckland

and associated companies in
Beirut Berlin Ibadan Mexico City Nicosia

First published as Part Two of the trilogy
A London Family 1870–1900, 1946
First issued as an Oxford University Press paperback 1978
Reprinted 1979, 1980, 1982, 1985

British Library Cataloguing Publication Data

Hughes, Mary Vivian
A London Girl of the 1880s
I. Title
London—Social life and customs
ISBN 0-19-281243-2

Printed in Great Britain by
Richard Clay (The Chaucer Press) Ltd.
Bungay, Suffolk

CONTENTS

PREFACE

NONE *of the characters in this book are fictitious. The incidents, if not dramatic, are at least genuine memories. Expressions of jollity and enjoyment of life are understatements rather than overstatements. We were just an ordinary, suburban, Victorian family, undistinguished ourselves and unacquainted with distinguished people. It occurred to me to record our doings only because, on looking back, and comparing our lot with that of the children of to-day, we seemed to have been so lucky. In writing them down, however, I have come to realize that luck is at one's own disposal, that 'there is nothing either good or bad but thinking makes it so'. Bring up children in the conviction that they are lucky, and behold they are. But in our case high spirits were perhaps inherited, as my story will show.*

DON PEDRO. *In faith, lady, you have a merry heart.*
BEATRICE. *Yea, my lord; I thank it, poor fool, it keeps on the windy side of care.*

I

An Ordinary Girl, 1881

§ 1

Your father, dear old chap, is always so anxious about you, and afraid of your becoming an ordinary schoolgirl, with an ordinary schoolgirl's tricks and mannerisms.

THIS sentence is part of a letter from my mother to me in 1879, when at the age of twelve I was spending my summer holiday in Cornwall. The term 'old chap' was merely one of endearment, for he was only a little over forty, and to us children more like an elder brother than a father. He never worried us about our behaviour, so that any hint he let drop was the more significant. And when a few weeks later in that same year he met with a fatal accident, it was natural for us to treasure everything that we remembered about him. The particular hint quoted above was occasioned by a letter I had written home with several postscripts and facetious turns of phrase. I knew quite well that what he meant by 'ordinary' was the silly attempt to be extraordinary, and that he wanted me to be as simple and straightforward as possible. The same idea had been rubbed in by my four elder brothers, with less delicacy. So, paradoxically, I tried to carry out the wishes of these my household gods by being as ordinary and as little conspicuous as I could, suppressing a child's desire to shine by using grand words and witticisms—all that the boys summed up in the dreaded phrase 'trying to be funny'.

My mother's ideas for me gave a healthy make-weight. She was for encouraging any scrap of originality in anybody at any time, and allowed me to 'run free' physically and mentally. She had no idea of keeping her only girl tied to her apron-strings, and from childhood I used to go out alone in our London suburb of Canonbury, for a run with my hoop or to do a little private shopping, and once even went to Cornwall by myself. Her precepts were extremely few and consequently attended to. 'Never talk to any one in the street except to tell them the way.' To back this up, lurid stories were told me of children offered sweets by a 'kind lady', or taken for a ride in a gig by a 'kind gentleman', and never heard of again. The mystery of their fate was alluring, but deterrent enough. When a little older, I was warned, 'If out late, walk fast and look preoccupied, and no one will bother you.' Why I should be bothered I had no idea, but adopted the line of conduct without question. One striking instance of the potency of fewness in commands comes to my memory. Mother came in rather agitated one day; she had seen some 'very dreadful pictures' in a shop in a side street not far away; she begged me not to walk down that street ever. Although curious enough to know what the pictures could be, I never dreamt of going to look. She showed even greater restraint in refusing to give advice; when I applied for such help she would nearly always say, 'Use your own judgement'.

Another policy of my mother's was not so commendable. She wished to make me indifferent to my personal appearance, provided only that I was tidy and had no buttons missing. She snubbed me once quite severely for remarking that I thought I looked nice in my new dress: 'It's no business of yours what you look like.' She told me that the moment any one put powder or paint on her face she was taking the first downward step. This was not from a moral point of view, but self-regarding. 'You have to keep on with it more and more because you look queer without it, and then when you get older you look like poor Miss Dossit.' This was a dressmaker who served as a helot in another direction, too: she was never punctual, and we had to say that a dress was required three days before it actually was, in order to get it in time. My mother drove home the moral, concluding with the remark, 'The Queen is never unpunctual'.

By common conspiracy, as I discovered in later years, all of them, father, mother, and brothers, kept me from any knowledge of the evils of the world. To-day this seems ridiculous, if not dangerous, but there was some wisdom in it after all, for my life all along has been fresher and jollier for being free from fears and suspicions. As for little points of *savoir-faire* I picked these up unconsciously from hearing the boys' comments on the behaviour of their numerous acquaintances. The characteristics of the girls who came to the house were freely discussed in the family circle, and I easily discovered some types that were not popular. There was the extravagant girl, who was always wanting to be taken out, making serious holes in pocket-money. There was the managing kind, who knew how to deal with men. There was the empty-headed silly giggling kind, bearable for only a very short time. The wonder-struck girl with big eyes, who said, 'Oh, Tom, fahncy!' to everything he said, lasted only a little longer. Then there was the intense and interesting type—'all right, you know, mother, for a chat, but not much as a companion for life'. Least popular of all, I gathered, was the aggressively sensible girl who was never taken in.

The family tea-time, when such opinions were let loose as we all sat round the table, was a pleasant and I think useful part of our education. The main work of the day was over and the family pooled what gossip they had got from school or books or friends, discussing future plans and telling the latest jokes. Mother, pouring out at the head of the table, liked us to chatter freely, but I, as the youngest, seldom got a word in and was often snubbed when I did. Thus, after venturing, 'I did well in French to-day', I had the chilling reminder from Charles, 'Self-praise is no recommendation'. If I related a joke, 'We've heard that before' would come as a chorus. Once when I confided to Dym that we had begun America, he called out, 'I say, boys, at Molly's school they've just discovered America'. In short, I was wisely neglected.

I say 'wisely', because at the private school to which I trotted off every day I was a person of importance. I shared with another girl the glory of being *dux*, as our Head called it. We took places in class, and the one who was top at the end of the morning wore a silver medal. This nearly always fell to Winnie Heath or me. She and I were good friends and shared a hearty contempt for our teachers. The only things they taught us quite thoroughly were the counties and chief towns, dates of the kings, French irregular verbs, and English parsing. Since these were immutable and mainly irrational, they were unsullied by explanations and remained useful possessions.

One day Winnie came to school all flushed and excited, took me aside, and said, 'I've got an idea. Let's work at something for ourselves. Yesterday I came across in a book all about the different races and languages in Austria. You wouldn't believe what a lot there are—so jolly. And I thought, why not get the things we want to know out of *books*?'

'Splendid,' said I. 'Why, I've got lots of books at home. My brothers will show us where to find some things worth learning, and you and I can lend books to one another.'

We set about our new plan at once, and soon became quite intoxicated with this furtive pursuit of information and all our learned notes and diagrams. We would come to school bursting with news about such things as the cause of an eclipse, what the Renaissance was, the effect of climate on national character, the legend of Barbarossa. Dym lent a hand on the science side and Charles on the literary, although I had to warn Winnie that Charles was more imaginative than reliable. One evening Dym brought me a grand note-book of blank paper that he had bought for Optics, but didn't really require (so he said). This became for Winnie and me a joint magazine of treasured notes and illustrations, boundless in its range of subject. It seems ludicrous that at the age of fifteen we should have attacked knowledge in general in this way. The modern attempt to make use of this desire to dig for oneself seems to have erred in being over-organized and thus to have destroyed the mainspring. If Winnie and I had been presented by the school authorities with a full programme of work, lists of books of reference, access to a library, and proper time and place to work in, with judicious assistance always at hand—most of our zest would have melted. More in line with our method was that of a schoolmaster who fostered a love of history in his boys by putting some attractive books on a high shelf and asserting that they were 'too difficult at present'.

As it was, we taught one another and 'heard' one another in odd corners of the school and playground, sometimes sitting on the stairs. In those old-fashioned private schools no one minded what you did, nor when nor where. Winnie was good at arithmetic, and at last made me able to face a complicated simplification of fractions, and indeed to get fun over seeing it come out. But we were both unable to fathom the reason for turning a division 'upside down and multiplying', although Barnard Smith explained it at length. We laughed and agreed to 'never mind but just do it'.

A few weeks later it was I who came to school brimful of an idea. It had been suggested to me by my eldest brother, Tom, who had seen that we were wasting energy by lack of any system. 'Winnie,' said I, as soon as I could get her alone, 'let's go in for the Oxford Senior Local.'

As I expected, she stood aghast, but under my pressure she soon caught my enthusiasm, and we approached the Head with our ambition.

'What, dears? What is this you say? The Senior Oxford? I fear this is quite beyond your reach. However, I can but write for particulars and then you can see for yourselves . . . far out of your depth.'

In a few days' time we were handed with a pitying smile the 'Regulations for 1882'. How queer the date looked, as if it were in the next century; and regulations for it seemed almost impious. We took the pamphlet to a quiet corner and eagerly ran our fingers through the many injunctions in types of varying emphasis, muttering them aloud and occasionally exclaiming, 'Not really impossible!' At last we reached the set books. 'Only a play of Shakespeare's and some Addison—Coo! We can do that. I know a good bit of Macbeth already. Infirm of purpose, give me the daggers,' I cried, seizing the Regulations and waving them in the air.

There followed crowded hours of joyful acquisition. Mother

helped with French in the evenings, Dym worked out for us any specially bad problem, and Tom gave us some learned views on the character of Lady Macbeth that we could 'lug in' as he called it.

Few of life's scanty triumphs have exceeded my reception of the parchment decaring that I had 'satisfied the examiners in the Rudiments of Faith and Religion', and (on the back) had satisfied them in several other large-sounding things, including, yes arithmetic.

'Hm! they're easily satisfied,' was my brother Dym's comment on this last item. He was a mathematical scholar of Jesus, so of course ... but the other boys were unstinted in their admiration of how their little Molly had been able to hoodwink the examiners in so many different things. I pictured these examiners, grave and reverend *signiors*, all bearded, gazing at my answers and leaning back with complete contentment—satisfied.

I was now an ASSOCIATE IN ARTS OF THE UNIVERSITY OF OXFORD. How those capitals delighted me, and it seemed that I was entitled to put A.A. after my name. We were down in Cornwall when the glad news arrived, so that my many cousins were duly impressed. As I had left school at the end of the summer term, I returned to London that autumn with the idea that life's summit had now been reached.

§ 2

But mother had begun to think a bit, as mothers will, and when October brought my sixteenth birthday she took me seriously into the dining-room and began thus:

'Listen, dear. Now that the boys will soon be all scattered at their various work we shan't need such a big house as this. And we needn't be tied to London. Suppose you and I were to go and live together in a cottage down in Cornwall? Somewhere by the sea, such as St. Ives or Marazion—within reach of Tony at Reskadinnick?'

She paused, giving a chance for these magic names to take

effect, and then added: 'You could work at literature and read French with me. We could do lots of sketching. In fact we could do whatever we liked. You could have a horse and ride to all those parts of Cornwall that you've always wanted to see—Mevagissey, Zennor, Tintagel. Perhaps we might travel abroad, to Italy, Norway, Spain.'

'But how could we afford to——' I broke in, knowing how limited were our means, but she stopped me with,

'I have already talked to the boys about the idea, and they have assured me that we shall always have enough to live on— they will see to that.'

Then, looking away from me out of the window for a few moments in silence, she turned and said in a dull, careless tone, 'Or—would you rather earn your own living?'

I hesitated. Rosy visions of Cornwall and its romantic villages, possession of a horse (always a passionate desire), the sea, Italy and Rome, floated in my imagination. It must have been a bit of my father's blood that made me say,

'It's awfully good of the boys to say that, and I know they mean it, but I would rather be independent.'

Mother smiled and admitted that the 'lady of leisure' idea had been the boys' and not hers. I know now that she must have hoped for that decision; for it was habitual with her to load the dice in favour of the result she least wanted, for fear of influencing the choice.

In those few moments the current of my life was definitely set towards hard work and uncertainty, and although these two have been my constant companions, and several times I have been in very low water, never have I regretted my choice.

The next point to consider was how the earning of a living was to be done. In those days it was not considered the thing for a girl to 'earn', although she might toy with a little work. Any other career than teaching was practically unknown. For me it would have to be teaching in a school, since the word 'governess' had become a grim joke in our family. During my last term at school one of the girls had told me that a friend of hers knew a girl who had actually become a B.A. We had both been awe-struck that a woman one might meet could attain such glory, but we neither of us connected this pinnacle with an ordinary teacher in a school. Indeed, I fancied that one just 'took up' teaching in the same casual way that I had taken a Sunday-school class last summer in Cornwall.

By the way, that bit of experience might well have given me pause. My cousin Lucy had been distracted by the vast number of children committed to her care on Sunday afternoons, and implored me to come and take a class. The section she assigned to me consisted of some forty children, aged from three to twelve, herded in a stale-smelling room, and supposed to be seated on long wooden forms. However, the only restriction to their jumping up or crawling about was the tightness with which they had been sewn into their Sunday clothes. Not even the death of Jezebel (the lesson appointed for the day) had any appeal, and my efforts to draw what moral I could from this story were continually interrupted by such remarks as 'Please, teacher, stop Tommy crawlin' on 'is best trowsies' and other intimate requests requiring immediate personal attention. Of course, truly Cornish, they wanted to know where I had come from, why I had had my hair cut short like a boy's, and what I had paid to have it cut. I was foolish enough to admit that I had come from London. This started a new excitement, and I was asked if the pavements were really made of gold, and whether there were lions there. Seizing this last as a godsend, I abandoned Jezebel and spent the rest of the lesson in the Zoo.

I suppose it was the memory of this at the back of my mind that made me say to mother that I felt a bit young to teach in a real school.

'Yes, exactly,' she replied, 'and it is only this morning that I've had a letter from Tony suggesting that you should go to the very best school that can be found, and that she will pay the fees, no matter how high.'

Tony was mother's favourite sister in Cornwall, an aunt who never knew how to do enough for us. She had been told of the birthday choice to be put before me, had guessed how I should decide it, and was determined that her present to me should consist in a proper preparation. 'I know what she will say,' ran the letter, 'so look sharp and find a good school.'

Now it chanced that as I used to go along Highbury New Park to my school I had frequently met a girl on her way to the station, carrying books and obviously going to school herself. After a while we used to smile on one another and then came to saying 'good morning', and finally used to stop for a few moments' gossip.

'Where do you go to school?' was of course my first inquiry.

'The North London Collegiate, the biggest school in England, and the finest. You must have heard of it, and of its famous headmistress, Miss Buss?'

No, I hadn't, but I was not to be squashed, and she had to listen to my glowing description of our Prize-day.

'You call that grand!' she exclaimed. 'Why, who do you think gave away *our* prizes? The Princess of Wales!'

I had been duly impressed with this and with later information about the hundreds of girls, the examinations they were going in for, and the great assembly hall. I hadn't given much thought to these glories, but they came to my mind when we were wondering what school would be best for me. So I recounted to mother all I could remember about this big school, whose name, 'The North London Collegiate', had remained in my mind, as well as its locality—Camden Town. I also recalled the name of the head, Miss Buss. Mother thought that she might venture a note to ask for particulars. A reply came at once to the effect that I might enter the school, provided that I passed the entrance examination, that I obeyed all the regulations, and that my fees were paid in advance.

'Entrance examination?' said I, 'Won't it do if you tell them I've passed the Senior Oxford?'

'Apparently not, dear, for I mentioned it in my note.' I felt that I was indeed up against something big. What would they expect for their entrance examination?

An afternoon was fixed for me to attend, and taking the

train from Highbury to Camden Town I found my way to
the school—a formidable-looking building. Seeing some steps
labelled 'Pupils' Entrance' I went down them, told the first
person I saw the reason of my appearance and was ushered
into a room in the basement. Here I was provided with paper,
pens, and ink, and various sets of questions which I could
take in any order.

Keyed up as I was for something stiff, these papers seemed
to me pifflingly easy. As for an explanation of the tides, I knew
much more about them than men of science do to-day, and
drew beautiful diagrams to show how the water was piled up,
in Biblical style, with no visible means of support. A blank
map of Africa was to be filled in with 'all you know', and I was
still busily inserting rivers and mountains, towns and capes,
when all the papers were collected. I had floored them all,
even the aritmetic, and sat back in a slightly supercilious mood.
The very large and motherly official (addressed as Miss Begbie)
who swam towards me looked a little surprised as she gathered
up my stack of answers, and was almost deferential as she said,

'Now, dear, just make a buttonhole before you go.'

This was a quite unexpected blow. I confessed that I
hadn't the faintest idea how to set about it, and thought that
buttonholes just 'came'. Up went Miss Begbie's hands in
shocked surprise.

'What! A girl of sixteen not know how to make a buttonhole!'

'Can't I come to the school then?' I asked in dismay.

'Well, possibly, dear. We shall see. But you must go
home, learn to make a buttonhole, and come again this day
week to make it.'

Mother was watching at the window for my return, and as
she opened the door I exclaimed, 'I've failed.' How heartily
she laughed when she heard of my disgrace. 'A buttonhole!
Why, I'll teach you to make one in five minutes.' So indeed
she did, and I practised the trick so assiduously all the week
that even now I can make a buttonhole with the best. Meanwhile mother made me a little case to hold needles, cotton,

scissors, and thimble, to take with me, 'to look businesslike'. On the appointed day I appeared, was given a piece of calico, made my buttonhole, and went home. It seemed absurd to take the railway journey just for that, but it was a rule of the school that no girl should enter who couldn't make a buttonhole.

A few days later mother received a notice that I had passed, and might enter the school in January. On hearing this, a friend of ours gave me an introduction to a doctor's family living near, for the eldest daughter, Mary Worley, was one of the head girls of the school, and could tell me more about it. She very kindly called on me, asked me to her house and was friendliness itself. But as to the school she was vague. She had been there for so long that nothing struck her as unusual enough to mention, but she was sure I should like it all right. Although she was going to Girton, and must have been stiff with learning, she was so simple-minded and jolly that she gave mother a happy impression of the type of girl with whom I was to associate. We had many long walks together talking of this and that, but nothing definite about the ways of the school could I extract from her. She was pleased to find that I had done a good bit of Latin by myself and with my brother's help; she thought it would come in useful, and at her suggestion we read some Livy together. The book was laid open between us, we read silently, and the one who reached the bottom of the page first sat back and waited till the other turned over. She went slowly for my sake I am sure, but always sat back first, and I pretty frequently turned over before I had actually reached the bottom. She also said she enjoyed it. Altogether she was one of the best.

§ 3

The close of the year was a time of excitement not only for me but for the family at large, for the boys were at home, and usually during the holidays one or other of them would be suffering from 'purple fever'. This was the name we gave to the periods of post-seeking, because Messrs. Askin and Gabbitas reproduced their notices in purple ink, and each one that was delivered by the postman brought on a general rise in temperature. Thus for instance one day, 'Listen to this,' Charles called out to the breakfast table, 'here's a fellow wants some one to teach mathematics, some French, to play the organ in chapel, and should be good at games. Where on earth is Rosscarbery? Fetch the gazetteer, Molly. It's somewhere in Ireland.' This was followed by a chorus of comment: 'You don't know beyond the First Book,' 'You hate games,' 'Yes, but he can play anything on the piano' (this from me as I pored over the map). For my part I thought each one that came a most desirable post, and had no doubt of my brothers' ability to undertake anything that was wanted. And my natural belief in their powers was increased by their testimonials. It fell to my share to copy these out, and I hardly wondered that the boys objected to this job, for the praise was fulsome. As we had no reproducing device I had to copy them all many times in my neatest handwriting, and soon came to know them by heart. The only one I can now recall is our old doctor's effort with regard to Tom. Evidently put to it to find something useful to say, he described him as 'a man of parts'. Tom was not allowed to forget this gem.

It was a standing marvel in the family how Charles ever managed to be appointed to anything. True, he had never failed in an examination, but then he had never been in for one. His form of application was extremely bare, and he expressed his age, not as twenty-one, but 'next year I shall be in my twenty-third year'. But if he could secure an interview he was all right. Tall, dark, and good-looking, extremely serious in manner, he could impress any stranger as being widely learned and experienced in life. I have never met any one who could make a wee bit of knowledge go so far. Of course he didn't attempt to deceive the family, and gave us amusing accounts of the tight corners he had negotiated. He once undertook to teach a boy Greek, and while the pupil was struggling with the early letters of the alphabet the master was busy acquiring the later ones. But where he came out really strong was in anything to do with music or drawing and painting. Since the average school-master of those days was a blank in these matters, Charles was a useful man to have on the staff, and was allowed a free hand to teach as he liked. He had taught himself to play the organ by practising in the little Cornish church of Penponds, employing a small 'stamps' boy to blow for him. His first post was in that little Irish town of Rosscarbery, where the combination of school-chapel and parish-church was no less than a cathedral. Here he managed to get some music out of an organ, which was little more than an old broken box, with the swell destroyed, only two pedals that worked, and nearly all the stops gone.

My brother Dym was the exact opposite. Unless he knew a thing thoroughly he wouldn't teach it. Magnificent on paper, after continuous successes at school and Cambridge, he was poor at an interview, having not an atom of push. I remember his coming home once, a mixture of rage and mirth, to pour forth his feelings. He had been to see a headmaster who seemed dissatisfied from the first, and at last burst out,

'No, no, you won't do at all. You're too young, you have no experience and no degree.'

'No degree!' gasped Dym, 'but surely, sir, you noted in my application that I was a Wrangler?'

'Well, I don't care. I wouldn't have you, not even if you were a Senior Optime.'

In addition to his modesty Dym had the family drawback of looking much younger than his years. One day he called me up to the study to show what he had done to counteract this. He had actually got a post, and knew he could manage the work, but how impress the boys? I found him robed in his gown, with a pince-nez on his nose, flinging about the room, banging his board on the table, and throwing exercise books at imaginary boys, all accompanied by horrid frowns and vituperations.

'How's that, Molly, for looking grown-up?'

'Splendid! You'll frighten the biggest boys. But how can you see with those glasses on?'

'Oh, they are only plain glass. I got them for sixpence at Pocklington's; they're a kind of toy; I can keep taking them off and on, and wiping them, like this—gives me a gesture.'

It was a large school near Plymouth, and after a day or two he went to have his hair cut in a local shop. On asking the price he was told 'It's a shilling, sir, but we do the young gentlemen from the school at half-price.' Dym paid his sixpence, glad of at least one advantage of his youthful appearance.

He quickly gained the boys' respect, more on account of his cricket than his mathematics no doubt. But one great hulking boy was troublesome and had an admiring following of small fry. Dym waited his opportunity, and after some bit of veiled impudence from the boy, told him in very quiet tones to leave the class. As Dym had foreseen, he looked surly and remained seated. With lightning rapidity Dym stepped up to him, seized him by the collar, dragged him to the door, and slung him out far along the passage, resuming the lesson as if nothing had happened. He never had any more trouble nor the boy any more following.

My youngest brother, Barnholt, had methods entirely his own for getting on in the world. After being at sea for a year or two and passing his various examinations in navigation, he was at home for a brief spell in the throes of getting another ship. Quite content with a job he had secured, he had just signed on when an uncle offered him a far better position in the Pacific Steam Navigation Company. Was Barnholt annoyed at what he had missed? Did he call the family together to share his chagrin? No. He immediately went back to the captain who had taken him on, entered the presence in a deferential manner, and said with becoming hesitation,

'Excuse me, sir, for troubling you again, but mother thinks that before I join your ship I ought to have some reference as to your personal character, because——'

The sentence was never finished. It would not have got so

far but that the captain was rendered speechless for a moment. The gist of his reply (never fully reported at home) was that he wouldn't take Barnholt—not as ballast. Looking surprised and hurt, Barnholt got out of the office and wired his uncle that he was ready for the Pacific job at any moment.

Nothing ever perturbed Barnholt. We used to say that if he were told that St. Paul's Cathedral was walking down the street he wouldn't get up to look at it. And his curious mixture of self-depreciation and fastidiousness is shown by the following talk:

'Ever been in love, Barnholt?' I asked.

'No, Molly, and you may lay that I shall never marry.'

'But why?' I replied, surprised at such a determination, for he was a prime favourite with everybody.

'Well, it's like this—any girl who was fool enough to have me would not be intelligent enough for me.'

§ 4

During the Christmas holidays of '82 it occurred to the boys that I ought to have a little relaxation, in view of the rigorous time I was likely to have at my new school. How would I like to go to a theatre and see a real play? My experience of acting had been confined to home and school theatricals. I had never been even to a pantomime. A scrap of doggerel summed up my knowledge of the auditorium:

> *Silence in the gallery, order in the pit,*
> *The ladies in the boxes can't hear a bit.*

Mother was consulted, and thought it wouldn't do me any harm, especially as Dym said he would choose quite a small theatre and a funny farce—*Betsy* at the Criterion. Tom and Charles said they couldn't stand such rubbish, but would go somewhere else and join us at supper afterwards. The play itself has faded from my memory, but the accompaniments are still vivid. An anxious farewell from mother, as Dym and I stepped into a hansom, sent us off.

'Where to, Sir?' came a voice through the cabby's little window.

'Criterion.'

'He'll think we are out on the spree,' said I.

'He'll *know* it,' said Dym.

Mother had put me into my nearest approach to an evening dress, which Dym approved, so that I was not too shy when I sat in the dress-circle, and walked into the grill-room after the play. This was full of cheery people and a pleasant hum of enjoyment and hurrying waiters. I felt it to be like something in the *Arabian Nights*. We had hardly been bowed to our seats when Tom and Charles walked in and joined us. A low-toned chat with the waiter followed, while I looked with amazement at the wide array of knives and forks by our places.

'What can all these be for?' I asked Charles.

'You'll see. I'll tell you which to use as we go on; and remember you needn't finish everything up; it's the thing to leave something on your plate.'

Such a meal as I had never dreamt of was then brought along in easy stages. Never had I been treated so obsequiously as by that waiter. When wine was served I began to wonder what mother would think. It gave that touch of diablerie to the whole evening that was the main charm. To this day I never pass the 'Cri' without recalling my one and only visit to it, with those adored brothers.

I was to have one more treat before the holidays were over. Charles took me to German Reed's to see Corney Grain, who sat at the piano and chatted to the audience in a most intimate and engaging way. His description of a honeymoon-couple on board a steamer still comes to my mind when I am embarrassed by a public display of affection. They were sitting opposite Corney at the lunch-table, were holding one another's hands and gazing into each other's eyes. In order to avoid looking at them without turning too markedly away he had to aim his food into his mouth as best he could—with some casualties.

Corney's manner was solemnity itself, and his remarks about

the inconvenience of his own fatness were made with such
serious concern that some ladies near me seemed quite annoyed by my laughing over it.

'Don't you mind those people,' said Charles, 'Corney likes
to hear you laugh. That's what he's here for. I noticed him
just now turn towards you and give a little smile.'

II
Under Law, 1883

A<small>ND</small> now for my first day in the grand new school. I was as proud of my season-ticket from Highbury to Camden Town as any girl of later days with her latch-key. On it was inscribed 'with the privilege of alighting at intermediate stations'. This amused the boys, for the only intermediate station was Barnsbury, where no one ever went; Tom said it was only poets and railway-passengers who 'alighted'. With this talisman in my pocket I was able to pass the booking-office as though it didn't exist, and mutter 'season' in an off-hand manner at the barriers—a taste of life indeed.

As I walked up Camden Road I indulged in rosy dreams of all the brainy people I was about to meet. Mary Worley would have gone with me, but the new girls had been told to arrive an hour later than the rest. Consequently Prayers were over and the school was absorbed in the quietude of work, when some fifty of us new-comers were ushered into cloak-rooms and thence into a large theatre-shaped room, to be instructed in the ways of the school. A melancholy official began to read aloud a number of regulations. She had only read a few when she suddenly stopped, pointed at a girl in the middle of us, and exclaimed,

'Take off that locket, dear.' (By the way, I soon noticed that every remark to a girl was followed by the word 'dear'.)

I can see that poor girl now, very red in the face, fumbling with the chain of her locket. It seemed that there was a rule forbidding any unnecessary ornament. This didn't trouble me because mother had kept me severely puritanical in this line, even reproving me once for wearing a ring out of a Christmas cracker. School uniforms were then unknown, so some restric-

tion in dress was no doubt needed, but the lack of politeness
to that poor girl gave me a shock.

A gracious welcome was certainly not the note of this preliminary harangue, the main object of which was obviously
to chasten our spirits, in case we should think the place a free
and easy affair like the régime of the despised private gover-
nesses or schools to which we had been accustomed. 'No nonsense here' was the key-note. It certainly had an imposing
effect on me, and I was impatient to get to work, although a
little dazed by the many instructions. At last we were dismissed, with orders to go to the various Forms to which we
had previously been assigned by letter.

'Whereabouts is the Upper Fourth?' I asked.

'You must not speak without putting up your hand, dear.'

'Sorry,' said I, and repeated my question with my hand
hoisted.

'You should say "please" at the end of your question, dear.'

I tried again in proper style and was told,

'You will find the name of the Form on the door, dear.'

We dispersed in various directions, and presently I found
myself alone, and quite lost. The passages were deserted.
Through the glass door of each room I passed I saw serried
ranks of girls at work. Nowhere could I find a room labelled
'Upper Fourth', although there were several other species of
Fourth. Presently I caught sight of a little white-haired old
woman, cap on head, and dressed in black rather the worse
for wear. Some caretaker or cleaner or something, I thought,
but she may possibly have noticed the names of the classrooms; I can but try. So I hailed her in a manner I thought
appropriate.

'I say, am I going right for the Upper Fourth, do you
happen to know?'

Glaring at me she exclaimed, 'Do you know who I am?'

'I haven't the faintest idea; I've only just come.'

'I am Miss Buss!' and standing back a pace she drew herself
up to mark the effect on me. It was not at all what she expected, for I cheered up and said,

'Oh, then *you* are sure to know the way to the Upper Fourth, and I do so want to get there.'

At this suddenly her face changed, and with a little gay laugh she said, 'That way, child, down the stairs, the first door you come to at the foot. Run along with you.'

Thus, oddly enough, it was in my first encounter with Miss Buss that I saw several different phases of her strange personality: her insignificance of stature and attire (*natura et arte*), her pomposity when she desired to impress, her kindly good temper, and her instantaneous and delighted recognition of any one who was quite at ease with her. These points didn't strike me at the moment, of course, but on recounting the incident to a seasoned schoolfellow afterwards I learnt that Miss Buss positively loved any one who was not afraid of her, who would look her in the eye and speak out.

At the moment I was far more intent on the Upper Fourth than on the headmistress. I was craving to see those wonderful girls, as low down in the school as the Fourth, to whom the Senior Oxford was a bagatelle.

Well, I found that Upper Fourth, and the very word gives me a mental shudder even now. After my dreams of cultured teachers and keen-brained girls—how humiliating was the drop! An empty desk among some thirty others was pointed out to me, with a hurried 'Sit there, dear.' Something that seemed like geography was in progress, and the girls were being questioned round out of Cornwell's Geography, a textbook only too familiar to me. After an astonished taking in of the dreadful reality I relieved my feelings by a contemptuous remark to the girl in the adjoining desk. She placed a warning finger on her mouth, but was too late. The teacher had heard an unwarranted voice and beckoned me to her desk. Thrusting an open exercise-book towards me she said,

'You must sign, dear.'

'Sign? Sign what?' I asked in bewilderment.

'Write down "I spoke in geography" and sign your name, dear,' she replied, hurriedly resuming a question on the Welland canal.

Soon there was a mid-morning interval, and I asked a girl
what on earth this kind of thing meant. She explained that
we had to write down what we had done wrong and sign our
name every time we broke a rule.

'Yes, and then what happens?' I asked.

'Oh nothing more than that. We just sign.'

'Is that all? How my brothers will laugh!'

'Your brothers may, but *you* won't when your parents see
at the end of the term "Reported for breach of Regulations—
23 times". So look out.'

In what deep dejection I got home that day and tried to hide
my bitter disappointment from mother! But mothers always
scent low spirits, and she refrained from asking too much. I
was glad that Tony was in Cornwall and need not know that
she was paying such high fees for so little. I showed mother
the list of Rules that had been presented to each new girl (as
well as posted at intervals about the building). It was in small
print and double columns, like the blue by-laws in the trams.
Mother laughed and thought them 'rather excessive'.

Those were the permanent rules, but almost every day a new
one appeared in a corridor, in large sprawling home-made
lettering—such as: 'Broken needles must not be thrown on the
floor.' They were so many that they ceased to attract attention
and got caught up into the decorative scheme. 'I can't possibly remember all these,' thought I, 'so I shan't bother about
them.' A few of them, however, still remain in my memory:
Every book had to be covered (a different colour for each subject). No girl might bring a pen to school (was this to avoid
ink-stains?). We were forbidden to get wet on the way to
school, to walk more than three in a row, to drop a pencil-box,
leave a book at home, hang a boot-bag by only one loop, run
down the stairs, speak in class. As for speaking, it would have
been easier to enumerate the few places where we were permitted to speak than those where talking was forbidden. The
ideas were sensible, but why make rules about them? One
felt that if a girl were to knock over the blackboard by mistake
there would be a rule against it the next day.

Arriving early one morning I was alone in a corridor and chanced to drop my pencil-box. 'Thank goodness,' thought I, 'there's no one to hear it.' Hardly had this crossed my mind when the voice of Miss Begbie came from some distant cloak-room, 'You must sign for that, dear.'

The book in which all these crimes were recorded had an ominous title—'The Appearing Book', smacking not a little of the Day of Judgement. As the culprit was left to state her own crime, some amusing things were entered in the book that may well puzzle future students of nineteenth-century education. 'I marched with the wrong foot' was the way a girl expressed her failure to keep step. 'I was four in a row', 'I spoke in French', 'I called out in Latin'. A technical distinction appears here; to *speak* was to talk to another girl, while to *call out* was to answer before you were asked. 'I left my heart at home' referred to a diagram for physiology.

On the rare occasions of a Form's going half a term without a signature, it was awarded a Gratification. This was a half-hour to be spent in any way the girls chose. Only once did this boon come my way, and there was much hesitation among the class, and searching for some noble idea in the way of recreation. In a pause I exclaimed loudly, 'Well, *I* should like a romp.' Amid much laughter the others then confessed to a similar wish, and blessed me heartily as we all trooped off to the gymnasium and let ourselves go.

Now and again a girl who had collected too many signatures would have an imposition, a piece of French to write or learn, but this was so rare that I only once observed a girl doing it. And anyhow it was nothing to what might befall any one at any moment: this was what the boys called a 'jaw'. But I don't believe any boy since the world began has ever known what a jaw can be. It needed Miss Buss to give a full content to the term. I never experienced it myself, but heard tales enough of poor girls reduced to sobs and almost hysterics as they bent under the storm that went on and on and on.

In that big building there was one small room, near the front door, dedicated entirely to Miss Buss. Here was held the Inquisition, for to this would be summoned any case of naughtiness with which a Form mistress had failed to cope. A narrow, dark passage led to it, along which no unlicensed person dare go. One day, during some nondescript English lesson, we were suddenly told to stand, and then 'pass out in lines after me'. Such orders were familiar enough, and we only surmised that the lunch interval was a bit earlier or something. Our curiosity was roused, however, when the long file headed towards the front door. We glanced at one another (there was no rule against this) conveying the idea, 'We surely can't be going into the street hatless?' Curiosity sharpened into amazement when the conducting mistress led us down the sacred passage. Searchings of conscience began. What had we done? Anyhow, it was the whole form, so together we could stand up to it. We were ushered, or rather squeezed, into the little room and managed to stand in respectful files. To our relief there was no sign of Miss Buss. But doubtless she was coming, for there was certainly something up. But no, and the mystery deepened as we stood in silence. I concentrated on the clock, as if it would throw some light on the matter, and it soon began to take on that fantastic look that any object does if you stare at it. Suddenly it seemed comic, and I was on the brink of a *lèse-majesté* burst of laughter, when fortunately from the door came the sharp orders, 'Turn. Pass out. Go back to your form room.' We returned to our English lesson as if nothing had happened, and no reference was made to our expedition. The most accepted theory in our lunch-time discussion of the affair was that it had been just idle ordering about, in the same spirit that induces odious people to command their dog to lie down, beg, 'die', and so forth, for no reason at all. We had forgotten all about it when, at the next English lesson, a few days later, we were told to write then and there a description of what we had observed in the room during the three minutes we had spent in it. It was a clever exercise, because we had no means of aiding one another's memory; but as a test of observation it was useless because we had been in too agitated a dread of what might be in store for us to observe anything. I had to spin out all I could about the clock, but the girl at my side was writing busily. This was Bessie Jones, who was never known to do anything wrong. Her conscience had been so clear that she dreaded nothing, and as she had always been a Bluebeard's wife in her curiosity about the sacred room, she had spent her three minutes to some purpose. Her substantial essay was read aloud to us, while we others were held up to withering scorn for our lack of observation.

But not even the righteous could always escape. Even Bessie Jones was once summoned alone to the sanctum, and went off light-heartedly, *conscia recti*. 'She'll make you cry,' said her companions. 'Nothing shall make me cry; I know I haven't done anything' was her stout reply. A letter of complaint had been received from a parent, accusing Bessie of leading her daughter to loiter on the way home. The girls had taken one side of a square while the mother went to meet them on the other and became annoyed at missing them; there had been no lateness. Was Bessie allowed to explain this? No, the storm broke. 'I won't cry,' she kept saying to herself, 'I won't cry, let her abuse me as much as she likes.' But Miss Buss had a trump card; remembering that a few days before Bessie had brought an excuse for being late owing to her brother's sudden illness, she exclaimed, 'And fancy your behaving so disgracefully in the street while your poor brother is lying ill!' Now Bessie's brother was everything to her, and at this mention of him she collapsed and broke into sobs. That was all Miss Buss wanted, and she dismissed the 'penitent' without more ado.

The iron discipline of the school made things easy for those in authority. Every moment, almost every movement was ordered. Where supervision was impossible we were put on our honour. This was far worse, for to a sensitive conscience it was torture to decide whether the mutter of 'pardon' on knocking against a girl by mistake was to be reported or not. And often it roused a bitter sense of injustice. I wonder that any of us retained a rag of conscience, for it certainly did not pay. For instance, one afternoon a week we stayed at school for a two-hour drawing lesson—a Pacific Ocean of boredom. We copied dusty cones and cubes in endless variety, but I can remember no single point or principle that was taught me. We were allotted ten marks, not for what we did in drawing, which mattered nothing, but merely for not talking. Thus, if you said 'thanks' automatically for a loan of india-rubber you took off one mark. But two girls who sat near me carried on a conversation all the time, yet took off only one mark. They salved their conscience by counting it as only speaking *once*.

Talking appeared to be the main evil, and of course the absence of it made the school seem an ideal of good order and 'teaching' an easy job. But the continual restraints and fuss had worse results than actual overwork. Even when we got home we were not free. There were little printed time-tables on which we had to enter the hour at which we began to work, the hour we finished, and the total time taken. We had to fill them in with pen and ink, to prove that they were done at home, for no ink was allowed at school. Then the parent signed them as a voucher of their being correct. Every morning they were collected, looked over by the form mistress, and filed for reference. The cupboards were crowded with them. The conscientious girl was fidgeted beyond belief, and certainly beyond hospitality if a visitor interrupted her work and put out these tiresome calculations. A slow worker came in for continual scolding for taking too long over her sums or what not. Meanwhile many put down just what they thought would look well, and needless to say the average mother signed it without bothering. I had an eye-opener one morning as to the simple procedure that passed muster. I noticed a girl going stealthily past the teacher's desk, taking a dip of ink and returning to her own desk to fill in her time-table.

'That's not much use,' said I, 'without your mother's signature.'

'Oh, that's all right,' she blandly replied, 'I'm signing it myself; mother's name is the same as mine.'

There was no rule against forgery, of course, and it is

interesting to calculate how Miss Buss would have acted if this girl had been caught—perhaps no more severely than if she had been seen running downstairs. I am sure that the excessive attention required for trifling duties blinded teachers and pupils alike to the weightier matters of the Law. Common sense and kind-heartedness often had to give way to some pettifogging rule, as the following incident will show.

One day our form-room door was flung wide open and Miss Buss entered. We all rose, and she addressed us thus: 'Now, girls, you are going to have a lesson from a stranger. I expect you to attend well and be on your very best behaviour. Of course no one will fidget, or drop a pencil, or speak unless directly asked a question.'

Turning to the door she then graciously invited a young teacher, a girl of about twenty-two, on to the platform. A solemn-looking man with a beard followed and was given a chair. Miss Buss gave the order for us to sit, and then took another chair whence she could eye us all. The form mistress hurried off to another class.

The young teacher then shot forth at us in breathless haste a lecture on Townshend, unbroken by the slightest pause, let alone a question or a writing on the board. We looked at the man and saw that he was absorbed in taking notes. He surely couldn't want to know about Townshend? Then it dawned on some of us that he must be a kind of examiner. We had never heard of a teacher's being examined, and we naturally concluded that it must be ourselves he was making notes about. So we looked intelligent and managed to hold on to a fact or two. After about a quarter of an hour the lecture came to an obvious end, and the poor lecturer stood irresolute; her matter was finished; what could she do next?

Now throughout the school there was a system of 'cards' —a packet for each form with the girls' names on them. This was a capital device for helping a new teacher, or a visiting one. After asking a question she could read out a name and the girl would stand up if she could answer the question. The packet was also handy for testing a large class fairly, because no one knew whose name would come next, and no one could be left out. It stood on each teacher's desk for use at any time.

When, therefore, Miss Buss saw that the lecture was ended she pointed out the packet to the young teacher and said with an encouraging smile:

'Now you ask any question. Then read out a name on a card and the girl will stand up if she can answer it.'

So the lecturer seized the packet hopefully and began, 'Where was Townshend born?'—following her question with the name on the top card. No one rose, so she tried another card, then another and another, but no one moved.

'After all, a man's birthplace is not very important. Can you tell me in whose reign he lived?' Name after name was called, card after card fell on the table. No response. Of course the lecture had been delivered so fast that it was quite excusable if these questions, and some others that followed, were unanswerable. But it was queer that no one attempted anything at all. The man went on taking notes, and Miss Buss was looking with disgust now at the teacher and now at us. In despair at last came the question, 'Can any one tell me any-thing at all about Townshend?' Again the cards fell without result and the poor girl looked on the verge of tears. Then to every one's relief the man rose and said that the time was up, and the visitors filed out, Miss Buss casting a withering look on the class as she left.

Fool-proof devices must be a special delight to Puck, for it enables him to come out strong. In this case, as may be guessed, he had popped the right packet of cards into the form mistress's hand as she was departing in hurried politeness, and substituted on the desk the packet of another form which she had brought in by mistake.

'But why, *why* didn't you say that they were the wrong cards?' she exclaimed, when we told her of the disaster on her return. She did not press the point, for she knew that it needed iron nerves to interrupt what Miss Buss had figured out to go smoothly.

Yes, smoothly and with the regularity of clockwork—that

was the ideal of Miss Buss, as she walked along the corridors continually, looking through the doors and seeing everything 'going on'. She told me (in later days) that she could tell even from such a passing glance whether or no the teaching and discipline were good. That very tidiness was a danger-signal, had she but known it; but there was no one to warn her, and her power was absolute. The danger lay not so much in our being fidgeted by small routine of externals, as by our being mentally fitted into a procrustean scheme. It was tidy for thirty girls to be all doing the same thing, and the chief enemy was the appearance of confusion (detectable through the door). As for confusion of mind, that didn't show so much and was overlooked. In my own case—fairly typical, I gather —hours of boredom were spent in listening to stuff I knew quite well; and yet at one time I was obliged for a week or two, owing to some time-table trouble, to attend a rather advanced German class, although I knew little more than *der*, *des*, *dem*, *den*. I was required to put a piece of English prose into German for homework. A kindly girl let me copy hers in the train, and so I rubbed along. It was no use for a parent to protest. Miss Buss had forestalled such a nuisance as this by making a rule on the Prospectus to the effect that the Head was the sole arbiter of what should be taught to any girl at any time.

'Taught' is hardly the word to apply to the text-book-and-water method that I endured for the first few weeks. At the same time I was kept so busy with one thing and another for 'homework' that there was no leisure for the least amusement. Several of us were high-spirited enough to find our own solace during our classes. One, a future artist, for ever chafing against the régime, developed a perfect technique; she would come early on the first day of term, secure a back desk, and then contrive to make her face look attentive while her mind was far away, and she left school after some ten years of this in the middle forms, 'quite unscathed' as she expressed it. She had acquired for life an enviable power of enduring boredom, and had always been 'good' in school hours.

We had no chance of pursuing any useful work during a

lesson, because the desks had to be clear of everything but the precisely needful. So I amused myself by studying the teacher's mannerisms in voice, movement of jaw, roving of eye, or nervous fidgeting with her brooch. Choice bits of careful English were also treasured, such as 'Commence at the commencement'. With imitations of these I regaled my fellows during the scanty times when we were allowed to talk. The girl who usually sat next to me would laugh on the slightest provocation, and it was my cue to upset her by moving my hand sideways in an impressive manner whenever the teacher said something more than usually fatuous. There was no rule against this gesture, though we amused ourselves by framing one that would meet the case: 'No girl must move her hand sideways in class.'

Marks were the life-blood of the school. No work whatever was done without them, so that a large proportion of time was consumed in assigning them, counting them, entering them in huge books, adding them, and checking them. Great precautions were taken against cheating, as if this were the natural thing to expect. Tests done in class were marked by one's neighbour. Each desk was provided with a board that could be fixed into iron sockets at the edge and form a screen, so that the next girl couldn't see what one was writing. After every test done in class there would follow a cascade of questions as to whether some answer might 'count' or not. Thus:

'Please will it count if 1488 is put instead of 1588 for the Armada?'

'Well, dear, give it a half-mark.'

One evening I spent an hour rather enjoyably in writing an essay. It was returned with one mark deducted for one spelling fault, from a maximum of two—no other comment. This injustice rankled long, although to work for no marks at all would have worried no one.

Of all the lessons French was the dullest. It is barely credible to-day that hardly a word of French was spoken. We had to buy an expensive and appallingly dull book by Van Laun, and prepare the French at home for his stupid exercises. When

we came to class we had to write out two or three sentences
selected to test us, which were taken in and returned corrected.
The bulk of the lesson consisted of so-called translation—a
muttering of bad English round the class from *Picciola*. I
hated that 'little flower' and cast a longing glance back at our
merry time in my private school over *Les Malheurs de Sophie*—
a book in lively French with funny illustrations all about a
little girl who did gorgeously naughty things.

The study of a play of Shakespeare's was simplicity itself.
We had to learn the footnotes given in our texts. These consisted mainly of foolish paraphrases of any lines supposed to
be obscure, and it was in these notes, believe me, and not in
the text, that we had to be word-perfect. However, in the
matter of Shakespeare there was a worse thing than boredom
—active irritation. So long as a teacher droned on with questions we could curl up mentally as soon as our turn was past.
But one teacher fancied her powers of poetic declamation.
Although we had the text open before us she would roll out
the lines in an exquisitely modulated, soft, pleading style.
Whereas with the dull teacher I could think of something else
or enjoy the joke of her folly, there was no escape from
this murderer of the old friends of my childhood—Rosalind,
Fluellen, Aguecheek, Dogberry. . . . The Saul of dullness may
slay his thousands, but the David of sentimentality slays his
tens of thousands. I always wonder how Shakespeare sur-
vives these energetic spouters, who are more rife to-day than
ever. *As You Like It* has never recovered in my case from that
poetical soul, who would clasp her hands in prayerful attitude
and incline her head from side to side, as she chanted the uses
of adversity.

From all this it may be supposed that mentally at least our
life was easy. But not so. During my first term I hardly ever
had a good night's sleep. Every morning before Prayers we
had to recite to the form mistress or one of the monitors a
piece of poetry—a different kind for each day of the week: on
Monday it was verses of a Psalm; on Tuesday, English; on
Wednesday, French; on Thursday, German; on Friday, Latin.

I can picture how this neat arrangement appealed to Miss Buss,
or whoever it was who invented the torture, for it was little
else. Singing a Psalm in church is easy, but try to recite one in
cold blood. The French was enjoyable, because mother learnt
it with me and got me to pronounce it properly, so that even
now some of the lines linger lovingly in my memory. German
was the worst; it simply haunted me until I had staggered
through it somehow, or signed for not knowing it. Only two
lines of Virgil were required, but it made no difference whether
one had done any Latin or not, and how most of the girls
managed to learn them is still a mystery to me. At that time I
supposed myself to be particularly stupid at learning by heart,
for I would spend nearly an hour over half a dozen lines of
Milton. But it was the anxiety that militated against memory,
for I have learnt plenty of poetry in later life without any
trouble.

Anxiety in some shape was always with us. In order to ease
it, and have a little leisure in hand if a friend dropped in, we
used to get our work 'forward' as much as possible. One girl
carried this to such an extent that she worked as feverishly at
getting forward as if it were for the morrow, and her only
reward was that she had nothing at all to do on the last evening
of the term. Miss Begbie told an amusing story of her little
niece, who was found late one night kneeling up in bed:

'Whatever are you doing, dear?'

'I'm getting my prayers forward for the morning, Auntie.'

§ 2

It was just at this turbulent time of my life that our vicar
called to persuade mother that I ought to be confirmed. She
was taken aback, having never regarded me as old enough for
that sort of thing. She had never been confirmed herself, as
the ceremony was not on the map when she was a girl in
Cornwall. Like the Communion Service, the Order for Confirmation was huddled away in the same small print as Forms
of Prayer to be used at Sea. My brothers appear to have been
confirmed at school, in absence of mind, all in the day's work,

for I can remember nothing about it. However, mother was quite willing for me to be 'done' if it was the correct thing, and it was arranged for me to attend at the vicarage once a week for preparation classes.

About half a dozen girls of the neighbourhood assembled round the old man's study table. His only claims to respect were a pompous manner, a kindly goodwill, and a long white beard. Nothing but platitudes ever fell from his lips. Owing to the solemnity with which he uttered the obvious, most of the energy of the class was spent in restraining nervous laughter, for none was required for thought. His main care was to make us word-perfect in the Catechism. This gave me little trouble, except the long paraphrase of the Lord's Prayer, which seemed to me so much more cumbersome than the prayer itself, and so absurdly unnecessary that my mind positively refused to take it in. So I escaped it altogether by looking as bright as possible when the demand for it was looming. Thus it was assumed that I knew it and need not be tested. We were obliged to learn and recite even the questions, and I had some bother to keep a straight face in addressing the old man thus: 'My good child, know this . . .'

One day he actually indulged in a little Gospel history, apropos of a clause in the Creed, and passed round the familiar map of Palestine for us to see where Bethlehem was. Disgusted, I looked ostentatiously out of the window as it came to my turn.

'Do you not want to know where Bethlehem is?' he asked, in pained tones.

'I know where it is,' said I.

'Ah, but we can never be too sure of these things. You had better look.' So to please him I gave a glance.

Very occasionally he probed our minds. 'What is meant by "Ghost"?' he asked the member of the class who was mentally deficient. 'It's something that frightens you' was the hesitating reply, but as this was not a promising approach to what he had in mind he gave a curious cough and passed on to something else.

'You do not seem to know your prayer-book very well,'

was his reproof to the same girl as she was fumbling in the Psalms in search of the Order for Baptism.

'It isn't mine, it's my sister's,' she answered with confidence, leaving him again defeated.

I think now that he was more nervous of us than we were of him. Far more. All the time he used to fidget with a quill pen, and at one glorious moment, as he was assuring us that we were all miserable sinners and emphasizing this startling idea by dabbing the pen on the table, the bewitched thing took a flying leap across the room.

'You must not smile,' said he.

This finished me, and we all abandoned ourselves to joyful laughter. He hurriedly rose to pick up the pen, but I noticed a distinct grin between moustache and beard. Even the ranks of Tuscany could scarce forbear. . . .

For our final class he asked us to write out for him any personal failings or evil tendencies of which we were aware, and especially our besetting sin. I accepted this task like a piece of school 'home-work', and set about it as if it were a French exercise. With earnest thought during the week I scraped up about a dozen failings. But which of them beset me I couldn't decide, so I let that point go. Indeed they were all flights of imagination, and I was not a little proud at having filled two sheets of paper about them, feeling sure that my list would be the biggest. It was.

When I handed it up to the vicar at our next class I was annoyed to find that not one of the others had got a list at all. And worse still they were on the high horse about it. To his inquiries they replied that their mothers had forbidden them to do it, one even muttering that 'mother thought it Romish'. And glances were cast at me as though I were a kind of Mary Tudor. However, we started our lesson and I hoped the affair had blown over. But as the class was dismissed the vicar laid his hand significantly on my paper, with the words, 'Kindly remain behind; I will see you alone.'

What followed is a black spot on my memory. Opening my wretched paper he very slowly rolled out my sins, one by one,

breathing after each, 'Ahh . . . mmm.' I have felt a fool often
enough, but never such a completely silly one as during the
rehearsal of those absurd 'sins'. Really it was he who was the
fool, for not one sensible remark could he find to make about
them. But the whole thing had one good effect. Never again
could I take seriously any sense of sin, or desire to confess, or
any such thing. The vanity had been purged, I had done my
bit in this line, and had attained a kind of freedom of the city.
If the mothers of the other girls had only known, they missed
a grand opportunity of putting their daughters off the fasci-
nation of the confessional for ever. I have come to bless my
own mother again and again for her policy of non-interference,
which was risky, but as effective as that of Charles II, whom
she used to quote: 'Don't hang him; give him rope enough
and he'll hang himself.'

When the day for Confirmation was fixed I inquired at
school whether one could have a day off for it. Then I learnt
that Confirmation was one of the two reasons that were valid
for absence, the other being the wedding of a sister; a brother's
wedding apparently was not of sufficient importance. All I
need do was to bring a note for Miss Buss to sign. It was
therefore with confidence that I joined the morning queue of
girls who daily brought excuses for lateness or absence owing
to illness. Miss Buss, seated on her throne in the Hall, received,
signed, and dismissed. I felt rather important at being a candi-
date for Confirmation, and expected a few words of pleasant
exhortation. What was my surprise to find my mother's note
received with a storm of abuse. Pushing it back into my hand,
Miss Buss burst out:

'What do you mean by bringing me a note in an envelope?
Do you suppose that I have nothing better to do than spend
my time opening envelopes? What would become of my
morning if all these girls brought envelopes for me to open
every day? Why, I shouldn't have any time left for the serious
work always piling up for me to do. Take it away. Go to the
end of the queue and bring it again—open.'

I was too upset to care what comment she made on my

being confirmed, and it was as well, for she made none, but merely seized the note, signed it, and turned to something else. Mother seemed to get a good deal of quiet fun out of the episode when I told her about it.

§ 3

Coming into the school at the age of sixteen I saw its glaring faults and absurdities. The whole seemed to me an elaborate machine for doing the minimum of useful things with the maximum of fuss. I didn't see then, as I saw later, that Miss Buss was faced by a herculean task. The endless anxieties she caused her pupils were as nothing to her own big anxiety. She was a pioneer, and almost single-handed, in getting some kind of systematic education for girls. She had no school to copy, no precedent of any kind. Her private school had been so successful that she found herself before long with five hundred girls —all to be taught something and to be trained along Victorian lines of good behaviour.

To be taught something—but what? Negatively the problem was easy. All the hitherto satisfactory ideals of accomplishments and 'finishing' must be wiped out, but what was to take their place? While the education of boys had been gradually shaped from ancient times, engaging the attention of philosophers, that of girls had as a rule no other aim beyond making them pleasing to men. This idea was to Miss Buss anathema, and she failed to see all its great possibilities when really well done. To be deeply pleasing to a husband, and widely pleasing to other men, seems to me as good an ideal as a woman can have. But instead of facing squarely the real needs of future wives and mothers, as the vast majority of girls were to be, Miss Buss seized the tempting instrument at her hand—the stimulus to mental ambition afforded by outside examinations. By this means the curriculum was readymade. And thus, for better or worse, the education of girls became a feeble imitation of what the boys were doing, for the public examinations made no distinction of sex, and no woman's voice was heard at the examination boards.

A more serious problem than the curriculum was the discipline. The girls came day by day from a great variety of homes, and never before had there been so many at work together. Here the example of the boys' Public schools was no help. Three essentials of their system were entirely lacking: games, effective punishment, and respectable learning.

I don't think it ever occurred to Miss Buss that games are far more than games, that they provide a vent for high spirits, develop natural obedience, and prevent mental overstrain. True, we had only a tiny yard of open space, nothing to call a playground, but there was a big gymnasium where games could have been freely played. All we did in it was Swedish exercises—bouncing balls or balancing poles—and marching round to music. Were they afraid that if we played free games we might start a riot? Even our short breathing-space of a quarter of an hour in the middle of a long morning's work gave us no freedom except to talk. We filed down into a basement room, bought a bun or a biscuit at a table as we passed, and then stood in *rows* till the time was up. I used to recall with a pang the jolly games of rounders in the grassy garden of my private school, whence we returned to work all hot and recreated.

Punishment as the boys knew it was impossible. Caning was out of the question, and detention was almost equally so. The bulk of the girls came from considerable distances, and the double journey for an afternoon school had to be ruled out. Consequently the lessons had to be over by half-past one, to allow time for getting home for dinner. But parents had complained that the girls had not enough to do during the afternoon and evening. Therefore, since hobbies were considered frivolous, the curse of homework was started. A detention would involve stopping at school for dinner, and an imposition would add to the already over-burdened homework, so neither of these was widely practicable.

Reproof, therefore, was the only form of punishment available, and it is hardly to be wondered at that Miss Buss had brought it to a fine art. It ranged from the mild disgrace of

'signing' to the third degree in the private room. Very rarely,
I believe, expulsion was used. The knowledge that there was
always a waiting list of pupils gave Miss Buss absolute power,
and this must always be dangerous for a woman. Now by
nature she was generous and kind-hearted, and did most
sincerely long for the loyal co-operation of her pupils in making
the school a success. To this end she delivered every week a
moral lecture, and would frequently enlist our cheerful com-
pliance with the innumerable rules. 'Multiply the results' was
her great slogan for deciding whether a rule was necessary or
not. She would point out that one girl running downstairs
might not be dangerous, but what if five hundred did? One
shoe-bag untidily hung doesn't matter, but five hundred look
bad. One girl talking makes no disturbance, but five hundred
do. The fallacy of this argument never struck her. Or did it?
and that's why she repeated it so often? I think that her sleep
must often have been broken by the nightmare of five hundred
girls all running amok at once.

Underlying all this iron discipline must have been the subconscious fear that the assistant teachers could not carry on
if there were much freedom for questioning and discussion
in class. Hard as it is to realize to-day, a well-educated and
cultured woman-teacher was extremely rare. It was in this
direction that Miss Buss made her greatest mistake. Instead of
searching far and wide for the best, she almost invariably chose
women who had been through the school and could be relied
on to follow her methods; no doubt from a subconscious fear
that those methods might be called in question by some lively
and original member of the staff. After all, fresh ideas are
always upsetting.

Not quite so easy to understand was the objection to the
teachers having any interests outside their work. Now it is
obvious that no teacher, and no parent, can inspire children if
he thinks too much about them; he must have some wider
outside interest about which they must be left guessing. But
for Miss Buss the school, the scheme, the orderly plan—this
was the one absorbing thought.

III

Bright Intervals

FOR the first week or so I was definitely under a cloud, disappointed with the work and disheartened by the atmosphere. But as it was almost a point of honour in our family to squeeze as much enjoyment as we could out of everything, I soon began to see some good things around me.

I shall never forget my excitement at first seeing the great assembly hall. It seemed to have something of the splendour of the Merchant Taylors' Hall in Charterhouse Square, where I had so often been present at my brothers' Speech-days. To Miss Buss I think it represented all her glorious aspirations, and she had thought out every possible means of investing it with dignity. She could not have the dignity of the M.T.S. hall, with its flavour of great age, heroic men, and eminent scholars. So she wisely struck out on a different line. Everything of importance had been 'presented' and bore the name of the donor with a date. On the high platform was the throne. Behind this rose the great organ. At the other end was the gallery, with a medallion of the Princess of Wales, to commemorate her having opened the hall. A stained-glass window, in memory of some one, gave a cheerful bit of colour when the morning sun poured in. The rows of folding desks and benches were kept spotlessly clean, a contrast to the roughly handled forms at Merchant Taylors'.

On my second day I was present at Prayers, and saw the Hall at its main function. The idea of prayers at school was quite new to me, and I was certainly amazed. The girls came in from cloakroom or classroom, one by one as into church, and took their seats in perfect silence, while a voluntary was played on the organ. As soon as Miss Buss ascended the platform every one stood up, and then followed a hymn, a short reading from the Bible, and a short prayer. A lively march tune accompanied our filing out in due order to our form-rooms. If Miss Buss had been content with these simple dignities we should all look back on that Hall with unmixed affection. But she required absolute silence in it, not only during Prayers, but also at any time during the day when pupils were casually passing through it, and they were in honour bound to report themselves and sign, if they had uttered a single word in the holy precincts.

During Prayers, however, a sterner vigilance was kept; honour was evidently not to be trusted; a teacher, prefect, or monitor was stationed over each form, to make sure that silence should be absolute. Now it chanced that the Upper Fourth had fallen to the charge of my prefect friend, Mary Worley. Imagine her dismay when she noticed that I made casual remarks quite freely to my neighbour morning after morning, while we sat waiting for Miss Buss to appear. Nothing would have induced her to order me to sign, but in the train on our way home she very tactfully approached the point:

'I'm a bit bothered, Molly, by the way you talk in Hall. The rule is quite a good one when you come to look at it. If they all talked there would be such a babel.'

'Of course there would,' said I, 'and I'll never do it again.'

My respect for Mary was enormous, and I kept my word, suddenly discovering that a good deal of fun might be got out of keeping all the rules, no matter how needless they seemed. Indeed, they were not much trouble when once you got used to them, and in this cynical spirit I became a model pupil.

One advantage of the school I felt immediately. Ever since my father's death we had been hard up. And I was quite miserably ashamed of it, in a way that modern boys and girls can't imagine. In those days people never dreamt of saying they couldn't afford a thing. Actual privations were as nothing to this wretched feeling. I didn't mind going without a summer trip to Cornwall or the sea-side, not having fires enough in the winter, never having a new dress (only 'passed-ons' from cousins), and dreading every order for a new text-book.

But I did bitterly mind that the girls in my private school should notice my poverty. For instance, one day the news had gone round that Mary Thomas had got a new dress, and I was elated, until one keen-eyed girl discovered that it was only an old one turned.

Now at the North London I sensed at once a different atmosphere. No one asked where you lived, how much pocket-money you had, or what your father was—he might be a bishop or a rat-catcher. Girls would openly grumble at having to buy a new text-book. The only notice taken of another girl's dress that I ever heard made a funny contrast to what I had experienced in the private school. I was told after I had left school that I had been a constant wonder for the length of time that one dress had lasted me, and that this had called forth admiration, not contempt.

Every now and again we were besought by Miss Buss, in her addresses on moral subjects, not to waste our parents' money by being extravagant with exercise paper or careless with books. One special delinquency in this line would rouse her to boiling-point. Since she couldn't track down the culprit she was obliged to pour forth her wrath on the school at large. A stall was opened every day on the premises for the sale of text-books, paper, pencils, and so on. Again and again it happened that a girl would buy a book, lay it down in the cloakroom while she did up her boots, and forget to take it home. A horribly efficient underling would find it and transfer it to the Lost Property Office. Here there always tended to be a great accumulation of goods, for one could only get anything out of it by signing twice—once for leaving it about, and again for not having a name on it. So naturally the girls preferred to sacrifice a good many articles. When Miss Buss saw an expensive new text-book among the unclaimed store she must have realized how some girl had cajoled her mother into giving her the extra money for another copy. 'Lying and robbery!' exclaimed Miss Buss in her moral lecture. But as long as the foolish rules existed she was beating the wind.

In my new-born enthusiasm for keeping all the rules 'for

fun' I discerned some practical advantages. I made a habit of getting everything ready overnight, so as to be unflustered for the start in the morning. Much wear and tear, physical and mental, have been spared me throughout life by always being 'ten minutes ahead of schedule'. Waste of time from being occasionally too early for an appointment has been amply compensated by peace of mind.

The advantage of strong discipline, too, was brought home to me during my first term. Some kind of theatrical display was being given in the Hall when suddenly the top part of the temporary stage began to give forth smoke. As this was before the days of regular fire-drill in schools, there was no recognized procedure. We all sat like graven images, glaring at the outbreak, frightened of the fire, but still more frightened of Miss Buss's wrath if we showed our alarm by moving or 'speaking in Hall'. As it was, the fire was quickly got under and the play proceeded. But Miss Buss seized the chance at her next moral lecture to praise us for our self-control, and to point out the dreadful consequences of any one person's showing fright in a large assembly. 'Sit tight and look calm,' she said, 'no matter how frightened you really are.'

Any incident from school life, or the newspaper, would be pressed into the service of those moral talks. It was the period of tight waists, when girls were vying with one another to get the smallest girth. One young society woman (Miss Buss told us in a solemn undertone) pinched her waist so much that her liver was completely cut in two! I always longed to know how they found this out, and whether she 'died on them'; but the story was sufficiently alarming anyhow.

The fallacy of the slogan 'Spending money is good for trade' was brought home to us by a hypothetical case: Little Tommy bought too many jam tarts and was ill. The confectioner was encouraged by his 'demand' to make more jam tarts. More little boys bought too many tarts and were ill, and so on. 'Who then,' asked Miss Buss triumphantly, 'was benefited?' The question was rhetorical, or we might have suggested both the confectioner and the doctor. But we gathered that the fewer sweets we bought the more sweet-makers would be driven to some nobler work, and to this day I buy sweets with a sense of guilt.

It was not long after term began that I went home one day in almost a cheerful frame of mind, full of the news that we were to be taught some quite new subjects. Mother was properly impressed by the title 'Political Economy' of which even she had never so much as heard. But she was to learn a great deal of it before she was much older. Another subject called 'Domestic Economy' puzzled her still more, but sounded as if she would be quite *au fait* in it. However, she became meeker when I began after a time to talk familiarly of hydrogenous foodstuffs and carbohydrates. 'Foodstuffs!' she exclaimed, 'what a funny word!' The lessons were entirely theoretical, as there was neither kitchen nor laundry at our disposal, and I darkly suspected that our teachers had never entered such places. Now I could make a rice pudding blindfold, so mother and I were greatly tickled at my having to write down and learn a recipe for it. Her notion of a recipe is best shown by a conversation I heard one day. A dropper-in to lunch had enjoyed her pudding and began:

'How do you manage to get such good rice puddings, Mrs. Thomas? My cook is so uncertain—one day we can swim in it, and the next day we can dance on it. Do tell me exactly how you get it just right like this.'

'You take a pie-dish.'

'What size?'

'Oh, the ordinary size. Put some well-washed rice in it.'

'How much?'

'Enough to cover the bottom. Then add a bit of butter.'

'How big a bit?'

'As big as a walnut. Then add salt and sugar.'

'How much?'

'Oh, as much as you think will do. Then bake in a *very slow* oven.'

'For how long?'

'Until it seems to be done.'

The curious part about this recipe was the complete satisfaction shown by the visitor, who nodded her head at each item of information, for mother took care to emphasize the really important point. Nothing whatever remained to me of those recipes at school, nor of the elaborate menus for a family of seven, and I never had any idea whether my sons were consuming nitrogen or carbon or what.

Another new subject called 'Laws of Health' was far more attractive, for it involved lots of drawing. We had to draw lovely skeletons and lungs and hearts, with tubes in red and blue. Underneath we could put neat little 'keys' to show the observer what A,B,C, a,b,c, stood for. One day there was brought into the room a life-size model of the human trunk, which took to pieces. A bit was lifted off and behold the stomach with appurtenances. After a short exposition another bit was lifted off, with still more intimate revelations. Notes were dictated, but when we were told that the intestines were thirty feet in length I wrote down thirty inches, arguing to myself that thirty feet was an impossible length to get into one's body. When my note-book was corrected, the 'inches' was allowed to pass, but a mark was taken off for the spelling 'intestins'.

The one thing I remember from those lessons is the way in which the blood managed to get up the veins. Valves seemed to me a most ingenious device of the Creator. In doing my diagrams with such loving care I little thought of the use to which they would be put. Some years later I found that my brother Tom had captured my note-book, and with its aid had been able to give some lessons in physiology to a pupil in a Yorkshire town, where that same pupil is now a leading doctor.

Needlework should naturally have been included in the Domestic Economy course, but very little attention was paid to it. Whether Miss Buss, like my mother, had been so overdosed with it herself that she did not care to inflict it on the young, or whether she considered it a feminine and feeble pursuit, easily picked up at home, the result was joyful enough for me. And yet, much as I hated the sight of a needle, sewing was the cause of some of my pleasantest memories of the school. Turning her back on the frivolities of embroidery, Miss Buss encouraged both plain sewing and Christianity by ordaining a Dorcas meeting once a month. To most of us it was a treat, providing a change from the usual routine. It involved a lunch at school and staying for the afternoon, with a possible game in the gymnasium thrown in. Surprise packets were prepared by our mothers and eaten, picnic fashion, in the dining-room, rousing envy among the girls who were enduring the school lunch. Since the work was more of a good deed than a lesson, we were allowed to talk a little within reason while we sewed. The only thing we had to sign for was forgetting to bring a thimble. I generally forgot mine, but Bessie Jones could always be relied on to have brought a few spare ones, in order to meet such cases.

For two hours we sewed horribly coarse cotton, of a dull biscuit colour and queer smell, with little blackish threads poking out of it here and there. It was to become in time chemises for the poor. We were not taught how to cut them out, for our mistakes would have been wasteful. Our duty was to join long stretches of stuff together. It seemed to me much the same as hemming, but the expert girls called it running and felling. Where did the pleasure come in? The reward for our noble work consisted in being read aloud to by the form mistress. As she was not required to improve us, she chose some jolly book that she herself liked, and we were encouraged to discuss any little point that arose in it, even while we sewed—a delightful change from the usual procedure of a lesson. Two of these books are still vivid in my memory, always recalling those cheery afternoons: *The Autocrat of the Breakfast Table*, giving us a taste of a new kind of humour, and Aristotle's *Ethics*.

Even here marks pursued us. Since they were not to be taken off for talking in this blessed instance, ten or less were allotted for the amount of sewing we had achieved. At the close of the time the mistress went round to examine and award. During one reading of Aristotle my whole output was some twelve inches.

'This is very little, dear, for two hours.'

'Ah, yes,' I replied, 'but the book was so interesting that I had to stop to think.'

'Ten marks,' said she with a grin, passing on to give my neighbour only five for an enormously greater stretch of sewing. But we looked at one another and laughed, for the Dorcas marks never 'counted'.

These joyful afternoons came only about twice in the term, but there was always some little excitement going on. Fully aware, no doubt, of the mental limitations of the rank and file of her staff, Miss Buss obtained the help of occasional outside lecturers, who gave us real contact with the science and art of the day. Lantern slides were then a rare treat, involving the darkening of the hall, a pungent smell and the joyful possibility of an accident, or at least a hitch of some kind, when the lecturer would call out 'next please' and get either no response or the next slide upside down. A man called Proctor gave us a course on 'The Birth and Death of Worlds' and 'The Life Story of the Moon'. As my ideas in these matters had been confined to those of Moses I found the new knowledge entrancing, its only drawback being that we had to write an account of each lecture afterwards.

Henry Blackburn, the editor of *Academy Notes*, gave us a course on modern art, far more fascinating to me than the astronomy, for instead of using a lantern he made drawings for us then and there, illustrating his remarks on good composition, perspective, the use of figures, and so on. I was able to jot these down, and mother and I went over them eagerly when I got home.

A certain Captain Speedy had just returned from Abyssinia, and gave us an amusing talk about it, dressing up, like a quick-change artist, as a general, a priest, a merchant, a courtier, and so on, and throwing in some amazing details of their religious rites, wedding ceremonies, and methods of commerce. He won our gratitude, too, by saying: 'I understand that you girls have to write an account of my talk to you. Well, the very word Abyssinia means confusion, because the races are confused, the religion is confused, the mountains and valleys are confused, the climate is confused, and I know that I am confused in addressing so many girls. So the more confused your accounts are, the better they will represent the country and the lecture.'

The father of one of the girls was a sculptor, so he came to give us the story of how a lump of marble is gradually turned into a statue—a mysterious business on which we were completely ignorant. My chief pleasure in this consisted in the little bits of marble that he distributed among us with the hint that if put in the sugar-bowl they would cause much innocent mirth when a visitor stirred and stirred in vain.

These are only samples of the outside lectures that were liable to occur at any time, and hardly a week went by without one. But in addition there were two men who were habitués of the school. They were so unattractive that some of us fancied that Miss Buss had imported them to show us what men *might* be like. One of them came once a week to teach the upper forms composition. He seemed to use the lesson for venting some secret grouch. At first a few of us who were new to his ways took the trouble to write some interesting essays on the themes he set. But he seemed to derive pleasure from reading bits aloud and sneering at us for 'trying to be clever'. What else did he expect us to try to be? However, we could have borne the ill-tempered remarks if he had shown us how to improve, and had not mixed his remarks with a mouthful of biscuit which he was continually munching. We were quite glad when he washed the crumbs down with some of the sherry that always stood on the desk for him. One day, to the general astonishment, an essay received high praise and was read aloud to us all.

'How did you manage to get at all that stuff in the time?' we asked the writer of it.

'I copied it straight out of an encyclopaedia, just to see what he would say.'

That was enough, and thenceforth we copied from any book that we could find and took no more trouble with him. Round this man I have since woven an absurd fancy that it was a case of blackmail, put into my head by one of the Sherlock Holmes stories in which a teacher holds his post by this means. Miss Buss blackmailed by a sinister-looking man who drank sherry opens up exciting possibilities.

While this man aroused dislike and contempt, the other produced a boredom that was of a vintage unsurpassed by any that I have tasted since. For the last half-hour (1 to 1.30) every Wednesday the school assembled in hall to hear a sermon from him, preceded by a collect—always the same one, which ever since recalls to me, and probably to hundreds of others, the figure of a tall, thin, long-bearded, dark, cadaverous-looking clergyman, who spoke, all on one note, about Christian Evidences, possibly with the aim of making them so dull that we should never question them again.

During the last period of morning school we could stick to hard work fairly well, but to listen to dreary talk was another matter. Most of us had breakfasted before eight, and it was considerably past two before we could reach home for dinner. Bessie Jones has told me that she used to get back in such an exhausted state that she often had to lie down and rest before she could face her dinner. Well, one day during this sermon ordeal the girl next me fainted. I got her out as quietly as I could to some one who would attend to her, and then returned. When the address was over I was summoned to Miss Buss's presence.

'Why did you take that girl out?' she thundered.

'She fainted. What else could I do?'

'You meant well, my dear, no doubt, but you must never allow a girl to faint.'

When I looked my surprise, she added: 'Once I was in church with a pewful of girls. I noticed that one of them looked like fainting. I leant across to her, shook my fist at her and said: "You *dare* faint." And she didn't.'

The choice of that particular clergyman for our weekly

sermon was the more surprising because Miss Buss seemed
to take great pains to prevent our school-days from being
dull. Exacting and often stupid though the lessons might be,
there was always some little event on the horizon to look forward to. She gave 'at homes' to certain forms now and again,
and the Sixth would give theatrical displays to the Upper
School. But on two occasions in the year the whole school
spread itself for special enjoyment. The merriest and most
care-free day of the year was Foundation Day on April 4th.
Since daffodils are then in season they were chosen as the
school flower, and we were exhorted to bring as many as we
could. The hall, corridors, classrooms—every available space
was smothered in daffodils. How jolly the place looked compared with its usual severity. For in those days there were no
pictures to relieve the blankness of the walls or to distinguish
one room from another. No, that is wrong. In one room
hung an illuminated notice, headed LOST. In pretty and varied
lettering followed the information that there had been lost one
golden hour, studded with sixty ruby minutes, set in sixty
brilliant diamond moments. No reward was offered, for they
were lost for ever. I was driven by some kind of nervous
strain to read this again and again, and how I longed to write
underneath 'Then why mention it?'

Well, on Foundation Day we lost as many minutes as we
liked, and the day before was still better, for several of us
stayed at school to help decorate. We were given plenary dispensation to talk when and where we liked, got into a thorough
mess, and had an uproarious tea together, during which our
austere teachers became as frivolous as ourselves. On the day
itself the school was thrown open to parents and friends, for
whom the main interest was an exhibition of toys made by our
own hands and destined for a children's hospital.

While Foundation Day was mainly a gala for parents and
pupils, the authorities looked upon Prize Day as the more important festival. Miss Buss always managed to secure some
great personage for this—a member of the Royal Family, or a
Church Dignitary, or a Celebrity of some kind. It was a gay

scene. Parents (of prize-winners only) were huddled into the gallery and upper corridor, while the whole school, dressed in the brightest garments possible, white for choice, filled the hall. Tables on the platform were loaded with books, for there was never any stint of prizes. Proceedings began with a speech from Miss Buss, detailing school successes, and then the Grand Person spoke a 'few words'.

During my school career there were three of these ceremonies, and I remember each as though it were yesterday. In my first year (1883) it was the Duchess of Teck who had consented to officiate. That was very grand and pleasant, but had its drawbacks for *us* that the Duchess would never have guessed. For a fortnight beforehand we had a morning drill in the correct method of approaching and receding from Royalty. After Prayers Miss Buss seated herself on her throne to act the part of the Duchess. Each prize-winner had to mount the steps of the platform on one side, approach, make a deep curtsy, receive a book and then retire (rather perilously) backwards to the other side of the platform and descend, without once turning her back on the 'duchess'. Now I had never curtsied in my life, and Miss Buss, with many an impatient 'tchah', made me do it over and over again until I would willingly have foregone my prize to be delivered from this public exposure of my awkwardness. Mother was much amused over my description of it, and since she could curtsy as to the manner born she soon got me into the way of it. How the Duchess would have laughed to see mother and me practising at home.

The great day was very hot, and we were all packed into the hall in good time, so as to be on the safe side, because 'Royalty was always punctual'. But the Duchess was late, Miss Buss showed signs of fluster, and we began to think there had been an accident. At long last there was a stately ushering on to the platform and bowing and smiling. The Duchess was a dear, for she inflicted no speech on us and gave us our prizes without the least observation of our manner of bowing. Mother (in the gallery) was amused to note that my much-practised curtsy ended in a jerk from the waist and a hurried retreat foremost down the platform.

The broad homely accents of Bishop Temple warmed our hearts at a later Prize-giving. He assured us that girls were far cleverer than boys. 'Now my wife,' said he, looking round at Mrs. Temple as she sat nervously brooding over the piles of books she was to distribute, 'always says the right thing at the right moment. As for me, my efforts at speech-making consist of what the French call "staircase wit", or what you wish you had said as you go downstairs afterwards.' Every one must have rejoiced when this most human of bishops went to Canterbury. He deserved the highest honour, if only for his advice to the curates of his diocese. 'In making a sermon,' said he, 'think up a good beginning; then think up a good ending; then bring these two as close together as you can.'

It is absurd how an anecdote will stick for a lifetime when all the uplifting thoughts of a speaker are forgotten. In '84 our celebrity was Roby, of Latin Grammar fame. Perhaps he was none too good at mathematics himself, guessed what the average girl was like in that line, and so, faced by five hundred of them, he chose the following reminiscence (which I remember practically verbatim):

'It was during the Education Commission of '68 that I happened to be in the chair at one of the meetings. Sitting near me was Matthew Arnold, who had recently visited France to investigate the kind of education going on there. He was bubbling over with a New Method they had got. No matter what was on the agenda, he kept referring to it. It was a positively magical way of doing "Rule of Three" sums, called, so he said, the "Unitary Method", and was so simple that not even the dullest could fail to understand it. He explained it so fully to us that we got quite confused, and at last, in desperation at the waste of time I said, "Look here, Arnold, I'll set you a sum, and you *do* it for us by this new method of yours." "Good," said Arnold, "that will be splendid." So I set him a good long one, with plenty of trench-digging and men with

unusual hours (you know the kind, don't you, girls?) and he
retired into a corner of the room with it. We turned to our
business and forgot all about Arnold. In due time we broke
off to go downstairs for a tea interval. Presently a voice was
heard calling over the banisters: "Roby, Roby, is this a *real*
sum?"'

IV

Under Grace

IF the weather during my first term might be described as 'cloudy with bright intervals', one day shortly after the beginning of my second term the sky changed to 'set fair'.

A school official burst into our room and asked in an offhand way, as though expecting no response, 'Has any girl here ever done any Latin?' I put up my hand, the only one, as well as I remember. On further questioning, I admitted having read a good deal of Caesar, two or three books of the *Aeneid*, and some Livy. These points were taken down and the official departed. We were so used to such sudden questionnaires, demanding statistics as to our birth-place, full Christian names, father's initials (if dead, put 'none'), and so on, that I thought no more of it, not even mentioning the incident to mother, the ever eager listener to the smallest items of news.

Next day at the mid-morning interval we were lined up as usual in rows, and indulging in as much talking as we could squeeze into the time while we ate our halfpenny buns, when Miss Buss entered. There was a slight sensation in the ranks, for her presence in the dining-room was unusual, and a stormy petrel. An underling in her wake called out 'Mary Thomas'.

'Now you're for it,' said the girl standing by me. 'What have you been up to?'

'I can't think,' said I, as I started off.

'Mind you stand up to her,' was the parting injunction.

Miss Buss was evidently in one of her unpleasant moods. But I was fairly comfortable in my conscience and looked her full in the eye.

'What was your last school?' she barked at me.

'Oh, only a private school,' said I in a deprecatory tone as an attempt at delicate flattery.

'What is its *name*, I said. Answer my question.'

I gave her the name, but it obviously conveyed no idea to her, and I wondered why she wanted to know it. Then she shot at me almost venomously:

'How long have you been learning Latin?'

'I can't remember. Mother began me when I was about six, and I have been doing it off and on ever since, chiefly with my brother.' Then something in her expression gave me the clue to her ill-temper and induced me to add 'Not much at the school'.

At this a look of relief crossed her face and she visibly relaxed, but pulled herself up again, glared at me for a moment or two in silence and then snapped out:

'Go back to your place.'

'What was the matter?' was the inquiry of my neighbours in the line.

'Nothing much. She only wanted to know the name of my last school, and exactly how long I had been learning Latin, just to fill in some of those eternal forms, I expect.'

On our return to the classroom I was ordered to take the books out of my desk and go to the Upper Fifth. This must mean a sudden 'remove', and staggering mentally under the idea and physically under the books I made my way to the room that was actually next-door to the Sixth! Here I was cordially welcomed by the form mistress and helped quite graciously to a vacant desk. A lesson was in progress on the derivation of French words. I found this amusing, for it was quite a new idea to me that other countries had 'derivations' for their words. I gained much kudos from being able to contribute several Latin words in the accusative, which appeared to be in great demand. Towards the end of the morning one of my new comrades was told off to show me what the home-work would be for the next day. I went home on the wings of an eagle, giving mother the full dramatic scene as I ate my dinner.

She and I turned with anxiety to examine the new home-work, and found it difficult in some ways, but not beyond our joint efforts. Mother came out strong over a tricky bit of French composition, and the exhilaration of my 'remove' made everything seem fun to us. The mere look of the Cicero text (lent me for the day) was like the rattling of spears to the war-horse. 'Bless you, mother,' said I, 'for having started me in Latin so early, for that's what got me my move.'

The next day I felt more at ease and able to look round the room. The sight that attracted me more than any other was a girl with a mass of red-gold hair and, whenever I caught her eye, a jolly smile. We gravitated to one another in the lunch interval, and exchanged our names and gossip. This Mary Wood had known no other school, had been under Miss Buss since childhood, and thought everything perfect. She had reached the Upper Fifth as she said, 'in a proper and orderly way, not like you "by the earthquake".' I was glad she knew her *Alice*, and we soon found many books and tastes in common. When I demurred to so many rules all over the place, she told me that it was nothing to what they endured in the lower part of the school. Here a wooden instrument called a 'clacker' was in use for giving commands—to stand, put pencils down, 'hands away', pass out, and so on. It was used even for punctuation in a dictation exercise: one clack, a comma; two clacks, a semicolon; three, a colon; four, a full-stop. I had heard this clacker clacking in the distance and had wondered what it was. But I gathered that as one went up the school the discipline was relaxed bit by bit, and to my relief I found that learning daily portions of poetry was not required in the Upper Fifth.

There was an announcement one morning that Mary Wood was to have a day's absence for a sister's wedding, and would some one volunteer to send her the particulars of home-work by post? I immediately offered, and stepped up to my new-found friend to get her address. Only recently, while writing this book, I recalled this incident to her, and she said, 'Yes, indeed I remember it well, and the angry tears I shed at being obliged to stay away from school for even that one day.' Surely the oddest of reasons for tears at a wedding.

When the half-term holiday came mother asked me whether I would like to invite a schoolfellow to tea.

'Very much,' said I. 'There are lots of jolly girls, only I have no idea where any of them live.' Then suddenly remembering that I had Mary Wood's address in my note-book, I looked it up and decided that it couldn't be very far, for it was in Camden Road itself. So off I started to fetch her. But Camden Road seemed to stretch endlessly, and the numbers on one side bore no relation to those on the other. I persevered until I reached No. 267, and found it to be an imposing house with a large garden. Rather shyly I knocked at the door, little thinking how often I should come to it, how dear all its inmates were to become to me, and how I should be married from it.

Mary was more than willing to come back to tea with me, and insisted on bringing her shoes to change, in spite of my assurances that our family didn't mind mud. Mother was much struck with this bit of thoughtfulness, and took a great liking to Mary at once. There was a special tea for us, and Mary was delighted with the boys' study, and Charles's pictures and our family magazine. Thus began a friendship of over fifty years between our families, that has had no break nor even suspension.

§ 2

On the very first day of the next term we were informed that there were two vacancies in the Sixth, and the official added, 'Mary Wood and Mary Thomas, take your books and go.' Almost helpless with excitement and nervousness we stood laden with our books outside the sacred door of Room No. 1. 'You go in first', we exclaimed simultaneously, and pushing each other forward we fell in together, for the door had given way unexpectedly, and our books were scattered over the floor. The form mistress, Mrs. Bryant, was much amused and made some reassuring remark about such an energetic entry being a good omen.

From that first moment we found the atmosphere entirely

different from that of the rest of the school. We were privileged beings and felt that the whole place belonged to us. We were expected to behave properly, for, as Dr. Abbott said of his own Sixth, we were under Grace and not under the Law. Or, as Mrs. Bryant pointed out to us, the attitude of 'liking what you do' comes to the same thing as 'doing what you like'.

And certainly we did like what we had to do. We were considered capable of discussions in class and having opinions of our own. The history specialist made the subject quite a new thing to us, all about people who really lived, and 'policies' that acted or didn't act. As her Christian name was Sara she was dubbed 'the divine Sara', not so much in fun as in genuine admiration.

Our main comic relief was provided by a weekly French lesson. The grammar was assumed to have been 'done', and the chief business was conversation, carried on almost entirely by Mademoiselle herself, punctuated by *oui, oui* from us. A terror in the lower forms, to us she was just a lovable old thing. I think she was of a great age, for she wore a black wig, with grey hairs showing beneath it, and was extremely wrinkled. She liked teaching the Sixth, for there she could unbend without fear of disorder. Coming along the hall she would herald her approach to the room with shrill cries of 'Qui est-ce qui parle? Qui est-ce qui rit?' On entering she would throw up her hands in feigned amazement as she saw (what she expected) my broad grin—'Hélas! c'est la petite Miss Thomas!'

Her one bit of serious work was a *dictée*, in which we had far more words wrong than right, but that didn't seem to surprise or worry her. At the close she would say 'Qui veut épeler?' and always picked me out, no matter how many others offered. I stood by her desk, facing the class, and spelt out the French letters without any pause.

'Doucement, doucement, petite', she would insist every now and again, grasping my arm as if putting on the brake. Pretending to think that this meant 'softly', I lowered my voice still more every time she repeated it, but still went as fast as breath permitted—much to the joy of the class. When I looked

round panting and triumphant at the end, her face was always
wreathed in fatuous smiles. I think now that this was the only
approach to a joke that she obtained from her stolid English
pupils, although she assured us that the *dictée* was always a droll
anecdote.

Indeed, with nearly all the teachers I enjoyed something of
the privilege of a court jester, for not only did I look absurdly
young for my seventeen years, but I had my hair cropped like
a boy's instead of being 'done up' like nearly all the others, and
my famous dress came only to my knees.

It was in the Latin work that I felt the greatest advantage
from my move. In the Upper Fifth the teacher had kept a crib
on her lap for even the syntax sentences, and we were not
allowed any variety of rendering. A fair copy placed boldly
on the desk would have been respectable, but a crib on the
lap, hidden (supposedly) by the desk, was quite another thing.
Now in the Sixth we encountered a Classic mistress who was
a mental aristocrat. She seemed not only superior socially to
the bulk of the staff, but she knew her subject, and, more
remarkable still, she knew the business of teaching. She might
have stepped straight out of a public school or a tutor's room
at the university. When we made a howler she just stopped in
her tracks and looked bewildered: 'Surely, Mary, you would
not use the indicative there? Of course . . . Have you any
precedent for it?' Slips in gender and such trifles she treated
with the polite disregard one would mete out to a coffee-spill
at table—quick remedy with no fuss. She certainly, more than
any one else, gave the Collegiate touch that justified the title
of the school. She was the daughter of the R.A., who had
executed the medallion of the Princess of Wales, and no doubt
her artistic upbringing had heightened the effect of her natural
good looks and vivacity. Meeting an old schoolfellow the other
day I asked what she remembered of the school. 'Nothing,'
was her reply. ' I can recall nothing except my admiration for
Miss Armstead; we used to watch what she had on, because
she dressed in such good style.'

More attractive to some of us was Mrs. Bryant, who was by

no means a clear teacher, but had the rare quality of inspiring us to work and think things out for ourselves. With her Irish sense of humour and kindly sympathy she gave a good balance to the masterful spirit of Miss Buss. Now and again, too, she would give us glimpses of her subversive political views. We had in the form a girl from Ulster, conservative to the bone, and it was very pretty to see a passage of arms between her and Mrs. Bryant, all the more entertaining because neither dared to be entirely outspoken. The spirit of *camaraderie* that existed in the Sixth between teachers and taught was quite a new thing to me, and all the delightful dreams with which I first approached the school were more than fulfilled.

The autumn term was to end with the Cambridge Locals. This was a different business from my Senior Oxford of the year before. A mere pass was nothing. Scholarships were awarded to the girls who got the highest places, and we aimed at distinctions. The scholarships took the form of remission of school fees. Now it chanced that my aunt Tony was in one of her low-water periods, owing to the vagaries of the price of tin, and although she would have screwed out the money somehow for me, mother and I were determined that she should not be allowed to. I knew, therefore, that I must win one of those scholarships or leave, and the competition was severe. Mrs. Bryant said years afterwards that we were the best Sixth she ever had. Anxiety, however, could not sit on me, and I gave myself up to the exhilaration and amusement of the whole proceedings.

The school presented so many candidates for Junior and Senior that it was a Centre in itself, and 'Cambridge Week' was an annual festival. The desks in the Hall were provided with inkwells, pens, clips, heaps of lovely new paper, and, of course, the dividing boards to prevent cheating. All candidates were required to sign a solemn declaration that during the examination week they would open no school-book, visit no friends or place of entertainment, go to bed at nine, and take the school dinner every day.

Easy—all except the last item. No doubt it was well to

ensure that every one had a substantial meal, but it was the fly in the ointment for me. Substantial that school dinner undoubtedly was. Instead of mother's home-made pasties or dainty sandwiches I had to face pieces of meat (animal unknown) swimming in straw-coloured water, with two soapy potatoes and a lump of warm greens, followed by a slab of suet pudding with treacle. The girl next to me on the first day had had previous experience of these meals, and had come prepared. On her lap she had spread a sheet of paper, and ever and anon she would transfer to it a lump of the pudding. She told me that it got bigger in her throat and swallow it she could not. 'I don't mean to try,' said I, and sat back. Presently an official bore down upon me.

'You must eat your pudding, dear; it's a rule of the school that nothing must be left on the plate.'

'But I can't bear those bits of suet that seem to ooze out and look at you; and I loathe treacle.'

'Then you should not have taken it, dear.'

'Well, they planked it down in front of me without a word; but thank you for telling me what to do. To-morrow I will refuse it.'

I was fortunate enough to be able to carry out this plan, and supplement the meat course with apples and pears provided by mother, eaten in secrecy and shared with my neighbour of the paper-scheme. I say 'fortunate', for if my refusal had come to the ears of Miss Buss there would have been an unpleasant time for me. Let alone fainting, she would not permit any symptom of illness or even weakness anywhere. Her demand for endurance and self-control was carried to a cruel extreme. Coughing was strictly forbidden, and small tortures were endured by both teachers and pupils in their efforts to prevent it. One morning I put a little handkerchief round my throat, as it was slightly sore. It met the eagle eye of Miss Buss. 'Sore throat! What nonsense!' she exclaimed, and pulled it from me. Any suggestion, therefore, that a girl couldn't eat what was put before her would have set the school rocking. I am inclined to think that the official who upbraided me preferred to keep the matter to herself, for in a big storm no one knew who would get the blame.

Among the minor pleasures of life few can equal the excitement of being presented with a fresh examination paper, when you feel at home in the subject. Our set play was *Henry V*, full of pleasant associations with my father, who used to read to us the glorious brush between Fluellen and Pistol, giving us the Welsh intonation. And quite recently the bombastic speeches had been made lively for me by Mrs. Bryant. It was not her subject, but one morning she had undertaken to hear some of the memory work, and it fell to me to declaim 'Once more unto the breach'. I had hardly begun when she said 'Louder'. I started again. 'Louder' said she, in the same quiet tone. I started again. 'Surely Mary you can speak more loudly than that?' Well, thought I, she shall jolly well have it, and I rolled forth the words with all the strength of my lungs, expecting to be immediately hushed, for the noise must have penetrated into the hall. But there sat Mrs. Bryant, smiling and nodding approval, and the whole class looked round at me as I warmed to the work, and when I roared forth 'God for Harry, England, and St. George' they all clapped.

Full, then, of the play and its delights, what was my dismay to see the first question: 'Give the action of the play.' Just that, with no illuminating chat about it. I had not the remotest notion what it meant. Action seemed to mean 'doing', and all through the play they were doing something. I let it go and devoted myself to the explanation of queer words and contexts that examiners seem to like.

The writing of an essay under examination stress is always a severe trial. But Tom had given me two good hints: always choose the dullest looking subject, because the examiner will be so bored with the others that he will be grateful for the change; and then think up your two opening paragraphs, and scrap the first one, which is naturally dull. The subject 'Names' looked the dullest on the list, so I chose that. My first paragraph was to the effect that names threw a light on the history of the people, my second was to illustrate this by Cornish names. So I scrapped the first and went straight to Cornwall, pointing out the effect of the Wesleyan revival on the names. I made great play with an old miner called Mahershallalhashbaz, always known as 'Lal'. And I made up a good deal else, reflecting that the comfort of an examination essay lies in the fact that you cannot be pressed for evidence of your statements.

I was one of the very few who took Drawing, and they set a grilling test—to draw a chessboard with four men on it. It sounds much easier than it is. But after all, my only real dread was the Arithmetic. Little hope was held out by the form at large that I should get through. 'Concentrate,' they all advised me, 'on one or two that you *can* do, and make sure that they are correct.' The paper was even worse than I had imagined, full of talkative sums telling you to neglect brokerage and things like that. But one stood out in simple honesty—a very long row of figures whose cube root had to be found. Now in my private school we had been shown how to do this by putting 300 on the left, 30 underneath it, and 3 underneath that. It made a pleasing pattern, and by patient attention to detail (which escapes me now) the answer unfolded itself in due course on the right-hand side. It would take time, I knew, but I went doggedly at it, and it came out! I fancy the examiner must have had a bit of a surprise, for I have never met any one since who could do this trick. When I told Mrs. Bryant of my triumph she exclaimed, 'Mary, you *never* did!' Then she added, 'I hope it has pulled you through, for if you have passed you shall begin mathematics with me next term.'

The joy of saying good-bye to arithmetic was tempered by fear of the unknown. What if mathematics should turn out to be worse? The completely unknown is never so fearful as the partially known. At my private school we had 'begun a little algebra'. This involved spending some two hours a week in turning complicated arrangements of letters into figures, with preliminary notes that a stood for 5, b for 7, c for 3, and so on. When the turning was done we added and subtracted as required and got an answer. One day I asked the teacher why they bothered to use these letters when figures were just as good, and there were plenty of them. She told me I was impertinent.

My brother Dym was at home for the Christmas holidays, and as he knew all about mathematics I confided my fear to him, saying that as far as I could see algebra seemed to be a great fuss over nothing.

'Fuss over nothing!' he cried. 'Why, it's simply glorious. You'll never want to do anything by arithmetic when once you've smelt algebra.'

Never had I ever wanted to do anything by arithmetic, and was relieved to hear that it could be done without.

'Look here,' said he, 'I'll show you how useful algebra can be, even when you know very little of it.' And seizing a book he opened it at some problems, passing over with a gesture of contempt all the torturings of letters in the early chapters. Then he introduced to me the meaning of an equation, 'only a balance', and x as only the answer before you had got it. The questions about people's ages, price of pounds of tea, time taken to get anywhere—he worked them in a twinkling. It was sheer magic. Amused at my enthusiasm, he promised to give me a lesson every day. 'Just a little algebra and a little Euclid, so that you shan't go back to school a perfect blank.'

By the time the new year had set in I could solve any simple equation, however long and involved, by merely applying Dym's three steps: (1) Clear of brackets and fractions; (2) Collect all x on the left; (3) Divide by the coefficient of x.

But I soon perceived that it was the *making* of the equations that was the real difficulty, when you were faced by a long problem, and I asked Dym if he had any simple tricks in this line.

'No. For that you must use your common sense, if girls have such a thing. But I'll give you a tip that will carry you through a great deal: never forget that space equals velocity multiplied by time, and that the area of a triangle is half the height multiplied by the base.'

Geometry gave me little trouble because you could see what was happening. It was only when they proved the too obvious

that my reason tottered, as in that nightmare business of showing that one line standing on another makes two right angles,
or else enough to make two. Dym, seeing my misery, said I
might skip that, and I got on swimmingly enough through
Book I. I was impatient for term to begin. 'Just for a last
treat,' said Dym, 'I'll show you a funny thing. Do you think
you could draw a circle through any three points I chose to
give you?'

'Of course not. How absurd. Why, I might put two of
them here on the study table, and the third at the North Pole.
You said "anywhere", you know.'

'Quite, I shouldn't mind,' and fetching out a big sheet of
brown paper and spreading it on the floor he said, 'Now put
your three points wherever you like.'

When I had placed them as nastily as I could I watched him,
entranced. 'Quite easy, you see, but you won't get to that
until the Third Book.'

Then the blow fell. Results of the Cambridge Locals were
out. No, I had not failed, I was among the top girls qualifying
for a scholarship, and had got three distinctions, one in Latin.
But there was a little after-note from the school secretary: 'We
regret to tell you that your daughter cannot receive a scholarship since she has not been the regulation time in the school
(two years).'

'Well, dear,' said mother, 'I'm afraid you must leave. But
I think that as you have done so well they will probably allow
you to leave without exacting the fees for the next half-term,
which seem to be required if you go without notice. I shall
go and see Miss Buss about it.'

I suppose the sight of my face made mother start at once,
and she was back again much sooner than I expected, since
I knew the difficulties of approach to Miss Buss.

'It's all right, darling, you are to go next term' were her
first words before I had got the front door fully open, and
then, 'Your Miss Buss is a marvellous woman.'

What happened at that interview I never entirely discovered,
but from the scraps that mother conceded from time to time

I had curious glimpses of the two women, both of whom were accustomed to being treated with subservience and dread by their inferiors. Apparently the two Victorians immediately understood one another and entered into one another's special difficulties. Mother had been shown in at once, and the matter of the scholarship was dismissed in a few words: 'Of course Mary shall have the scholarship; we have a fund to meet such cases.' Then I fancy that mother must have thanked her very warmly, spoken highly of the school and of all that it had meant to me, and among other things said:

'What a delightful type of girl you have here!'

'Oh, *have* I!' exclaimed Miss Buss. 'You should see some of them! Mary's friends are the pick of the school.' Here some confidences followed that mother didn't pass on to me, but I guessed why certain girls who were rather noisy on the railway journey had mysteriously disappeared. The interview ended with Miss Buss embracing mother and saying, 'Mary is our link.'

At tea-time that day, when the episode was related to my brothers they showed great pleasure at my good fortune, but unanimously agreed that the 'fund' was no other than an invention of the moment on the part of Miss Buss.

'But she told me,' said mother, 'that an old pupil, now very well off, and grateful for all that the school had done for her, had given a sum of money to enable any girl who was hard up to stay on for an extra year.'

'A very clever touch,' laughed Tom. 'Miss Buss has the tongue of the ready liar.'

Quite shocked, I said: 'She would never tell a direct lie like that!'

'Oh, wouldn't she though,' said Tom. 'From all you say of her, she's far too good a sort to boggle at a little thing like that.'

I never heard all that passed in that fateful interview, but some time afterwards mother told me that Miss Buss had said, 'You won't keep Mary long.' This seemed to both of us supremely funny. And a curious by-product of mother's visit was that whenever Miss Buss came across me in a corridor or on the stairs she would envelop me in an enormous hug. A group of girls who once witnessed this pretended to be alarmed —'We thought little Molly Thomas was gone for good.'

§ 3

I began that spring term in the highest spirits, wondering especially what might befall me in the mathematics line. In the usual bustle of rearrangement of divisions there was some hesitation as to where I should be placed, as there were no other actual beginners. But for the first morning Mrs. Bryant said I might as well come along into her division 'as a visitor' until a better niche could be found for me.

'Just sit with the others for to-day, Mary, and we will see what can be done to help you. I am glad to hear that your brother has been giving you a few lessons.' She smiled on me encouragingly, and then announced that they were about to attack Book III, adding in an aside to me that it would be quite beyond me, but that I could just listen.

'We will begin the subject of circles with a nice little problem. Can any one tell me how to draw a circle through *anny* three points?' (Her Irish pronunciation of 'any' made it seem extremely wide.) So saying, she planted three reckless points on the board and sat down to await replies. Puzzled looks everywhere, incredulous smiles, shakings of head, and my heart beating with excitement. Emboldened by the silence I held up my hand.

'No, no, Mary dear, you keep quiet, this is quite beyond you.'

'Yes, but I've got an idea how it could be done.'

'Well then, since no one else has a glimmering, you can come up and have a try.'

Walking up to the board amid the indulgent smiles of the class, I took the chalk and said:

'I think I should begin by joining up the points.'

'Good, so far. Do it.'

Having done this I stepped back for consideration and then,

'Next I should find the middle of each of these two lines.'

'Good!' exclaimed Mrs. Bryant, and the whole class leaned forward. After further consideration I ventured:

'I should draw lines upright from these middles.'

'Yes, yes, the proper word is perpendicular,' put in Mrs. Bryant eagerly.

'Then you see, where they meet would do for the centre of the circle.' Hands were now waving in the class, so I retired to my seat and left the proof to them.

That was a lucky coincidence, but it had its unlucky side, for I was expected to go on all right without any extra indulgence. But I thoroughly enjoyed the struggles over riders, and as for algebra, Bessie Jones was good at it and a tower of strength to weaker ones. A special charm of the Sixth was the licence we had to help one another. We could be trusted not to ask or give injudicious help, and marks were no longer of great importance. Consequently there was a general atmosphere of friendliness amongst us all, and a readiness to pool our resources. One of our number, however, was too unnaturally clever to be a great favourite. She knew every fact, could recall it at will, and use it to the best advantage. Once I remember she was dumb during a very interesting discussion of some question in history. In the cloakroom later she said to me, 'I knew a lot more about that business in India that Miss Burstall was discussing with us.'

'Why didn't you bring it out then?'

'I had been reading an article on it in the *Nineteenth* and knew several points that she didn't.'

'How splendid,' said I, 'but why didn't you bring them out?'

'I didn't want the others to know, because they'll come in useful for the examination.'

A better example than this could hardly be found of the evils of competitive work. Fortunately the bulk of the prizes in the school were 'standard' ones, that is, they were awarded to all who attained a certain percentage of marks. But a few were competitive, special prizes awarded on the result of an examination. Now to this girl, Emily, marks and prizes seemed to be meat and drink. She always got every possible standard prize and usually the competitive ones, too. On Prize Day she used to stagger off the platform steadying the pile with her chin. As long as it was standard work she was able and willing to help any lame dog, and we were all proud of her attainments. There was a rumour that she could repeat the names of all the Popes, and backwards, too, if necessary. In short, she was our show piece.

One of the subjects for a special prize was Political Economy, with which I was fascinated. I taught mother all about rack-rents and diminishing returns, and between us we demolished every fallacy we could lay hands on. I got her to cut out illustrative paragraphs from the newspaper to paste in my note-book. Lessons with Mrs. Bryant were full of excited argument, and we all looked forward with pleasant confidence to see what the examiner could possibly ask that we didn't know. I may add that the few 'laws' still lingering in my memory have all been exploded now. This prize was the only one I ever worked for, and I was one of the favourites for the race. On the eve of the trial my backers gathered round me with the request: 'For goodness' sake, Molly, do come out top, we are so tired of seeing Emily getting everything.' I needed no urging, and felt like a Derby jockey being encouraged by the shouts of the crowd. The paper was an interesting one, and I felt to have floored it quite comfortably. Sitting back a few minutes before the end I glanced at Emily, who happened to be at the next desk, separated by the usual board. To my dismay she was still writing feverishly, and sure enough she beat me by four marks. Looking back half a century I am amused to think how much sweeter to me was the disappointment of the Field than any prize could have been.

I did once try for a holiday prize, but it was not competitive. Books were lavishly given to girls who did anything in the holidays, so great an evil was mere idleness considered. Mary Wood and I were looking at the list before the holidays and saw 'Needlework Prize'.

'Let's go in for that,' said Mary.

'Me! Needlework!'

'But look, there's a choice, you can make either a frock or a chemise. Surely even you could do a chemise?'

'Well, after all our Dorcas times I *could* do *that*.'

So we entered our names, she for a frock and I for a chemise. Since there was a regulation that the work must be unaided, I couldn't ask mother how much material to buy or how to cut it out. I guessed at the quantity of stuff, and imagined that cutting out must be quite simple; after all a chemise hasn't much shape, and you just cut it out. Laying the material fully out on the study table I slashed away with confidence, and showed the result to mother with some pride.

'I'm afraid, darling,' was her comment, 'that you haven't allowed for turnings. It will be a very small garment.'

Indeed it seemed to get smaller and smaller, for I had to keep cutting off bits to make both sides alike; but I put exquisite work into the actual sewing, literally spilling blood in my fervour. Charles's comment was pointed when he saw the small result, 'For the future, I take it?'

I managed to wash off the marks of blood, wrapped my treasure in tissue paper, and then in brown, tied it up firmly and gave it in. Mary arrived at school *in* her holiday task, a pretty brown woollen frock. When I told the boys they said what a good thing for me it was that such a test as appearing in it could not be applied to my chemise. Anyhow I won the prize, and chose Brachet's *French Dictionary*, which is a constant witness to my sons that I could sew once.

§ 4

Although we were all very friendly together in the Sixth, Mary Wood's was the only house that I visited. She and I used to spend any half-term or odd holiday together, she with me and my brothers or I with her and her sisters. I had no sister, she no brother, so it fitted well, and all through life she has been more of a sister to me than any one else. We were never very emotional in our friendship, and that is perhaps why it wore so well. Her people came from Shetland, and that always seemed romantic to me. Her mother used to tell me of the ways of the country people there, and these had the same tang of reality that we had in Cornwall. The inhabitants of Lerwick, she said, are not at all Scottish, but speak a mixture of English and Norsk. When my aunt Tony was staying with us she hailed Mary ecstatically:

'Why, my dear child, you are thoroughly Norsk—the shape of your head, your peculiar type of golden hair, yes, and your ready laugh.' It was a disappointment to Tony that Mary could not speak Norsk, for they could have conversed together —the rarest of treats for Tony.

Of Mary's sisters I was rather in awe. The eldest was an artist who exhibited regularly in the Academy; but she was very jolly to us younger ones and amused us with acting and reciting. Another sister had been to Girton and was reading for a medical degree, and to this day I have not quite overcome my original fear of her. Mary also had a twin sister, whose chief ambition was to leave school and pursue her art studies. She never expressed the least interest in any school subject, having remained in the same slough of despond into which I fell on my first arrival, although (by some scholastic hydraulic pressure) she reached one of the Fifth Forms. But for the grace of God, I thought, or rather for my mother's starting me in Latin, there goes Mary Thomas.

The person I ought to have been frightened of was their father. But I have never felt alarmed at a man, and although Mr. Wood was in aspect and manner quite forbidding, I took great delight in him, and I think he was surprised and amused to find any one to treat him so cavalierly. Full of fierceness and severity of criticism, especially against radicals and nonconformists, he would break his brooding silence at any moment with some caustic remark. At breakfast, buried behind *The Times*, he would read out a bit of the less cheerful news here and there. If Gladstone's name occurred he would mutter in brackets, 'Damned old scoundrel'. One morning, in a specially morose mood, he read out to the family the statistics of the inmates of the workhouses: so many agricultural labourers, so many bank-clerks, so many plasterers. . . . Seeing the gloom round the table deepening, I broke in:

'Does it say how many barristers?'

At this he ran his eye over the list again, looked solemnly at me over his spectacles and replied, 'I see no mention of them. The truth is that there are so many that they gave up counting them'; and then he added that his net income during the past year had been fourpence-halfpenny.

When I was spending a week-end there he would take Mary and me to the Temple on Sunday morning, and before Service would take us into his chambers at No. 1 Hare Court. These were on the ground-floor and looking into the old court. Everything here had a peculiar attraction for me—the portraits of famous judges on the walls, the rows of Law books on the shelves, the musty aroma of the room, and, above all, the scope for imagination of all the fateful conferences and decisions that went on in 'chambers'. I made up my mind that if ever I married it must be to a barrister, little thinking that by sheer coincidence that very room was to be my husband's.

Mr. Wood's dislike of nonconformity was very much the same as my father's—an objection to anything openly per-fervid in the religious line, but unlike my father he fell in with the Victorian custom of assembling the family and servants for prayers every evening. They were conducted in the same off-hand style in which he used to look into his hat for a few moments before the Service in the Temple. We read round a verse each of the Bible, during which my interest was absorbed in watching for Libby's trouble with difficult words. Then followed a few short prayers, mumbled so hastily that I had the impression of his being ashamed to bother the Almighty and that he was hoping not to secure attention. A little girl on a visit there had been warned to be very quiet during the proceedings, and in the middle we heard a shocked whisper, 'Mamma naughty bo nose'.

Libby had been their cook for untold years, and seemed to rule the entire establishment. Her name was the children's corruption of Elizabeth, and with them she remained to her dying day. Mary and Ursula (her twin sister) and I were not considered old enough to be present at the family evening dinner, and had supper by ourselves in the study; but Libby would always sail in with some tit-bits for us, such as gooseberry-fool or lemon-sponge. We could also make a raid on the kitchen at any time, and be sure of good sustenance from an over-indulgent Libby. The housemaid had also been with them from babyhood, for there were stories of her sternness in giving the twins their bath, allowing no splashing till the end, when she would exclaim, 'Now waller'. Her standard of morality was high and she never laughed, while Libby, a devotee of Spurgeon, would break into joyful smiles on any provocation, and I gave her plenty.

§ 5

During the summer holidays of '84, mother decided that I looked in need of a change. We hadn't been able to afford an excursion from home for two years, and she said we would have a bit of sea air now, whether we could afford it or not. She had heard that rooms could be had at a little place near Walton-on-the-Naze, called Clacton. The name sounded comic, like something in Dickens, and far from aristocratic, mother thought. The look of the place appalled us when we walked out of the station. Bare. A few houses were trying to look as if they were in streets here and there, with encouraging names put up. Leaving our luggage at the station we set forth to look for lodgings, and soon found some, with a view of the sea. Indeed, the sea had nothing to hide it from any of the houses. We engaged our rooms, told the landlady that we would have our luggage sent up, and then added that we should 'lunch out', so as not to trouble her at once. At this she looked a little surprised, but said nothing.

'Now, Molly dear,' said Mother as we stepped forth briskly, 'let us look for some nice confectioner's.'

We made for the commercial centre of Clacton, and certainly

found a few shops—a butcher's, a fancy shop, a greengrocer's, an ironmonger's with some pink and white crockery ware, and some other nondescript shops, but the nearest approach to a confectioner's was a small baker's stocked with loaves and some weary looking jam tarts. After these the town seemed to cease and we were getting into 'country' and half-made streets again. We looked at one another in dismay, for it was long past 2 o'clock and we were violently hungry. Presently, at a corner of two of the projected roads I detected another thing that might be a shop. It had little red curtains and some uncooked chops laid out.

'Let's try in here,' said I. 'At all events there are some chops that they could cook for us.'

We were told that we could have the 'Farmers' Ordinary', and were given seats at a table with a sort of cloth laid. As it was rather late we were the only customers, and almost immediately there was brought a plate of food each. I had no idea that the Potteries made such enormous plates. Even so, the huge slices of beef fell over the edge. Potatoes, cabbage, and Yorkshire pudding were ranged around in decent plenty, while the whole was awash with rich gravy. 'If this is a farmer's ordinary,' said I, 'what must be his extraordinary?' How we laughed as we picked bits here and there and found it really good; and indeed it would have been princely if there hadn't been so much of it. What was our astonishment to find the charge only 10*d*. each. This is the meal I picture whenever I see 'Good pull-up for carmen'.

We did not patronize the circulating library, for we had brought with us for evenings or wet weather a most exciting book, called *Progress and Poverty*, by Henry George, lent to me by Mrs. Bryant. His main point was that since the sea and air were free for everybody, so also should be the land. He was indignant at the preservation of fish by the landlords. Why should it be theirs? Does a salmon carry a label addressed to the landlord 'with the compliments of the Almighty?' I forget all the rest, but remember my conviction that nationalization of the land was so obviously just that no doubt George's views would be put into force at once. Mother was not quite so hopeful on this point and seemed to think that it might take some time to carry out the idea.

What with our long tramps and our dip in the sea every morning before breakfast, we grew strong and brown and even a bit fatter. We returned after our fortnight to London to find Charles rather excited. He had left Ireland, where prospects were none too good, and had already secured a post at a school in Bedford, where he was to teach nothing but drawing and music. I little thought what difference that new post would make both to him and to me.

V

Maesta Abeo

§ 1

MOTHER and I had a little shock at the end of the summer holidays of 1884, on realizing that in October I should be eighteen. It was the buff form for the renewal of my season ticket that brought home the unpleasant fact. Beyond this age you were not allowed the scholar's half-price. While mother was exclaiming 'Fancy your being eighteen, and you hardly look fifteen!' I was thinking what a dreadful waste of money the full fare would be.

'I tell you what, mother, I'll *walk* to school.'

'Oh no, dear, you can't possibly.'

'Yes, I can. Lots of the girls come from long distances, and all I should have to do would be down Grange Road, through a bit of St. Paul's Road, along Holloway Road, and up Camden Road. I walked it one day with Tom, to show him where the school was.'

Mother was wavering, and then suddenly saw a bright side. 'I've got an idea,' she said. 'I always take a long walk some time in the day. I can easily go with you most of the way, or all of it, and then come home by any new ways I can find. Anyhow, we could try it and see.'

Except in really forbidding weather, that is what she did for the last year of my school days. Those walks were a real enjoyment to both of us, for she entered with zest into every detail of my work, and I was able to point out to her several of the girls and teachers of whom I had talked. She had a quick eye, too, for anything amusing that we came across during our tramp, and best of all she managed to see beauties in the clouds and shadows and perspective of the streets and buildings, translating everything into terms of her water-colour box. I think she was never bored when out alone. But I didn't leave her entirely alone when I went into school. When Charles returned from Ireland for good he brought back to Canonbury with him his much-loved Irish terrier, to whom he had given the absurdly grandiose name of 'Trevor'. On going to Bedford he had left Trevor in my keeping, since I had grown very fond of the dog and had taken him on all my walks in the neighbourhood. If ever I missed him I never worried, for he would always turn up in his own good time. So, of course, he went with us every morning on our walk to the school, and was jumping about in eager anticipation as soon as we got up from breakfast. And as I turned into school I liked to hear mother's cheery 'Come along, Trevor'.

On the rare occasions when mother was prevented from coming, Trevor would trot along beside me and beguile the way by making various investigations and bringing reports to me. At any point *en route* if I looked at him and said firmly 'Home' he would at once turn tail and trot back. I seldom took him the whole distance, but generally dismissed him at the Athenaeum, just before the last lap to school.

I found mother rather perturbed one day when I reached home as usual at about half-past two. Trevor had not arrived. She had been watching in the window, but——

'Oh, he'll be all right,' said Tom. 'Where did you see him last, Molly?'

'At the Athenaeum, about nine o'clock, when I told him to go home.'

'Then I'll find him,' said Tom, and started off. By tea-time he had returned with Trevor. He had found him lying quite patiently on the steps of the Athenaeum, and, of course, we never knew what had caused this break in his routine. It was in the following year that I took him out for a walk not far from Canonbury Park, missed him, but returned home, expecting him to turn up later. We never saw him again, and could never solve the mystery, for he had a collar, and was not valuable enough to be stolen.

The chief drawback to the no-train situation was the walk

back after school. I couldn't get away before about twenty minutes to two, and was too fagged to have pleasant mental occupation along the horribly familiar Holloway Road. I had Mary Wood's company for the first bit of the way, and used to cajole her to come a little farther, 'just to see the time by the Athenaeum clock'. This clock was painted a dark blue, as though to prevent its being seen, and this suited me because it involved Mary's having to come close up to it to see the time. Not, of course, that either of us wanted to know the time, but it was a good excuse for my having Mary's company for a few minutes longer. After that I had nothing to distract my mind from my craving for dinner. The halfpenny mid-morning bun had lost its effect and Holloway Road stretched endlessly. One of those days I remember absurdly vividly: Mary couldn't come on to the Athenaeum because there were friends to lunch and she had to get home at once. As I went up to her front door to say good-bye there floated through to me the smell of roast duck. No nearer approach to a barmecide feast has ever come my way.

One day I indulged in a tram along Holloway Road, so impatient was I to get home.

'You are back very early, darling. Have you been expelled or something? I'll have your dinner hurried up!'

'I'm so excited, mother; I've been made a prefect. We had an election this morning. We were all given slips of paper with the names of all the form, and we had to cross out all except the ones we chose, so that no one could tell who voted for which. There was a long talk beforehand, telling us not to choose our favourites, but the ones who would be best for the whole school.'

'But why the whole school?'

'You see, prefects are not like the mere form monitors, they help to keep the discipline all over the school at all times, and they wear a special badge with blue ribbon.'

That was about all I knew at first, but gradually I found that the prefects were a real power in the place. It was no doubt from the example of Arnold of Rugby that Miss Buss sought to govern her school and set its tone through their agency. Influence rather than power was what she chiefly desired; there was to be no 'Jack in office' spirit; and although the prefects had full power to order any girl to sign, I can remember no instance of their exercising this power. How fully I now realized the distress of Mary Worley at my breaking a rule when she was prefect over me in Hall, and how wisely she had used her influence. I think the two ideals nearest to Miss Buss's heart were her Hall and her Prefects. She lavished on the latter all the little privileges she could think of, guessing unerringly the kind of thing they would appreciate. They were allowed to speak anywhere at any time. They came in at the front door instead of the pupils' entrance. Every now and again they were summoned to a special 'Prefects' Meeting', to discuss some difficulty that had arisen in discipline or school arrangements. Once I remember we were consulted about a girl in the Fifth who had become over popular, was uproariously clapped on going up for a prize, and was having her head turned. Another time the point was raised: 'Should teachers come to school on bicycles?' I remember giving it as my considered opinion that such a thing was undignified!

Miss Buss was far more friendly and confidential with her prefects than with several of her assistants, and obviously respected them more. But neither her prefects nor her most exalted assistants dared to tell her an unpalatable truth, as the following incident shows:

The weekly moral lectures, already referred to, were given to the whole school in detachments, about three forms at a time, in the theatre-shaped room. The Sixth had the same lecture, but since they must not be mixed with other forms, it was given to them separately in their own room. Topics of a general nature were treated in a vigorous way—loyalty, truth, courage, idle thoughts, and such-like. They were never dull, but one week for a change it was an entirely comic lecture, full of gay reminiscences and good jokes (jokes that seem good even in memory to-day). We of the Sixth rose to it finely, letting ourselves go with bursts of laughter, and I excelled

myself by prolonged whoops that the others used to call
'Molly Thomas laying an egg'. At each fresh outburst Miss
Buss beamed with delight, and had some difficulty in keeping
her countenance sufficiently to read her manuscript, and this
totally new aspect of our austere head was a big joke in itself.
At the end, however, she straightened herself up and warned
us that such a frivolous lecture would not happen again.

But it did. Re-enter Puck. Next Monday as usual we were
all set for the weekly address when in walked Miss Buss and
announced that she had intended a lecture on 'Humour', but
thought it would be better to give a few examples of it
instead, and we settled ourselves for some kind of elevated
discourse with illustrations from great authors. To our utter
bewilderment we soon perceived that we were to have the
identical lecture of the week before. Still, we hoped that there
was some subtle humour in its opening in the same way.
But no, on it went with the same anecdotes and the same pauses
expectant of laughter. Well, I can laugh at most things, but
all merriment was frozen, and I knew that no sound is more
mirthless than forced laughter, or more easily detected by some
one telling a chestnut. I gave a side glance at Mary Wood,
and then at Bessie Jones, and they might have been at a funeral.
No propitious moment arose for us to jump up and explain.
Besides, there sat Mrs. Bryant, the form mistress and confidential friend of Miss Buss, looking as miserable as we were—even
she didn't dare to interrupt, although every now and again she
jerked her head at me as much as to say, 'Do for goodness'
sake, Mary, get up and stop it.' That was all very well, but
there were limits even to my audacity. So on went that
lecture, drained of all life, the jokes that were funny the week
before seeming stupid if not lugubrious. Miss Buss went on
doggedly to the final word (a specially funny climax), looked
round at us with disgust and swept out of the room. Mrs. Bryant
hurried after her, and inside a minute they were both back
and the storm broke. Miss Buss was never lacking in invective,
and there was a good deal of it hurled at us, of which the
burden was, 'Why didn't you stop me?' 'Why didn't *you*,

Mary?' was specially thrust at me, but Mrs. Bryant bore most of the brunt, deservedly I think.

Mother's comment on it was 'Miss Buss is such a great woman, what a pity she isn't a bit greater. If she had only come back into the room and had a hearty laugh over the mistake, what a real lesson in humour she could have made from it.'

'We were all dreadfully sorry for her, you know.'

'Sorry! That's fatal.'

§ 2

It was at the close of one of our holiday times, and Charles heard me boasting about my knowledge of the theatre.

'Pooh!' said he, 'why, you've only been once, and that was to a farce. You've never seen a real play.'

Annoyed at this, I asked him what he meant.

'In a farce you can hardly tell what's happening at the time, let alone afterwards. You can't remember the story of *Betsy*, can you now?'

I had to admit this. Then he added, 'you haven't seen what a play can be till you've been to a Shakespeare or a melodrama.'

'What's a melodrama?'

'It's difficult to explain exactly, but I'll take you to see *The Silver King* and then you'll know.'

Mother was very pleased for me to have this treat the last night before term; it would freshen up my brain. Charles was right on its being a perfectly new experience. Entirely unsophisticated, I hung on every word and gesture, completely entering into all the troubles of the hero, and I can remember the progress of the story to this day. How noble Wilson Barrett seemed when he pretended that he had signed the forged cheque! I understood then what Tom meant by 'lying well in a good cause'. As mother and I walked to school the next day I had to tell her the whole plot, and even now there is a bit of Camden Road that recalls to me the cry of the man who thought he had committed a murder: 'Oh God, put back Thy universe and give me yesterday.' Mother was impressed by this, or else pretended very well, for she never appeared bored by anything I related.

Not very long afterwards I had a good chance for indulging my love of acting. The time drew near for the Sixth to perform a play to the rest of the school. A committee meeting, with Miss Buss in the chair, was held in the Library, to settle the great question—what shall we act? In recent years there had been scenes from *Pickwick* and *A Winter's Tale*, and a play of Molière's. We wanted to strike out a new line if possible.

'Any idea, Mary?' said Miss Buss to me.

Yes, I certainly had. My love of the Greek stories amounted to an obsession. Saturated with Church's *Tales from Homer*, even as a small child I had imagined myself Achilles as I bowled my hoop along Grange Road, smiting the Trojans hip and thigh. So

'Why not do the siege of Troy?' said I.

'But how could we do the wooden horse?' objected some one.

'And the burning of the city?' objected another.

The idea had taken root, however, and soon some one suggested that we could make Hector and Andromache the leading characters, and arrange a complete story round them. This looked more feasible, and plenty of ideas were offered. But Miss Buss saw a serious difficulty in providing the poetic language needed to give the thing the right Homeric flavour.

'I have a very classical brother,' said I, 'who could do the language for us, and he knows a lot about plays and how to make them.'

Fearing that this might be thought cheeky, I was relieved when Miss Buss said, with sharp decision: 'Tell your brother to come to see me.'

Whereas mother had come back from her interview with Miss Buss full of admiration and affection for her, Tom came home bubbling with laughter. That many-sided woman had become quite a different person when confronted with a young

man whom she was predisposed to like. After he had heard
what she wanted done about the play and had promised to do
his best, she said:

'So you're full of the Classics, are you? And now I suppose
you'll be pitchforked into some school?'

Tom was greatly taken aback at her expression, and replied
that he supposed he would.

'And I suppose you have not the faintest idea how to teach?'

Tom grinned acquiescence, but said he thought he could
manage all right.

'You young men have an easy time. . . . Now that sister of
yours, if I don't rescue her, is destined to the dreadful career
of stopping at home and helping mother—dusting the drawing-
room, arranging the flowers, and other horrors.'

'I know,' said Tom, 'and mother and all of us want her to
do something better, and you can't think how grateful we
all are to you for all——'

'Yes, yes,' she interrupted. 'Now what I say is, Why did
the Lord create Messrs. Huntley & Palmer to make cakes for
us, if not to give our clever girls a chance to do something
better?'

Tom didn't tell us whether she hugged him, but I shouldn't
have been surprised.

Within a short time Tom had concocted a play for us, by
selecting a few dramatic episodes from Pope's *Iliad*. He
rounded it into a complete story by writing a Prologue, to
tell the previous events, and a final speech (to be delivered by
Cassandra) prophesying the Greek wile, the Trojan debacle, and
the burning of the city.

I bought a new exercise book, and took great pride in
copying out the passages from Pope that Tom had selected,
decorating them with drawings from Flaxman, to give the girls
an idea of correct clothing and posing. Tom's main job lay
in the Prologue and Epilogue, and for these he felt that blank
verse would be far more soul-stirring than rimed couplets.
Up and down the study floor he paced, slowly declaiming the
lines as he invented them, while I sat at the table taking them

down roughly, to be polished up and written out neatly afterwards.

The finished book created something of a sensation at school, as the girls crowded round Mrs. Bryant's desk to look at it. It was taken to Miss Buss, who presently had me summoned to her to receive her very warm approval and grateful messages to Tom. The next business was a meeting for casting the characters. Andromache was easily settled, for Ethel, Miss Buss's niece, was tall and beautiful, very dignified in bearing, and never known to laugh. Again, Hector was soon fixed, for Bessie Jones was not only tall and handsome, but had cropped curly hair, almost black—Hector's locks to the life. For the subordinate parts I was given first choice, and at once picked Cassandra, so that I might speak Tom's Epilogue.

Feverish work on the dresses was carried on in every available moment and spot. Even the sacred Library, where the head girls were preparing for Girton, had quiet corners of needlework industry. A Greek woman must have had an easy time with her toilet, for all she needed (so we were told) in the dressmaking line was a sack, open top and bottom, and provided with a couple of buttons and holes at the top so as to make three gaps; her head went through the middle gap and her arms through the side gaps, while the whole fell in graceful folds from the two buttons. With this hint we provided dresses for Andromache and all her maidens. The meaning of 'we' must not be pressed. My part lay in general encouragement, admiration, and advice, with a lukewarm offer to make a few buttonholes. A far more congenial task for me was helping Bessie Jones with her armour. The helmet was the worst, for it had to be strong enough to stand being taken off gallantly, and carelessly put on, and flashed about a bit to amuse Astyanax. What with donning and doffing we tested it so severely that it came apart, and had to be made all over again on a firmer basis. About this second one Bessie felt like Don Quixote—'so sure that it was sound and strong that it need be put to no second trial'.

The Greek 'sacks' were really beautiful in their varied

colours and materials. There was no machine available for the long seams, but the rate at which some of the girls worked filled me with amazement. One girl in particular, named Alice Codner, ran and felled absolutely like the wind, and merely laughed at my astonishment. When it came to Cassandra's dress Miss Buss herself went to Liberty's to select the material. She must have spent a good deal on it, for it was soft and glossy and heavy and of a deep saffron colour. When it was draped on me to get the right length I kept looking down to see the effect, for I had never been so gloriously clad. 'Hold up your head, silly,' said the girl who was measuring me, '*you* haven't got to see it.' My only contribution to it was to cut out in red material a border of the Greek key pattern, for some one else to apply to the edge. The idea was to make the whole as much like a flame as possible (in accordance with a kind of stage-direction from Tom).

Meanwhile, the rehearsing of the speeches was going on in other odd corners, and several times we stayed on for the afternoon to rehearse in the hall. I remember once coming suddenly on Bessie Jones lying prostrate on a form in No. 1 cloakroom, representing the corpse of Hector, while some of the best-looking of the Sixth were firing off their wailing speeches over her. The discomfiture of others gave me much amusement, for I was spared any rehearsing. I was not to appear at all until the end, had to speak by myself, without bothering about cues, so Mrs. Bryant said, 'I know you can fill the hall with your voice if you like, and if you break down from nervousness or forgetting the words, why that in itself will add poignancy to your speech.' So I only practised it at home to mother and Tom.

'Hector and Andromatch' (as certain of the Lower School called it when the bills were posted up) went without a hitch. Hector's helmet stayed the course, Andromache fainted on the wall in realistic style, the many maidens did their wailing so well as to draw tears from some of the audience, and Hector lay very dead, in spite of being maddeningly tickled by something on her up-turned face. Meanwhile, in the little room behind the organ, Mrs. Green, our make-up artist, was laying herself out to make me look as blood-curdling as possible. How abandoned I felt when I looked in the glass and saw the tragic effect produced by Mrs. Green's paint and cunning touches under my eyes! I felt that I actually *was* the prophetess doomed to speak the truth and yet never to be believed.

The moment came. My excitement was stronger than my nervousness, and I strode through the mourners to the foot-lights which lit up the flame-effect of my saffron robe; then I let loose on the assembled school my prophetic vision, ending with stretching wide my arms at the words, 'And Troy is all a-flame!' Mary Wood told me afterwards that she and the girls near her were genuinely frightened, for the speech had not been dulled by rehearsing and came with all its fresh force.

§ 3

The serious business of my last year at school was preparing for matriculation. In those days it was something of a peak of achievement, second only to an entrance to Girton. About a score of us were to go in, and scholarships were to be awarded to the six who should come out highest on the list. I was disappointed to find *Caesar* among the set books, for Latin was my strongest subject, and I should have welcomed a far stiffer author.

The actual days of examination in Burlington House were a pleasant excursion. On the first day Mrs. Bryant took us all in an omnibus in very cheery style, and as she was an invigilator, the whole thing seemed no worse than a test in our own form-room. The Latin paper was absurdly easy, but what was my chagrin to find when I got outside that I had left out a whole paragraph of the despised *Caesar*. There goes my chance of a scholarship, thought I, and it serves me right for being so cock-sure about the Latin. As for the mathematics, my only hope there was to scrape through. Geometry and Algebra were not so bad—you knew where you were—so far in Euclid, so far in Todhunter. But there was a mixed grill called sometimes Mechanics, sometimes Natural Philosophy, and this subject seemed to have no natural boundaries. A ladder against a wall, however, was always cropping up and could be understood, and the parallelogram of forces was merely common sense. But Dym had alarmed me by solemnly warning me never to confuse two things—mass and weight, I think they were. Anyhow, I was so confused about everything that mass and weight were mere flea-bites. My secret fears were as nothing to the paper that actually faced me. I gave a hurried glance through the page and a half of long-worded problems, of which not a single one seemed possible. A look round the room showed the other candidates applying themselves calmly. 'Scholarship! It's not even a Pass I'll be getting!' I shall never forget the dismal aspect of that room and how I dropped my head on my folded arms on the desk. But despair is a tonic and I braced myself for another look. After all, three hours are a good stretch, and I might manage some little bit of some question. As Livingstone appeared to Stanley, so did the word 'ladder' leap from the page to my searching eye. Yes, the good old friend was at the old stand of 60°. When put into plain English the examiner's demands about it were quite easy. It was just like the lions in the path in the *Pilgrim's Progress,* and elated with my success I attacked three or four more questions.

Determined to squeeze some extra marks in some paper or other, I had prepared a map of the Mediterranean. This I had practised until I could do it almost blindfold, with Italy sloping the right way and the coast of Africa and the Black Sea complete. 'Give the situation and modern names of the following', one question ran. Suppressing a whoop of joy I put forth my map, and with the coloured chalks I had secreted in my pocket I put blue round the coast-line and red spots for the required sites, adding foot-notes on the modern names. Tom had advised me 'always save the examiner trouble' and there it was, the examiner had nothing to do but glance.

There was no stint of time, and the three hours proved far too long for the French, and every one had finished by half-time. But it was one of Miss Buss's rules that we must not leave before the time was up, in case we should think of something we could add or improve. Envying the candidates from other schools who walked out early, we North Londoners stuck to our desks, stared at the dirty windows, and grinned at one another until the weary time came to an end, too sick of our papers to look at them again. A workman coming to wind the clock and having to walk rather perilously along a ledge made a welcome interlude.

One of those days at Burlington House stands out painfully in my memory. To bolster up my chance of a scholarship I had entered my name for an extra subject (Drawing, it must have been). Such degrading things were relegated to odd hours and sometimes shifted about. Whatever the reason, I found myself obliged to stay one afternoon when I had expected to go home to dinner, as the rest of the North Londoners were doing. The trouble was what to do for dinner. I had only just enough money for my return bus fare. I couldn't borrow from a stranger, nor could I mingle with the other candidates who were having a meal in the canteen, and pretend that I didn't want any dinner. I thought of sitting among them and saying it was one of my fast-days, or the doctor's orders or something, but I knew that the sight of food would be too great a trial. So I returned to the now deserted examination theatre, hid behind a remote pillar in a corner lest any one should see me and beg me to come for some dinner, and waited. After all it was already more than half-past twelve, and I could easily hold out till two, when the examination would begin. As soon as I had something to do it would be all right—it was the blank waiting that was so trying. Unfortunately the rules of the school had forbidden our bringing any book with us, so I had nothing to distract my attention from my hunger. I raked my pockets to see if there were a bit of biscuit anywhere. Nothing! By 1 o'clock I was ravenous, and thought with sympathy of the lions at the Zoo roaring punctually at their feeding time. By 1.30 I had ceased to care whether I got a scholarship or not, rushed out and made for home. Mother was greatly disappointed at my missing the examination, and as she plied me with food begged me to take a cab and go back. But I made out that it would be too late, for the expense of a cab all the way from Canonbury to Piccadilly was too great for me to stomach. Mother argued that an occasional expense never mattered, and implored me to go. But I stuck to my point about the time, too angry with myself for having wasted so much in that foolish waiting.

The appointed day came for the results to be out. Mrs. Bryant went to the University to get them and we candidates passed the time as well as we could until she returned. By a kind device the few who had failed were quietly drawn away and had the news broken to them privately, without the rest of us being aware of their absence. Then Mrs. Bryant came in with the remark, 'All in this room have matriculated.' Five of us were named Mary, so we were able to say that there was not 'one Mary Beaton'. We had had to stay till the afternoon for the news, but Mary Wood had promised to come home to tea with me, either to celebrate our triumph or to drown our cares. She had to call in at her own home on the way, first, of course, to tell the good news, and secondly to show me her new niece (the offspring of her sister's marriage aforesaid). We rushed up to the drawing-room to find Mrs. Wood 'in baby', and everywhere cluttered up with baby things. When we burst out with, 'We've passed the matriculation . . . we're members of the University,' we received the response, 'Yes, dears? . . . and did it love its Ganny den!'

'Oh, come on, Mary,' said I, 'let's get home to *my* mother, who knows what's what.'

Yes, mother had a big tea ready for us, with new saffron buns and apple-cake, and she kept on cutting bread and butter for us, and pouring out tea, and hearing all about everything to our hearts' content. I don't think I ever ate so much at a sitting in my life. I can see mother now, standing to her task of cutting and laughing at our continual demands for more.

A few days later I was told that I was high enough in the Honours list to be a Platt Endowment scholar, which meant that I was to carry on my education somewhere else—all very vague, but I didn't mind much, for life at school was very jolly while it lasted. Mary Wood was to stay on at school and work with the *élite* in the Library, for she was destined for Girton. She was doing Greek, and thought that I ought to begin it, too; so she used to come over to Canonbury and give me serious lessons in our study, 'hearing' me the verbs mercilessly. When I flagged, she warned me that one never knew when a thing would come in useful. Mother backed her up on this point, telling us how all her life she had regretted not having learnt to speak Norsk when she had the chance.

§ 4

Except Mary Wood, who was definitely fixed for Girton, we were all rather wondering about our future. Miss Buss took a personal interest in all her 'leavers', and had shrewd ideas about suitable careers. At this time a new opening for women attracted her attention—the instruction of the deaf and dumb. Clever and sensitive fingers were specially desirable for this work, and one of the girls at school in my time was well endowed in this way and seemed indicated as a pioneer. When approached on the subject, however, she repudiated the idea entirely. But Miss Buss was not so easily put off and pressed upon her again and again the glories of such a noble career. At last, annoyed beyond endurance, the girl burst out:

'No, I will not teach the deaf and dumb. I would rather be a. . . .' There was a pause and the expected word was 'hangman', but the word that came out was 'dentist'. This was a curious case of the subconscious mind getting a chance when one is in a temper; for she told us that on the way home, feeling calmer, she said to herself, 'A dentist? Whatever made me say that? Why, that is the very thing I should like to be!' She then went to Miss Buss to unfold her ambition.

'How absurd, child! There is no such thing as a woman dentist.'

Determined, however, to be a dentist if it were at all possible, the girl got her parents to make inquiries. They drew blank in England, but found that there was a chance of admission in Edinburgh. They managed to send her to Edinburgh, where she came out head of the list in the final examination. Miss Buss of course congratulated her, and also showed generosity by acknowledging her own stupidity in having tried to drive her into a career she disliked. Truly Miss Buss illustrates the saying that 'personality is a tissue of surprises'.

The majority of us who had matriculated faced the fact that we should have to become teachers. It seemed a fairly pleasing prospect, mainly consisting, as far as work went, in talking and putting red crosses on other people's mistakes. But we now heard that you could be *taught* how to teach—a funny idea. Soon a chance arose for me to hear more about it. Along with some other enthusiasts Miss Buss was trying to raise teaching into a real profession, like Law or Medicine. To this end they formed a Society, called eventually 'The Teachers' Guild'. Of course, the most irritating stumbling-block to such a scheme was the amused indifference of man-kind. My brother Tom seemed to Miss Buss a promising convert, and in the hope of getting him interested she invited me to bring him to one of the first meetings of the infant Society.

So he and I made our way to the appointed spot—one of London's gloomiest halls (in Farringdon Street, as well as I remember). About a hundred earnest-looking people, mostly women, were percolating into the seats, and in due time the platform was occupied by a few men of weight. A bishop spoke at great length, and was followed by two public school masters—not over-enthusiastic. The weather was dull, the audience heavy-going, and the speeches in sympathy with both. But Tom could suck fun from the most unpromising material, and the more melancholy the speakers became the more absurd they seemed, and the more sidelong glances Tom shot at me. At last Mrs. Bryant rose to speak, and put some life into the audience with a breezy talk. She evidently was speaking from deep conviction and a full heart; but she became so involved in a tirade against the indifference of the world at large to 'this great question', with many an 'if only' and 'if however', that Tom whispered to me in apparent alarm, 'She's forgotten her apodosis'. I believe the lady on my other side thought it was some part of her toilet.

Probably Miss Buss and Mrs. Bryant were disappointed with that meeting. They were doers rather than talkers, and a new scheme was fertilizing in their busy brains. 'Here we are,' they were saying, 'with a big school, and a deplorable deficiency of really good teachers. Let us pick a few of our best girls and venture some money in training them properly for their work.' The Training Colleges already in being did not satisfy their ideals, and they looked round for some appropriate place and for some appropriate person. Undoubtedly Cambridge, with its colleges for women as encouragement, was the right background for general culture. And a certain Miss E. P. Hughes, one of the most brilliant of Newnham's graduates, was the exactly right one to be the Principal. To her could be entrusted the entire working out of the scheme.

Of course I knew nothing at the time of all this activity behind the scenes. The first news of it that reached me was that I had been selected as one of the four North Londoners who were to be among the first students in 'a new college at Cambridge'.

VI

Breaking Fresh Ground, 1885

§ 1

CAMBRIDGE! From early childhood the word had borne a magic charm. It must have affected me somehow through mother, whose dream it had always been to have a son at Cambridge. I shall never forget her joy on receiving a telegram from Dym: 'Elected scholar of Jesus.' I feel sure she attributed that election to some heavenly preference. So when I came home with the news that I, too, was to go to Cambridge her enthusiasm took fire.

'Yes but, mother, it isn't like Girton or Newnham, it's quite a beginning place.'

'That's all the more fun. And anyhow it's a College, and you will be going UP.'

Unfortunately the boys were away, at work or on holiday, during the summer of '85; so that mother and I had to fall back on our imagination of what Cambridge life was like. A brother's communications are usually scanty, and all that Dym had ever waxed eloquent about was the rowing. He had frequently referred to Jesus as 'head of the river', and on my being puzzled about this had carefully explained the nature of a 'bump'. He referred to his 'rooms', to his having been mixed up in a row and being nearly 'sent down'; he gave me a silk scarf of Jesus colours (black and red), and told me of his trouble in coming across an unpronounceable name in the Old Testament one day when he was reading lessons in Chapel. This chapel I imagined must be a building like the horrible little Wesleyan chapels disfiguring the villages in Cornwall. That was all mother and I could actually recall of Dym's talk about Cambridge, but we knew that he had gone there a diffident and rather morbid schoolboy, and had become almost at once an animated and charming young man.

It was a great comfort to me that the unknown was not to be faced alone. Two of my special friends at school were of the chosen few—Bessie Jones and her own *fidus Achates*, Bessie Davies. We three had tried to extract from Mrs. Bryant, during our last few days at school, some idea of what our actual work at Cambridge would be. She was almost as vague as we were; all that she was certain about was a subject hitherto unheard of by any of us, called psychology. Was there any book on it, we asked. Yes, a friend of hers, a Mr. Sully, had written a whole treatise on it, but it was rather expensive. Now the Sixth were allowed to choose their own prizes, so I went to the school secretary and asked if she would lump two or more of my prizes together and let me have 'Sully's Psychology'.

'Wait a moment, dear, and I'll see what the price of it is', and so saying she pulled down her fat catalogue of titles and publishers. Idly looking on I observed her running her finger down the letter S, and muttering Sa— Se— Si. There was a closer perusal here, and it suddenly struck me that she was hunting not for the author but for the subject. Tactfully breaking to her that it began with a P and then went on to an *s* and a *y* and a *c* and an *h*, I saw that she was quite incredulous; so we both looked it up in laughter, and to her astonishment found it.

To such points as this mother gave no thought at the moment, for her energy was concentrated on the material side of my new adventure. I had been instructed to bring silver and bed-linen. Of both these mother had plenty, since all the old family stuff was on her hands—the remains of our palmy days when she had bought the finest linen she could find, and when there had been spoons and forks enough for a large family and visitors.

But my dress—that was the rub. I had no notion about it, having always put on whatever was assigned to me. Mother's theory was that *one* dress for each main occasion was the acme of comfort, since there need be no worry as to which to put on. She even envied our vicar's wife who wore but one style

always—a nun's costume. It was usual to have three dresses:
one for very best, for parties or any stately affair; one for
Sundays; and one for every day. These were known as
'hightum', 'tightum', and 'scrub'. Now obviously my historical
school dress, my 'scrub', was not possible for Cambridge, and
my Sunday one had got too small. Mary Worley had lately
gone to Girton and we called on her for advice. She was as
uninforming about Cambridge as she had been about school,
but we managed to extract from her that colleges always had
evening dinner and that one was expected to change for it.

This meant three new dresses at least—one for every day,
one for dinner, and one for Sundays. By sheer good luck at
this juncture my young aunt Fanny, well-to-do, of fashionable
tastes, recently widowed, sent me three of her coloured dresses,
hoping they might come in useful. They took ages to get into,
with their close-fitting bodices, endless hooks and buttons,
skirts to the ankle, and a kind of gathering-up behind called
a crinolette. But they fitted all right when once on, and the
pleasure of looking grown-up atoned for my diminished
mobility. Before long I developed a technique for getting out
of the everyday one; while each one of the little round buttons
down the front had to be done *up*, they could all be released
by a sudden jerk given to the bottom one.

A few days before I had to leave home, our old vicar paid
a call to say good-bye to the house and family before its dis-
solution. As his spiritual duties were now over he allowed
himself to be absolutely jovial, and I like to remember him in
his new and human light. He was a Cambridge man himself,
and though he could not think of anything useful about it to
tell me, he assured me that it was the only place in the world,
and at the same time gave me half a sovereign. 'I thought you
might have to buy John Stuart Mill, or some such book,'
said he. Mother expressed her surprise at his encouraging
such a heretic, and they laughed together, and I am sure that
he winked.

My trunk, bulging with everything mother could imagine
I might possibly want, on the model of the white knight, was

hoisted on a cab, and I was dispatched to Liverpool Street Station in the care of our one servant. Mother waved to me as lightly as if I were only off for a week-end with Mary Wood. It was not till years later that I realized how dreadful that parting must have been to her. Not only had I never been separated from her before, but the boys had all gone, with no hope of reunion in that house where she had been through such extraordinary changes of fortune. She was left alone to face the sale of all her furniture and the accumulated treasures of fifteen years. And she was going to live with her strait-laced sister Lizzie in a dreary suburb of south London. Is it a provision of Nature that young people cannot sympathize with the grief of their parents, or else they would have no reserve of strength to meet their own troubles later?

§ 2

It was late afternoon when I reached Cambridge, and dusk as I drove through the streets to Crofton Cottages (the address given to me). After a long drive the cab pulled up outside a row of mean little houses all stuck together, such as one might see among the less cheerful outskirts of London, with 'Apartments' in the window. The cabby asked me which house it was, and while I was hesitating and about to tell him that there must be some mistake, a tiny door opened, disclosing a brightly lit narrow passage, and a staircase to the side, on which one could immediately step. Then a welcoming voice:

'Is this Miss Thomas? Come in, come in. We heard the cab and guessed it was you. The others have all arrived.'

This was the first time that I had been called Miss Thomas. My long dress didn't seem so absurd as before, and the new title gave me aplomb. My welcomer was Miss Rogers, a large and genial Newnhamite, considerably older than the rest of us. As soon as the idea of the college had been adumbrated she had entered her name as a student, and for some time had been the only one actually on the books. She had been known in Cambridge as 'Miss Hughes's lamb'—the point of the joke being that she was quite twice the size of Miss Hughes.

When my trunk was landed I was shown my room. This
was some twelve feet square, on the ground-floor, with one
small window flush with the pavement, a narrow bed, a scrap
of carpet, a basket chair, one upright chair, and a bureau. A
bright fire crackled in the hearth.

'Is this *mine*?' cried I in ecstasy. I had always had a bedroom of my own at home, but that had been almost entirely
occupied by a big double-bed, a washing-stand, and a chest
of drawers. But here was a real sitting-room (for the bed
looked like a couch), such a one as Dym must have had, a
room in College.

Around me there was soon a small crowd of the earlier
comers, for of course every one was anxious to know how
many students there were and what the other rooms were like.
Miss Rogers, acting as M.C., introduced us all to one another
before dinner, giving rapid information as to whence each had
come, and hoping that we should like our rooms and get on
happily together. She told me afterwards that some of them
were painfully shy, and how thankful she was when I told her
in confidence that I was the scourge of any society into which
I was thrown. 'I needn't bother about Miss Thomas,' thought
she, 'I can put her among the assets instead of the liabilities,'
and she looked to me to help her make things *go*. There were
twelve of us that first night, and two more were to follow
in a few days. Half of us had to be out-students in neigh-
bouring cottages since the College could only accommodate
seven. It would amuse the present-day students in their fine
buildings in Wollaston Road to see those meagre beginnings.
Two tiny houses had been made to communicate by the
removal of party walls. There was nothing at all between
the door and the pavement. Stairs were so narrow that we
had to squeeze to pass one another. Sanitary arrangements
were of the most primitive, and a bathroom, of course, was
unheard of.

But no student's room or suite of rooms in the best appointed
university could possibly produce the pride that we felt in ours.
The main charm was our power to shut the door, or even lock

it, and put up a notice 'engaged' on it. I had a notion to give my room a name, and the other students followed suit. I called mine 'The Growlery', after a room in *Bleak House*, intimating thereby that any one wanting to growl could come in and laugh it off. This proved, as time went on, no empty invitation, and I had many visitors for the purpose. One of our number was an aesthete, and hung up a portrait of George Eliot, whom she resembled. She dressed in dull green velvet and was a free-thinker. Another had had mysterious romantic experiences, of which she spoke at length in an allusive manner, and would play on her piano and sing at any odd moment. Another was a Russian aristocrat of charmingly gracious manners; she was so strict a vegetarian that she refused on principle to pass close to a butcher's shop, and had some difficulty in getting along Silver Street because there were two butchers nearly opposite one another, obliging her to take the middle of the road. We were a strangely odd team. The only one among us who was really normal and proper shone forth as original by her very commonplaceness.

The first morning that I awoke to my new surroundings I saw a policeman passing my window so close that I could have summoned his aid with a touch. At breakfast I tried to break the rather nervous strain by relating the incident and pointing out the convenience of having the Force literally ready to hand. Miss Hughes overheard, and suggested that perhaps it would be advisable for me to get some curtains. This meant a visit to the town, and it soon turned out that everybody had something to buy—cups and saucers, cocoa, biscuits, condensed milk, note-books. Miss Rogers then offered to show us the way, and as soon as morning work was over we all straggled off. Straggling in twos and threes was necessary, because to go in a larger body was against the code. We were warned also by this unwritten code not to greet a fellow student in the street, and not to take a short cut through the same college more than once a day.

We were eager learners from Miss Rogers of these bits of etiquette, and of the usual pitfalls to be avoided. We learnt which was the freshman's church and which the freshman's college. We knew how many balls there were on Clare bridge, and why it was bent in the middle. Those first glimpses of the town were unforgettable. The curious little streets and passages reminded me of those walks through the hinterland of the City that my father used to take us children on a Sunday. But the University had a peculiar flavour of its own, and I was intoxicated by the cobbled courts of the colleges, the smooth lawns, the bridges, and the stately avenues. In those days there was no such thing as an excursion to 'see' a university town, and it never once occurred to either Dym or me to ask mother to come to see it; and how she would have gone crazy over so many sketchable bits!

The shops, too, were unlike any I had seen, even in London. Bookshops especially were wickedly tempting, and the crockery shops almost as bad. But curtains were the subject of my story, and resolutely I turned my face from anything else. I must buy them in Petty Cury; the name drew me like a magnet; here I found some cheap 'art' muslin of the brightest rose colour. 'That', said the young man who served me, 'will make your room always look as if the sun were shining.'

And he was right. With the new curtains the Growlery always had a gay aspect, even in the dreariest weather. This was as well, for otherwise the room looked very bare. While the others had been buying little ornaments and framed views of the colleges, my limited pocket-money kept me to the barest necessities. So I made a bold move by adopting the role of a hermit, and telling every one that I preferred my room to be severely plain, that this indeed was the latest fashion among people who really counted. Pictures, I maintained, distracted thought, and ornament merely for the sake of ornament was *démodé*. On a piece of cardboard I illuminated the words, 'Thou shalt think', and hung it over my mantelpiece. That would set the tone and prevent any tiresome remarks.

After the atmosphere of school the most striking feature of this new existence was its freedom. We were hampered by no restrictions, and it was assumed that we had come to work.

No one took any notice as to who was present at prayers before breakfast every morning, when Miss Hughes read a short passage from the Bible and a collect. Work usually began with a lecture from which no one was ever absent. We were advised not to work in the afternoon until 3 o'clock, and not to sit up late at night. Country walks were encouraged, as there was no chance for any other regular exercise.

The 'staff' consisted of three: Miss Hughes, a lady house-keeper, and a maid of all work. Obviously Miss Hughes had her time cut out. Not being at all satisfied with the kind of training of teachers hitherto in vogue, she had to create the whole curriculum along new lines. Nearly all the tuition was provided by herself. And she had to live in extremely close quarters with fourteen girls, one or two of whom were tempera-mental, not to use a stronger term. She told us later on that when the task was first proposed to her she refused it flatly, but that Miss Buss had pointed out to her that it was a grand opportunity, that she was cut out for it, that there was no one else to do it, and that she simply must. We North Londoners were well able to picture that scene. To this day I am amazed at her pluck. Psychology and logic had been her special subjects at Newnham, and these gave her no trouble, but she had to give us lectures on the history of education, hygiene, speech production, methods of teaching, and theories of discipline and school management in general, in all of which she was merely feeling her way.

Our 'lecture room' was a source of much entertainment to the Cambridge people who came to visit the new 'Training College'. In the top room of one of the cottages was placed a trestle-table covered with American cloth. Around this the fourteen of us managed to squeeze, leaving just room for the lecturer at one end, and a blackboard behind. There were no means of heating the room, and Miss Rogers used to sit with her feet in a muff. The difficulty of speech-training in so small a space was overcome by making the students go the length of the passage (not far) and declaim a piece of poetry through the closed door. I never hear the words 'The quality of mercy is not strained' without recalling the scene when our Russian student made them penetrate, in absurdly foreign accents, to the rest of us, doubled with laughter, inside the room.

Miss Hughes's style of lecturing was entirely her own. Although she gave us some definite principles and theories that were fairly well established, the greater part of the time was spent in practically working out some problem, in simple psychological experiments, in discussion, or in probing our own mental experiences. For instance, we had agreed one morning that one could always distinguish interior from exterior sensations, when the Russian student told us that on her first awaking in England she was distressed by a strange happening inside her, only to find later that it was the breakfast gong. I doubt whether any modern training college, endowed with every advantage of reference books and special lecturers, can offer its students anything better than we enjoyed in that little upper room. Whatever we did was real. Not one of us was allowed to take refuge in mere words, for every point one tried to make was pursued and considered or exposed as rubbish. Yet no one was ever snubbed. The supreme value to us was the contact with a lively mind—a lasting good in itself; so that in spite of the great advances in the study of psychology, we have had little to unlearn.

The only thing I regret is the cruel waste of time and energy in reading and trying to understand our one text-book (the aforesaid prize). I suppose Miss Hughes hardly liked to disparage the book, but it was enough to put any one off the study of psychology for good and all. One anecdote is all that remains to me of that heavy tome; and that only because it illustrated neatly an important point of mental workings: 'What do you do in a storm?' a passenger asked an old sailor. 'I couldn't rightly say, Sir, but when the storm comes on I does it quite natural.'

We were handicapped by having nothing remotely re-sembling a library—only a few books lent from one to another. Or was it a handicap? Books of reference are invaluable, but such a lot of earnest rubbish has been written on education

that I think we were the gainers by not having so many
bewildering treatises around us. One of our founts of wisdom
was a book by Fitch, which seemed to cover every possible
want, but much of it seemed silly to us even then, and we were
in the spirit to get as much fun as possible. A book on 'Class
Management' (which was apparently a special branch of
educational science) gave a great many hints, one of which
made me dubious about the rest: 'Avoid unconscious humour.'
How could one avoid what one wasn't conscious of? And
surely unconscious humour was better than none? Another
hint sounded splendid at first, and fired us with enthusiasm,
but led to absurdities in practice: 'Never tell a class what you
can get them to tell you.' Everything however trivial should
be 'elicited', apparently. Thus Miss Rogers, in describing the
people in Aix before the good news arrived, wanted to impress
the idea that they were getting anxious. 'What do people get
when they are expecting something?' she asked. A hand
waved. 'Please Miss, a telegram.'

There was no need for Miss Hughes to point out the folly
of such 'hints on teaching'. Miss Rogers was never exempt
from covert allusions to 'telegrams' and the joke did the work
effectively. The few worth-while books at our disposal we
were shown how to read sensibly, and how to make abstracts
of them. To me this was quite a new pursuit and had a fascina-
tion of its own. One day Miss Hughes chanced on me as I sat
at my bureau busily making an abstract on some footling book
I had found on 'Education in the Home'. Glancing over my
shoulder she said: 'Remember what Bacon says about books—
some to be tasted, some to be swallowed, only a *few* to be
chewed and digested.' The quotation sounds a commonplace
now, but coming pat at the moment it was wanted it made a
lasting impression on me. I saw at once that the book I was
'abstracting' was not even worth tasting, and the burden of
my childish conscientiousness of never skipping fell from me
like Christian's bundle. In fact Miss Hughes had the fine
teaching knack of making her students aware of what they
'needn't bother about'. Like the Yorkshireman's direction to

a stranger: 'Follow t' road till tha coomst to a cloomp o' trees. Now, tak *no notice* o' t' cloomp, but . . . etc.'

As a make-weight to our free and easy discussions round the table, we were taken to the Divinity Schools to hear *real* lectures. For these we had tickets, sat with real undergraduates in their gowns, and provided ourselves with special new note-books. The course on psychology from James Ward might as well have been delivered in Hindustani for anything I under-stood of it, for it was on the lines of his article in the *Encyclo-pædia Britannica*. We all took notes as fast as possible, trusting that the future life would make them intelligible, but not one of us faced them again. Bass Mullinger gave a course on the history of education, quite intelligible, thorough, and dull; sufficient to make us feel that we never wanted to hear any more about Great Educationists. Perhaps Miss Hughes had an inkling of the relief we felt in returning to our home lectures after these efforts. Mrs. Bryant came from London to give us a course on Ethics. We understood her better, or thought we did, and wrote long papers for her. What pages of rubbish I must have written on moral questions. I used to sprinkle capital letters to give point and dignity to my remarks, causing ribaldry among the others by speaking of the Infinitely Post-poned, in a passage that was read aloud by Mrs. Bryant with grave approval.

One of these odd courses in the town was on the Hebrew Prophets, by Dr. Westcott. He looked like one of those old prophets himself, his face all radiant as he rolled out passages from Isaiah, and I wrote full accounts of him to mother. When she happened to see Dym she said:

'Molly writes to me a lot about a man called Westcott lecturing to undergraduates at Cambridge. Did you know anything of him when you were there?'

'Did I know the old bloke!' was my brother's succinct reply.

To all these lectures in town we made our way in parties of two and three, and once a rearguard detachment heard a man say to his companion: 'There goes that wonderful Miss

Hughes.' She was a well-known figure in Cambridge, not only on account of her academic honours, but still more for her social charm. She could persuade anybody to do anything, and sometimes she would induce a real live don to come and give us a short course of lectures in our own college. I think these big people from their ancient and stately colleges must have been vastly amused by our little attic and the eager group round the table, ever ready to fire awkward questions at them in sheer simplicity. One of these visitors was big physically as well as mentally, so tall that he had some difficulty in getting into the room and ranging himself into position for his lecture. This was William Cunningham of Trinity. Miss Hughes had begged him to take any subject he liked, for as she pointed out to him the best preparation for teaching was to have *something* sensible in one's head. So he chose his special subject, a kind of historical political economy. It was impossible to be solemn in our tiny room, so he let himself go in a simple and merry way, inventing ludicrous illustrations of important points, and then joining in our ever-ready laughter, obviously enjoying himself. At the close of his course he went the length of asking Miss Hughes to bring a few of us to tea with him one afternoon. I happened to be one of the three she selected, and shall never forget my first experience of a don's tea-party. Far too ignorant of the kind of thing to be nervous, I determined to make the most of such an opportunity. I was too much impressed by the combination of comfort and odour of learning in the beautiful great room to notice what the actual tea was like, but when the great man came to sit by me for a few moments in his Orbit of Grace round the many guests, I seized my chance. In response to his smiling inquiry as to what interested me most in Cambridge, I replied:

'Oh, all the great thinkers everywhere; and now that I have you to myself for a moment I want to ask you what you think really happened at the Resurrection.'

The poor man might have been suddenly apprehended for murder, so taken aback was he. Perceiving that I had committed a social indiscretion I gave a nervous laugh. Then we both laughed a little awkwardly, and muttering something about a 'large question' he passed on to the next guest.

In Miss Hughes's eyes any one who was an expert in anything could help her students to be more efficient teachers. One day we had a talk from an actress, a Miss Shaw, who was taking the part of the Princess Ida. She showed us how to stand in front of a class with ease and grace, so as to make ourselves more impressive, and how to make effective pauses between the main parts of a lesson, and how always to 'set the important in silence'. 'If you want to make anything emphatic,' she said, 'you must do as a good actor does—*change* your voice. No need to raise your voice, it's often far more striking to lower it, but change is essential.'

§ 3

A far more arduous business for Miss Hughes than lecturing on strange subjects, or finding generous lecturers, was getting schools for us to practise in. Such as were available were situated in remote streets the other side of Cambridge, and one lesson a week for each of us was the most that she could get. For us it was enough. In order to get the utmost benefit from such scant experience, it was customary during our first week or two for Miss Hughes and *all* of us to attend every lesson. In the halcyon week before any of these lessons were started we were rather light-hearted about them. Give a lesson! Pooh! Any one can do that. But it seemed that we were expected to write *notes* of what we were going to say—an unforeseen nuisance. It was quite a new and rather shocking idea that a teacher needed to prepare a lesson; we thought that lessons just flowed forth.

The first ordeal was at hand, and an afternoon was fixed for two lessons to be given in an elementary school right across the town. Miss Rogers and I were selected, she because of her age, and I, no doubt, for my insouciance. She was to begin with an object lesson and I to follow with a grammar lesson, and we prepared and gave in to Miss Hughes elaborate notes.

When we reached the school we found about twenty young children in a block of desks, and in a similar block at the side we students were invited to be seated, while the Head and Miss Hughes sat on chairs to command the view. Miss Rogers stood forth and began. She produced a large piece of rock-salt, and held forth on its properties. She had become very hot with the walk, and still hotter with nervousness. I can see her now, perspiration streaming from her, as she talked ever faster and faster about this lump of stuff. Nothing coherent reached my mind, for I was sick with dread at the thought of my own ordeal to come.

The subject allotted to me had been the *Noun*—easy enough it seemed. I was actually able to remember my own first lesson on it, when my mother had shown me the list of the Parts of Speech, and then introduced me to the Noun as the name of all the things to be seen in the room or indeed anywhere. 'Everything?' I had asked: 'Well then what is the use of all those other words in the list?' 'That, dear, you will find as we go along', had been her reply. In making my notes I had foolishly thought to improve on this wise approach, and settle the meaning of a noun once for all. But I hadn't reckoned on the immense space of time that half an hour can be when you are faced by a mass of indistinguishable humanity, when you are incapable of asking a question, and are afraid to stop talking. So utterly gravelled was I to think of anything else to say about the noun that I plunged into philosophical remarks about the nature of 'things'. I heard myself saying, 'a thing is anything you can *think* about; that gas-bracket is a thing; you yourselves are all things'. At this I was horribly aware that the students were smiling. But unfortunately the children had evidently been told to behave, and no relief came from them; they merely stared at me, no doubt regarding the whole affair as a kind of gala performance. And like some dramatic background I was aware of the students busily taking notes.

We reached home, and after a merciful tea we packed into our attic for a 'criticism'. Remarks quite just and sensible were volunteered, but with the leniency one would expect from a condemned man for a fellow criminal. Many good points and a few weak ones had been observed in Miss Rogers, but when she had been 'done' Miss Hughes said: 'I'm afraid we must regard the lesson given by Miss Thomas as a failure.' The Headmistress had considered that I had a pleasant manner, but that was the only bright spot; the students' criticisms were given reluctantly, but all the more deadly on that account. I needed my Growlery, and retired to lick my sores there. After a bit there was a tap on the door, and who should appear but Miss Hughes.

'I was pleased,' was her amazing remark, 'that you made such a mess of your lesson.' Then to my dumb astonishment she added: 'I have noticed that people who are going to do really well—in almost any walk in life—nearly always start with a failure. I could tell from your notes that the lesson would be a bad one.'

'Then why didn't you . . . ?' I faltered.

'Why didn't I tell you to alter them? Well, you were beginning with a definition, instead of leading up to it. You could easily have recast your notes; but don't you see that then the lesson would have been mine, not yours? Success so gained would have been very bad for you. As it is you have learnt for ever not to begin with a definition. And a lot of other things, too', she added smiling. 'No, I mustn't sit down; no end of things to do—but I can tell you this, you will make an excellent teacher.'

The Growlery had justified its name.

It was a little later in the term that the room did its duty again. We were all of us ready to see the humorous side of everything. All except Miss Hay, the one student whose seriousness and matter-of-factness amounted to a joke in itself. She was neither foolish herself, nor did she see any folly in others, and gained the nickname of 'La Haye Sainte'. One day she burst into the Growlery, without even stopping to knock, collapsed to the floor and exclaimed in tones of real heartbreak, 'I am ruined'.

'Come, come,' said I, 'Go to! How now Reynaldo!' But

seeing that these encouraging noises had no effect, I hoped for something really exciting, and said, 'Tell me ALL'.

With great reluctance a girls' private school had granted us the privilege of giving a few advanced lessons to the eldest class, and Miss Hughes was to be the only critic present. Hygiene was the subject suggested, and several lessons had gone smoothly enough when it fell to Miss Hay to give one on systems of drainage. She had written elaborate notes and was confident, and was solemnly getting on with her lecture, when suddenly, while in full cry about some U-shaped trap, her ignorance of the subject and her daring to instruct people about it, struck her as ridiculous, and she began to laugh. It was the first joke she had ever really felt. In vain she sought for some excuse for her lapse from propriety, but drains don't lend themselves to amusing situations, and the more she tried to stop laughing the more incoherent with it she became. Miss Hughes rose and thrust a piece of paper into her hands, 'Oh, Miss Hay, I have just remembered a most important message; will you take this at once to this address. I will carry on with your lesson for you, and tell the girls the funny story that I know you had in mind.'

The address was of course only that of the college, and poor Miss Hay had rushed home expecting instant dismissal, and flung herself into the Growlery. What was her surprise to find that it was not only I that laughed at her tragedy, but all the others too, even Miss Hughes herself, who told us that the girls had been quite unsuspicious of anything wrong. That incident was the making of Miss Hay, who was never thereafter the dull piece of conventionality she had once been.

In most schools we came to be welcomed, and in one case we were actually asked for. An urgent message came one day from the elementary school in Eden Street; two of the teachers were ill, and could Miss Hughes spare two of her students to take their place for an hour or two every morning for the next few days? Immediately two of us were picked out—Bessie Jones as being tall and imposing, and I as being game for any adventure. As soon as breakfast was over off we started in high spirits, not knowing in the least what would be expected of us, but glorying in the fact that the shortage of teachers would mean that there would be no one to supervise or criticize us. It was a lovely autumn morning and we were exhilarated by our walk and our new sense of responsibility. Surely no two teachers ever entered an elementary school more gaily.

We were heartily welcomed by the Headmistress, who showed us into a big room, with two large classes, side by side, and asked us to arrange the work as we liked between us. A cupboard with various piles of books for reading and arithmetic was at our disposal, and a time-table hung on the wall. But we were told that there was no need to stick to the time-table if we wished to do anything else. Then Bessie and I had a hurried consultation, agreeing to keep to the subjects on the time-table, but to treat them as freely as we felt inclined. We also arranged to begin at once, and change over the classes at the interval.

Our great asset was our having to ask the children what they had been doing last, which put us at once on a personal footing. The arithmetic was not beyond me, and I won their hearts by confessing what difficulty I had had in mastering the rule they were doing, and showing them a little dodge I had invented for doing it quickly. After this a reading lesson was plain sailing, and I dared to ask questions, getting a forest of eager hands thrust up in response, with the incessant sound of 'teesh' to implore my ear. I glanced across the room to smile at Bessie, who was having a like experience. At the interval she and I considered that we might launch out more freely for the ensuing lessons. So I boldly asked my class what they liked best. 'Please Miss a story.' Thereupon I plunged into the Greek legends, and kept these going throughout our stay, discreetly wedging them in between bits of dictation and arithmetic. Bessie had found that reciting poetry to them had been equally entrancing, and for one joyful period she took the whole two classes together for a singing lesson. To this day Bessie and I look back to those hours of scratch lessons as a red-letter spot.

In order to increase our limited chances of practice in teaching we were given the task of lecturing to one another. One evening a week a student had to stand up in our attic and deliver a lecture of an hour's length, without a single note, to Miss Hughes and the rest. My subject was the eleven years tyranny under Charles I, and I spent so much trouble over it that I know quite a lot about it even now. The audience was more critical than any other I have experienced, but what a tonic the criticism was! Miss Hughes maintained that severe criticism was the highest compliment that could be paid to any one. 'The more carefully you prepare your work,' she would say, 'the more I can pull you to pieces, because you give me something to go upon.' And the value of simple clearness of style she brought home to us by relating what had been said of Henry Sidgwick: 'He has not only got to the bottom of his subject, but he has come up again.'

VII

The Furies Amuse Themselves

§ 1

THE worst blight on the teaching profession is the woman who can think and talk nothing but shop. Men are not so bad. But on the Continent there are to be met women by the score whose sole purpose in visiting Bruges or Venice appears to be to find material for lessons to the Upper Fourth. The disease was not so rife in the eighties, but the narrowness of outlook was a danger just the same, and Miss Hughes continually pressed upon us the prime necessity for a teacher to have some bigger interest in her life than merely passing on (however ably) her own acquisitions to her pupils. 'Nothing inspires children more,' she would say, 'than to be aware that their teacher is engrossed in some big subject that is beyond them; and nothing produces contempt more surely than the notion that her main interest lies in their little successes and failures.'

It was in accordance with this principle that so many visitors were invited to the college at meal-times, to mix with us in an informal way, as well as to give us a talk on their own besetting subject, with no ulterior motive of its 'coming in useful'.

All our meal-times, whether enriched by visitors or not, were entirely free from 'shop' and were occasions for general conversation and jollity. I can remember nothing of the food we had except the marmalade and the butter, around which there were legends. We were told that marmalade was called 'squish' and that every undergraduate was expected to eat his weight in it during his time at Cambridge. One of Dym's rare bits of information to me had been that butter was sold by the yard; but this I had put down to a mere leg-pull. What was my astonishment, therefore, to find it literally true, and to see on the first breakfast table little four-inch rolls about one inch

in diameter. Unfortunately the butter was not very good, and
we ate rather sparingly of it. Except one student (Irish, needless to say), who disliked it so much that she ate great chunks
of it in order to get rid of it! We pointed out to her that if it
disappeared like that our housekeeper would think we were
quite pleased with it and would buy still more. 'I can't help
it,' said she, 'I can't bear the sight of it.'

Newnham and Girton were naturally very hospitable to us,
owing to Miss Hughes's acquaintances in the one, and old
North Londoners in the other. My first visit to each was
memorable. At Newnham Miss Clough was Principal, and as
she had been one of the chief promoters of our little college
she looked upon us as god-children, and invited us all to tea
with her on our first Sunday. I took in little of the glories of
Newnham, being entirely absorbed in admiration of its gracious
Head. I was in that green condition when one fancies that a
poet must be dead, even if he ever trod the earth at all; and
here, handing tea to me and humanly smiling was actually the
sister of a poet whom mother had so often quoted to me. 'To
veer how vain, on, onward strain', and 'But Westward, look,
the land is bright' were running in my head all the time, and I
was impatient to get home to write to mother about my visit.

My first voyage to Girton was more alarming, because I
went alone and had a long walk to get nervous in. And the
big buildings overawed me. But dash it all, I thought, it is
only Mary Worley I am going to tea with, and I have done
that at home heaps of times. Of course she was just the same
dear old Mary Worley in her room at Girton as she had been
in Canonbury. 'I have invited the jolliest of my friends to
meet you,' said she, introducing a Miss Ramsay. Jolly was
the word for her, and I had not a rag of nervousness left.
Fortunately for our gaiety I had no idea of the ultra-distin-
guished classic she was to become—the only one in the first
class in the Tripos. Faithful readers of *Punch* will recall the
picture of her entering a railway carriage labelled 'First Class:
for Ladies Only'.

In order to cure us of nervous 'tongue-tie', every Thursday

after dinner two of us were selected to take coffee in Miss Hughes's private room, to meet one or more of her men friends. I was never put through this ordeal, and conclude that it was because tongue-tie was not among my failings, on the contrary I was always one of the few who were besought (before a lecture from a stranger) to think up one or more intelligent questions when discussion was invited; in short, to use Miss Hughes's own expression, to make fools of ourselves for the public good.

However, it was the apparently strait-laced Miss Buss who took the boldest step in giving us a chance to meet men in a social way. She gave a real ball. The guests in the main were her own old pupils at Newnham and Girton, and their brothers and friends who were 'up'. A hall in the town was hired with, of course, a dance-band, and *all* of us were invited. Alarm was our first reaction, for the question of what we could wear was a pressing one with most of us. But Miss Hughes assured us that our dinner-frocks would do quite well. Bessie Jones firmly refused to go. Her dress, by the wildest flight of imagination, could not be called an 'evening' one; but her ostensible reason for refusal was her objection to dancing; she was a nonconformist and had been brought up to regard it as sinful. But after Miss Hughes had made some convincing references to David's behaviour before the Ark, and a fellow student had shown how her dress could be transmogrified, she was ready to join the rest of us as we got into the four-wheelers. A dark rumour had been spread among us that it took four girls to extract a single word from an undergraduate. But as for myself I had had so much experience with my brothers and their friends that I had no fear of any young men, and hoped that by continual smiling and talking I should be able to distract their attention from my inadequate evening dress.

This was the first dance with grown-up and entirely strange young men that I had ever been to, and I found it most exhilarating. My knowledge of the right steps was confined to a polka and a schottische, for although we had had plenty of dancing at home I had usually been requisitioned to play the piano for the others. However, I managed to get on fairly well, and even ventured on a waltz with one young man, who assured me that he would take me round all right if I just gave to the music and didn't attempt to do the correct step. And lo, it was so. He then asked me to sit out the next dance. This Peterhouse man and I found so much in common and had such a lot to say that we sat out the following dance, too. While we were chatting another undergraduate passing us exclaimed, 'I say, Mary, how you are going it!' I suppose my partner noticed how uncomfortably I blushed, and guessed that my name was Mary, for he hurriedly explained, 'You see they call me Mary— short for my name—Marillier.'

When we got home the others teased me about Mr. Marillier, and I said: 'Well, I shall never see him again, so what matter?' By a strange coincidence I came full tilt upon him the very next day in Trinity Street as we were going to a lecture in the Divinity Schools. Out of sheer annoyance at having been teased I looked at him as though he were a complete stranger. I shall never forget his look of surprise, and often wished I could meet him again to explain. It was a healthy warning to me never to tease any one in that foolish way.

Later on Cambridge was all asplash about a Greek play, to be performed by undergraduates, with only one woman actor, a Miss Case, to take the part of Athene in the *Eumenides*. Miss Buss and satellites were coming up for it. We were told what a wonderful chance it was; a Greek play might never come our way again; education and all that. Seats, ten shillings each. I wrote to mother and asked if she could possibly raise it, or if she thought the play wouldn't be worth it anyhow. The money came at once with insistence that I must go. Throughout the performance disappointment, anger, and boredom seized me in turn. That anything Greek could be so dull was my first surprise; then as it got still duller, anger at the loss of mother's good ten shillings took the field; then boredom overcame all other feelings, at last became unbearable, and I fell asleep. I believe the others did, too, for they were peculiarly reticent about the play when we got home; all except Bessie

Davies, who had amused herself by counting the Eumenides, and found that they were fourteen—the same number as ourselves; and as they seemed to rush about to business or pleasure in the same sort of wild way that we did, we adopted the name, and ever afterwards referred to our little band as 'The Furies'.

It is greatly to Miss Hughes's credit that she took us for an expedition on the river. We could guess from the expression on her face while we were in the boats that her anxiety was extreme; and she admitted afterwards that she would never have so embarked, had not her determination always been never to allow her nervousness to prevent her doing what was worth while. We were asked which of us could row, and I immediately volunteered. I had never done any rowing, but it looked so easy; I had watched men on the river, and all they did was to put in the oar leaning forwards, lean backwards and pull it out. If Miss Hughes had known what mother used to say of me, 'She would offer to command the Channel Fleet if required', her nervousness would have increased. 'Crabs!' she cried soon after we had started, 'why, it's lobsters you're catching!' Fortunately a few of us did know how to row, but even so, how those two boatloads returned in safety is a standing marvel to me.

Our everyday relaxations were really more enjoyable than those carefully planned for us. In all kinds of weather we would be out between lunch and tea. In groups of two or three we would explore the colleges and the Backs. I gained a certain respect from having had a brother at Jesus, and showed the others its grounds and chapel as if they belonged to me. We looked with awe at any Dons walking about, and once a man was pointed out to us as 'the only one who is able to imagine a fourth dimension'. I thought to myself, How do they know he can imagine it? They've only his word for it; I might just as well say that *I* could. We looked with curiosity at Oscar Browning, for we knew the famous quatrain beginning, 'O.B. oh be obedient. . . .'

More attractive even than the Backs and the bridges were the real country walks—either one that took an hour, or a

longer round that took more than two hours—called respec-
tively the Little Grind and the Big Grind. From these we
would come back hot and healthy, laden with branches of
autumn berries and leaves to decorate our rooms. One afternoon, when the weather had grown colder, Miss Rogers suggested an expedition to climb the Gog Magogs, and six or
seven of us fell in with the idea. She appointed a meeting-
place on the other side of the town, and there we all met after
percolating through the streets in driblets. I had heard a good
deal about mountain climbing, and was looking forward to
some tough work. Leaving the town we agreed to walk in a
comfortable bunch together, and so make a merry party of it.
To beguile the way one of us suggested a new kind of game.
Each in turn selected a fellow student, and told her quite
plainly her besetting fault. It grew exciting, for many an un-
suspected foible was brought to light. If there had been such
a word then, we should have called our game 'psycho-analysis'.
There was much fun over little tricks and mannerisms, but
after a bit I sensed that some of us were feeling a little sore, so
I hailed Miss Rogers—'Where are these Gog Magogs that we
hear so much about?' 'Why, we've been over them some time
ago,' was the reply, 'and are now well on our way home.
Didn't you know that to see the view in Cambridge you need
only get up on a chair?' I never look at those poor little hills
now without recalling my disgust at their size, and the fault
of character that was usefully brought home to me that afternoon.

Miss Hughes never came with us on any of these rambles,
but she managed during our first term to take each one of us
for a long walk alone with her, on some pretext or other, in
order that she might get to know us intimately. We gathered
this to be her motive, for she slipped out one day that there
was no revealer of character like a long walk.

§ 2

Our indoor recreations were for the most part confined to
the period between ten o'clock and bed-time, when we paid

visits to one another for a good-night chat. Quite untram-
melled by having read any philosophical works, we brought
fresh minds to the deepest problems, and found no trouble in
deciding the origin of Evil and little points like that. We had
a shock of delight on discovering that there is no such thing
as Time: the Past was gone, the Future hadn't come, and the
Present appeared to be no more than a kind of decimal point.
Then some one started a theory that every object had a soul
of its own. It commended itself to me except in respect of my
clothes-brush, which was soulless in its way of hiding when
wanted, or to use mother's favourite expression from St. Paul,
it had 'no bowels'. But Miss Rogers thought otherwise. 'You
see,' she said, 'the brush has a soul all right; it only follows
the law of the total depravity of all inanimate objects.' Miss
Rogers was always ready with a pat saying that dissolved our
arguments. The value of introspection was once on the tapis
when she broke in with, 'Surely you know how to conjugate
the verb "to be resolute?" It goes like this: "I am firm, thou
art obstinate, he is pig-headed".'

Of course, politics and religion were discussed as freely as
anything else, but I can't remember that we ever grew acri-
monious about them. As we none of us knew the exact
religious denomination or political party of the others, no
one had a 'label' and we were thus free to adopt any opinion
we liked, comfortably far from what our people at home
would think. Probably most of us had been brought up to
regard Gladstone as the prop of civilization, and as immortal
an institution as Queen Victoria. However, Mr. Wood had
given me a glance of the other side of the picture, and the
M.O.G. initials had lately been supplanting the G.O.M. in
many minds. One morning the first lecture was excused in
order that we might all crowd into Miss Rogers's room to
hear her read aloud his now historical Home Rule speech.
Bessie Davies was the only one to get really worked up about
it. She took this kind of thing more to heart than the rest of
us; on St. David's Day she appeared with an enormous leek
fastened to the front of her dress, and although she pretended

it was a kind of joke, I think she might have been as touchy as Fluellen if we had tried any funny remarks.

Fortunately we never took ourselves too seriously, for everything we undertook or talked about seemed to be shot with humour, and even the stern admirer of George Eliot would occasionally unbend into a hollow kind of laugh, although we were never sure at exactly what she was laughing, and suspected that sometimes it was at the emptiness of life as a whole.

Every Saturday night we made a point of going entirely silly. It was customary for one of us to give a 'cocoa' in her room to all the rest. At ten o'clock each guest arrived with cup and saucer, spoon, cushion to sit on, a bit of sewing, and some kind of contribution to the entertainment—a song, story, puzzle, or what-not. When the student with a piano was the host we had songs from Gilbert and Sullivan and some good old sentimental ballads. Bessie Jones was our only good pianist, but she could only play if she had the music to read. Incredible as it seems now, she had been brought up to think it morally wrong to play from memory. On what scheme of ethics can this have been based? What we all enjoyed most were cumulative rounds, and recitations from Edward Lear, Bret Harte, *The Hunting of the Snark*, and the Breitman Ballads. Readings from *Uncle Remus* and *Rudder Grange* were in constant demand. It was this last book that Miss Hughes introduced to us, and she could hardly read it for the laughter of herself and all of us. She entered with gusto into all our fun, and seemed to have a bottomless store of anecdotes, either true or *ben trovato*, from her own life or her desultory reading.

There was one item in these meetings that gave me no pleasure, and that was the bit of mending that it was considered respectable to bring. Not from any lack of mending to be done; my skirt got torn by brambles, frayed round the bottom and needing new braid, and often loose from its gathers; and holes in stockings were always with me. Mother had provided me with needles and cotton and 'mending', but she couldn't supply the constant service with which she had always spoilt me. I could do anything with a needle except sew with it, my bits of mending accumulated, and I soon learnt at least one piece of psychology, that you forget to do what you don't want to do. So I conceived the plan of arriving at the cocoa with my mending, spreading it out ostentatiously, and beginning to do it more clumsily than I need have done. No expert can endure to watch work being bungled. As I foresaw, my neighbour offered to do it for me. I protested properly, but was eventually persuaded to hand it over to her. After a week or two this device of mine became matter of comment, but as it struck every one as a joke it got caught up into the general fun, and I believe the two Bessies would have been disappointed if there had been no response to their cheery greeting, 'Well, Molly, what have you got to-night that wants mending?' They little knew how great was their boon, for I kept to myself how I had once in a desperate hurry been driven to my childhood's trick of painting with indigo the bit of my leg that was showing through a hole.

One of those Saturdays I specially asked to be the host, without stating the reason. It was my nineteenth birthday, and Tony had promised to send me a big tin of cream and a batch of saffron buns. These made a grand addition to the customary fare of biscuits. Mother had sent me a new dressing-gown of bright blue, and as it was usual to wear dressing-gowns at these parties, the gift was more than welcome. I had never owned such a garment before, and had hitherto appeared in my day dress. Perhaps it was my new gown, or my high spirits, or the cream . . . but they soon guessed that it was a special occasion, and did their best to make the party go off well. I can still remember some of the contributions. Miss Rogers led off with 'The Heathen Chinee', reaching the crisis with a preternatural solemnity.

'I looked at Nye, and Nye looked at me.'

Bessie Davies gave us 'Barbara Fritchie' in mock elocution style, making her teeth disappear as she imitated the old woman's 'Shoot if you must this old grey head'. Miss Mears read us Uncle Remus's story of the Deluge, which even then

we felt to be a masterpiece. By this time all had been well
plied with cocoa and Cornish fare, mending was brought out,
and we looked hopefully to Miss Hughes.

'I expect you want a story,' she said. 'Well, I have an old
one that may amuse you: Long ago, in the days of King
Solomon, there was a little robin—a specially happy little
fellow because his wife thought all the world of him. When
accounts reached him of Solomon's wonderful new Temple
"Pooh!" said he, "I have but to place my claw on the top of
it for a moment and the whole affair will collapse." His wife
told the neighbours with great pride what her husband could
do. By degrees the little robin's boast reached the ears of
Solomon himself. "Send him to me," said the King. "My
dear," said the robin to his wife, "King Solomon has summoned me to his presence." "Oh, I hope he has not heard of
what you have been saying." "I have no doubt that he has, and
desires a conference with me on the subject." When he reached
the royal presence—"What do you mean," King Solomon
asked, "by saying that you could destroy my Temple?" Rather
alarmed, the little robin thought it best to make a clean breast:
"To tell you the truth, Sire, I only said it to impress the wife."
"Oh, I see," laughed the King. "Enough! Wives need that
kind of thing, I know. But your kind of talk goes too far.
Don't do it again, you understand." On the robin's return
his wife was anxiously waiting for the news. "What did the
King say to you?" "He begged me not to do it, dear."'

After this the demand was insistent for another story, and
looks were turned on me for an account of one of the wild
tricks of my brothers when we were children at home.

'I've got quite a different story to-night,' said I, 'one that
I came across somewhere—in some magazine, I suppose. The
accuracy of the story was not vouched for, but I think you
will say that it has truth stamped upon it.' Amid incredulous
smiles I began:

'Many years ago two Englishmen, Brown and Robinson,
were engaged in a tiger-hunting expedition in India. Shortly
after their arrival Brown went out for a sun-down stroll by

himself. It was a beautiful evening and beautiful scenery, and he was tempted to stray afar, and was attracted by a narrow terrace-path winding along between the hill-side above and a precipice below, and each turn of it gave him a fresh view of delight. A greater surprise was in store for him. Rounding the next bend, some ten yards ahead, swinging along, was a huge tigress. With the wit that flies to our brain in tight places, he squeezed himself as flat as possible against the hill-side and kept as doggo as his agitation would let him, holding his breath. With awful slowness the beast swung along towards him, apparently enjoying the evening air as he had been doing. She drew alongside, yes, she was actually passing him. But the tension and the sudden relief were too much, and his nerve gave way. Giving her haunch a mighty smack he exclaimed "Gee up, old lady!"

'Next thing he knew he was hanging over the precipice supported by the tigress, who had her teeth in his clothes. She was pulling him up on to the path. He knew that his only hope now was to sham dead, and he lay on the path as limp as possible while she began to sniff him all over. Now he always carried snuff in his pocket, and some of it had been shaken out over his waistcoat in his fall. Presently the tigress gave an almighty sneeze, and bounded off in haste. "A lesson to you, my boy, not to venture out so far without your gun," was Robinson's comment on the story. A week or two later the two friends were walking together when Brown pointed to the very turn of the path where it happened. "And look, here's a fair find," said Robinson, aiming his gun at a tigress stretched out on a rock below, with her cubs by her. "Stop!" cried Brown, pulling his arm down, "Don't shoot her. That's *my* tigress. She saved my life."'

This story tickled Miss Hughes greatly, and frequently she would hail me at any odd time as I was starting off somewhere with 'Gee up, old lady!'

Sundays were always pleasant for us. With the plethora of places of worship in Cambridge we could sample any kind we liked, and no one remarked on what we did. Before we left school Miss Buss had summoned us few North Londoners for a serious talk and advice. She told us that Cambridge was a hotbed of infidelity, and that we must not be tempted away from our faith, but nail our colours to the mast. This led me to suppose that any college chapel was of the hotbed kind and must be avoided. As I had recently fallen under the spell of E. A. Stewart of Holloway and his too emotional eloquence, I determined to attend the church in Cambridge that he recommended to me. Off I marched by myself to this very low church (I forget its name) near the junction of Petty Cury with Sidney Street, supported through its quite exceptional dullness by the consciousness that I was doing a lot of nailing to the mast. On the third Sunday I suppose I looked a little disgruntled at lunch, for Miss Rogers came to me afterwards with:

'You might come with me to King's this afternoon; I should be so grateful for your company; you can go out if you don't like it.'

I respected Miss Rogers and felt sure that she wouldn't go anywhere that was too much of a hotbed. So I agreed. She made no reference to the chapel on the way, but talked of this and that. Never shall I forget my shock of delight as we stepped in. The afternoon sun was streaming through the warm colours of the west window. Then we went farther in, all among the deep cool blues of the windows beyond the screen. When we sat down my eye caught sight of the vaulted roof. In spite of my long acquaintance with St. Paul's Cathedral and occasional visits to Westminster Abbey, I felt that I had never seen anything so lovely. And the anthem finished me; not even St. Paul's choir could equal the singing of 'Lord, how long wilt Thou forget me'.

We barely spoke on the way home, for Miss Rogers had the sense not to 'pat' the impression by remarking on it. As our walk was ending I said, 'Thank you for bringing me. In church this morning they sang the hymn, "There is a fountain filled with blood", and I felt I couldn't stand it any more.' 'You needn't thank me,' said Miss Rogers. 'I saw your face in King's, and it was ample reward.'

After that there were no more ordinary churches for me. While you are in Cambridge, see it, was henceforth my slogan. Consequently I seized the chance to go one evening to Trinity chapel, as we were told that it was one of the sights of Cambridge. It certainly was a strange sight. Of the Service I remember nothing. What impressed me was the mental agility of the men who 'told off' the undergraduates as they came in. Hundreds of young men in white surplices, all of them looking to me exactly alike, and there were the 'tellers' pricking each one off as he went in. Apparently this pricking meant that the young men *had* to attend whether they liked it or not—a new and uncomfortable idea to me.

From a religious point of view I found a visit to the University sermon at St. Mary's far more inspiring. Not so much the sermon itself, as to see the church packed with undergraduates who had not been compelled to come, and to hear the volume of sound when they burst into 'All people that on earth do dwell'. This had always seemed to me a very tame hymn, but given forth like that by so many voices it took on a kind of majesty.

Perhaps Miss Hughes had suffered from sabbatarianism as a child, for she took good care that our Sundays should have no dreariness. In the evening we were always invited to her room for a reading and discussion. Sometimes it was Emerson, sometimes Robertson of Brighton, sometimes modern poetry. There was a vogue for Browning just then, and we all enjoyed trying to understand him—the obscurer the poem the better. How worked up we all were over 'Bifurcation'! Miss Hughes had a solution of it worthy of Sherlock Holmes: the girl was suffering from tuberculosis, and the man couldn't make up his mind to marry her. I thought I saw the idea once, but no fresh reading will bring back to me Miss Hughes's idea, or indeed any other.

The number of new ideas, new friends, new experiences, all coming to me in a rush, made this time at Cambridge seem very long in retrospect, in fact a large slice of my life. I can hardly believe that it lasted only two terms, from September '85 to April '86. To make the utmost use of such a short course Miss Hughes arranged for us to pay visits to different types of schools in the neighbourhood of our homes during the vacation. She gave us personal introductions to the Heads and asked us to write our impressions for her to see. This proved one of the most useful bits of our training, for the Heads took quite an interest in showing us round. One of my expeditions was to Croydon High School, where I was told: 'We have no rules and no punishments.' This staggered me, after the rigours of the North London. 'Oh, it works all right,' said the charming Headmistress, 'the girls behave quite well without them; after all, nobody *wants* to forget books or to be untidy, and really there's no fun in being unruly if you're not punished for it, is there?'

A visit to a London Training College was a very different experience. I was allowed, along with several other visitors, to attend a 'Criticism Lesson'. A large number of the students, lecturers, and visitors were seated as in the auditorium of a theatre. A class of children occupied the 'well', and the student to be criticized stood in front of them and held forth. By no stretch of the imagination could it be called teaching, in such conditions. When the half-hour was up the children filed out, and the lecturer in charge (a well-known educationist) took the floor. He then called upon student after student to give her criticism of the lesson. It was bad enough for the poor young teacher, but it was almost worse for the critics, whose merciful little remarks were held up to scorn. The strain was almost more than I as a mere onlooker could bear. How thankful I was that my lot had fallen in a pleasanter place, as I thought of our informal criticisms at Cambridge; and I hardly wondered that Miss Hughes gave up quite early the practice of having more than two or three critics at a lesson.

§ 3

Those Christmas holidays were an unhappy contrast to all the previous ones I had known. My father's death had destroyed the extreme hilarity of our childhood, but mother had always done her best to keep the season as gay as she could make it. But now Canonbury with all its jolly associations was a thing of the past. I know now that mother must have been eating her heart out while I was at Cambridge, living with her sister Lizzie in Lee, in a small house in a respectable road—the kind of road that has artistic architectural ornaments, but if you forget the number you can't tell which house is yours. Fortunately Charles came to spend part of the holidays with us, and enabled us to see the funny side of things. Aunt Lizzie herself was the main source of our amusement, from her adamant seriousness. Religion as ever was her absorbing hobby, but at this time it took the form of high anglicanism, for she had fallen under the spell of a young curate who had gone all ritualistic. His name was impressed on my memory, for she could never advance an opinion without introducing it with: 'As I was saying to Mr. Owen the other day'. It must have been out of sheer weariness of having this young man pushed down our throats that mother and I went to a nonconformist place close by. Lizzie, in spite of her many flirtations with non-conformity in the past, was distressed at such falling away.

'We get something to think about anyhow,' said mother.

'Of course the hymns are too emotional and the praying a bit *outré*; but that man Critchley has some fine ideas.'

'Oh!' cried Lizzie in horror, 'you don't mean to say that you listen to *him!* I'm told that if it weren't for the look of the thing he would be a Unitarian!'

'Come now, Lizzie, tell us what doctrines you hold that this man is likely to upset.'

Lizzie was nonplussed for a moment, and then said with great solemnity, 'I subscribe to all the Articles of the Church of England', and mother was merciful enough not to ask her if she had as much as read them.

Christmas Day was the nadir of that holiday. In all my experience of London weather I can recall no worse fog than the one persisting throughout those wretched hours. I remember counting six of them that I spent reading Sully's *Psychology* by gaslight. Charles found his painting impossible, and mother had got hold of a realistic novel. Not even Lizzie could venture out to church. Dinner was the worst, for rich food without wine or merriment is more lowering than a vegetarian cutlet. I can quite see why we remember the pleasant things of life, and also the tragic, but can never fathom the reason for the lingering in the mind of mere dullness.

Charles was a real godsend during the blessed week that he spent with us, delighting mother with the sketches he was doing or planning, and me with his stories of his colleagues at Bedford.

One young master had difficulty in keeping discipline. 'Make a boy stand on a form if he is troublesome' was Charles's advice to this poor fellow. A few days later he came into Charles's room in distress: 'Look here, I've got *all* the boys standing on the forms; what do I do next?' Charles strode into the room and said 'Sit'. The boys sat down at once and Charles went out again and said to their master, 'There you are; now go in and carry on.'

One conversation in those holidays became memorable from later events. Looking idly through Charles's birthday book one day I saw another signature by the side of my own. 'Hullo!' said I. 'Who is this Arthur Hughes with the same birthday as mine?'

'Oh, he and I are great friends. He is the mathematics man at Bedford. But he is only doing teaching for a time. He is reading for the Bar.'

'The Bar. That's the best thing of all.'

'By the way, I've told him a lot about you, and your being at Cambridge, and reading Browning, and all that kind of thing, because he is great on poetry himself. So he wanted to know what you were like, for he has never met a girl yet who can cope with Browning.'

'I suppose you told him all the worst things about me that you could think of.'

'Oh, rather. And he's taken quite a fancy to that portrait of you as a little girl that's hanging in my room. He often puffs his pipe at it and says he wonders what sort of woman you'll grow into.'

'What's he like?'

'A dark fiery Welshman, who thinks there's no country like Wales. And he lays down the law already about everything.'

'I like any one all crazy about his own country. I should like to meet him.'

'Well, I've promised to get you to meet one another some time soon. Where are you going to be after Cambridge?'

'No idea, Charles, anywhere from Land's End to John o' Groats.'

§ 4

This business of where we were to go next began to press upon us about the middle of our second term. With no experience, and training not much believed in, but rather despised by those who had never had it, our main chance for getting a post was Miss Hughes's recommendation. Headmistresses were occasionally visiting Cambridge and seeking assistants, and several of us were dispatched for interviews. This word didn't seem half so humorous at first-hand as it had seemed when it concerned my brothers, and when my turn came for enduring an interview I had to summon up the kind of courage I used for going to the dentist—by five o'clock it will be over —a paraphrase of Macbeth's idea. Like Dym, I suffered from looking much younger than my years, few as these were; and my hair was cropped short; and my nervousness always took the form of grinning and saying foolish things. 'That's better than being tongue-tied like some of the others,' said Miss Hughes, 'and to help you through with moral support I'll lend you my bonnet.' I had never had such a thing on my head before, even for a charade, and the strings of it were enough to check any tendency to laugh. A group of the students made encouraging remarks to me as I set off. The appointed house was on the other side of the town, and I walked with the utmost care lest the bonnet should develop a list. Fortunately it was late afternoon and the light in the room poor. I answered lots of questions and heard myself declaring ability to teach subject after subject, including, I fear, arithmetic. It was all in the future, anyhow, and the most pressing need of the moment was to keep the bonnet on. Once out, I hurried home, and to judge by the laughter of those who saw me arrive I must have looked a strange figure. But I was offered the post, and I am sure it was the bonnet that did it. All the others got posts too, so that the only drawback to the pleasure of our last weeks was the misery at the idea of their coming to an end. We tried to make the Saturday cocoas as lively as possible, and I did my bit with Charles's stories of the boys at Bedford. Of course these suggested anecdotes to Miss Hughes. She knew of an instance something like the poor fellow with the boys all standing on forms; only that in this case the teacher showed a ready wit. She had prepared an interesting lesson and was rather dashed to find on going into the classroom that the girls were all sitting with their backs to her desk. Instead of courting disaster by ordering them to turn round, she began her lesson as if there was nothing unusual; but she picked occasion to draw some illustrations on the board, and noticed the furtive attempts of several to turn round for a look. At last someone laughed, then the teacher laughed and suggested that they would all see better if they turned round, which they did amidst good-tempered general laughter.

For our final cocoa Miss Hughes herself was the host, and in order to keep us from getting melancholy she decreed fancy dress. And we were to keep our dress as secret as possible, so as to spring a surprise on the rest. Since my complete inability to sing in tune was one of the standing jokes, I determined that my contribution to the entertainment should be a song. To heighten the effect I would get myself up as a German student and render a very sentimental ditty in broken English. I was forced to get Bessie Jones's help in making a pair of black knickerbockers, and to apply to the housekeeper for some tow to make a wig. But my chief 'property' was to be a pipe, and this I meant to acquire in great secrecy. Not knowing in the least where to get one, I started off by myself one after-

noon to the district remote from Newnham Croft, away over
Magdalene Bridge. Not daring to enter a respectable tobacco-
nist's, I found a little combination shop, where they sold
papers and birthday cards as well as tobacco—indeed, what
mother used to quote from an old notice, 'mouse-traps and
other sweetmeats'. I went in boldly and bought some acid-
drops, and while the man was weighing them I confided to him
that what I really wanted was a pipe—a large wooden one,
'not to smoke,' I hurriedly added, 'but for a fancy dress'. He
smiled and disappeared under the counter, emerging after a
prolonged hunt with the very thing, a pipe with a big bowl
and a stem a foot long.

'But how much will that be?' I asked, fearing that such a
beauty might strain my resources.

'You shall have it for nothing, Missy, and welcome; it's
been lying by here for ages.'

Then I told him what I was going to do with it, and he
encouraged me by saying he thought it a fine idea, and he
showed me how to handle it effectively, stuff tobacco in with
correct gestures, and so on.

Thus armed I was game for any folly, and drew forth joyful
laughter as I made my unexpected flights from key to key in
my song, 'Mein Jacob Schmidt, ver vas you?' For an encore
I rendered the most sentimental ballad I knew—'Some Day'.

We had clubbed together to give Miss Hughes an oak chest
as a parting present, and her letter of thanks to us contained
the following:

> '*My dear Furies, you may rest assured that that chest shall be
> the last thing that goes to the pawnshop. It shall stand in my room
> as a memento of that happy year which I so much dreaded, but
> which (thanks to you) I have so much enjoyed.*'

VIII

My First Post, 1886

§ 1

'POLAM, Darlington.' These two words were all the information I had about my new work; for when I was in that bonnet I took in very little as to my duties. Mother was all alive at the idea of coming with me and seeing new kinds of people. 'Very outspoken' was the characteristic she had both heard and experienced of the north country. We could not actually live together, since it was a resident post, but the headmistress recommended to us a trustworthy landlady not far from the school. So with this name and address we started off together from King's Cross in good spirits. On our arrival in Darlington we drove first to mother's lodgings.

The word 'lodgings' casts a gloom over most people, but to me it brings a memory of a large sunny room in West Terrace, and of an old lady and her daughter of gentlest nature, who laid themselves out to have mother well-fed and tended. Indeed, I gathered that a real affection grew up between them, for Mrs. Steele used to have heart to heart talks with mother about times and customs that were past; she was too old for much active work, and I think Miss Steele was grateful for mother's friendliness with her. Her stay with these people was one of the really happy periods of mother's life, for she was free from cares, had time for reading and sketching, and had my daily visit with school gossip to look forward to.

By another stroke of luck it chanced that my brother Tom, who had not long been married, came north at the same time that we did. As classics master in Middlesbrough High School he was within a short railway journey of Darlington, and very seldom a week passed when he didn't manage to run over to see us.

Polam was not a private school, but was under the management of some kind of Church Trust, about which I was never clear. 'Polam' was the name of a large house in extensive and well laid-out grounds, including lawns, woods, and a good-sized lake. Schoolrooms had been added as a kind of wing, beyond the conservatories; the pupils numbered about seventy day-girls and over a dozen boarders; the staff consisted of the headmistress, who did Arithmetic and what she called 'a little mathematics', a Fräulein for French and German, visiting masters for Music and Drawing, and me for the rest.

What appalled me was not the number of subjects assigned to me, but the elder boarders. I met these girls at supper on my arrival, and barely slept for fear of facing them in class on the morrow. Big girls they were, in long skirts and with their hair done up, looking older than I did, or felt, and apparently far more women of the world.

My first lesson was with a younger class, and it passed off without much trouble, but for the second hour I was faced by two rows of those formidable young women for a geography lesson. Few animals are more awe-inspiring than a group of English schoolgirls who are taking your measure. I had had no opportunity for preparing a lesson, so it was with assumed nonchalance that I asked: 'What country are you to be taking next?'

'Italy,' was the lack-lustre reply.

'Oh, then we shall want a map,' said I as casually as I could, but thanking my stars for that map of the Mediterranean I had practised for the matriculation. With careless ease I turned to the board and executed the western half of my masterpiece. When I looked round the class had come to life, and amazement sat on the previously disdainful faces.

'Did you do that out of your head?' exclaimed one girl.

At this I spread out my hands, to show that there was no book or atlas near me, and said, 'No deception, ladies and gentlemen.' When a laugh greeted this my nervousness had entirely gone, and we all set out to fill up the map, as by a kind of dentistry I extracted a few of the 'natural features' from the class. While the Alps were being laboriously chalked in, I muttered 'Poor Hannibal!'

Overhearing this the girl nearest me said, 'Hannibal? That's a funny name—it's what our old horse at home is called.'

'Funny name!' I said, 'but surely you know who Hannibal was?'

Not one of the class had so much as heard of him, and when I looked shocked and said, 'Why, he was one of the greatest men that ever lived' there was an urgent demand, 'Do tell us about him.' Only too glad to get away from the products and industries of Italy (which I felt to be approaching) I plunged into Hannibal's boyhood, and took those girls with genuine excitement from Africa through Spain, over the Rhône (with a sketch of an elephant thrown in), across the Alps and down to victory in Italy. Then pacing up and down the classroom I acted Fabius, wintered in Capua, made a crescendo to Cannae, cursed the authorities in Carthage, and was hesitating about attacking Rome when the bell rang to the accompaniment of groans.

I had taken my first fence, but there was another to be taken that I had not even suspected. During those first few days one after another of the elder boarders would come up to me at any odd time of the day to ask me the meaning of something—anthropomorphic, bicentenary, protoplasm, and other long words. I gave the meaning briefly, but one day it was 'upanishad'.

'I have no idea what that means,' said I, 'fetch the book where you came across it, and we shall be able to give a guess at it from the context.'

The expectant group looked uncomfortable, and then confessed that they hadn't got any book, but had picked it out of the dictionary. Then they told me that my predecessor had always explained a word if she knew it, but if she didn't she would not admit her ignorance but would say, 'Don't bother me about a mere word, look it up in the dictionary, dear.' This sport lost its zest as soon as I admitted ignorance, and we laughed together at the absurdity of pretending to know everything.

After this we were friends, and sincerer friends than those few elder girls I have never had. They began to take an interest in their work, and induced me to join in their play, which chiefly consisted of tennis and rowing on the lake. They had the north-country outspokenness and were extremely matter-of-fact; their intelligence and interest in almost any topic gave a real fillip to my daily round. One day the eldest came to me, with the others attendant, to say, 'Miss Thomas, dear, we think something ought to be done about your hair.' Ever since leaving Cambridge I had been trying to look more grown-up by cajoling my hair into a knob with hairpins, but with the utmost pulling I could produce nothing much bigger than half a crown. So I asked these girls to try their hand at it. After several efforts they came to the conclusion that it would be better cropped short. When I saw Tom at the week-end I consulted him on the point. 'Well dear,' said he, 'you may as well have it cut, for you couldn't possibly look worse than you do now.' And on this hint I cut.

While all lessons with the elder classes were sheer pleasure, those with the younger ones gave me more difficulty. Soon it became clear that 'giving lessons' as we had done in the Training College, when each one was an adventure, was a different matter from teaching day after day the same children in subjects that were already dull to them. Instead of giving them plenty of jolly and simple things to do, I was foolish enough to try to explain things. I have come to the conclusion that children are endowed with some protective instinct that smells an approaching explanation and leads them to curl up like a cat in a thunderstorm till it is over. However, one day I really got the attention of the class to what I proclaimed as one of the most important things in life; and then I made clear what 'transitive' meant to every Christian eye. I wound up with a challenging '*Break* is a transitive verb. You can't break without breaking something. You can't give me a sentence with *break* in it unless there is something that you do break.' Hardly were the words out of my mouth when I thought how they might quote Tennyson at me, but a glance at the class reassured me on that point. One little girl, however, appeared to be in mental struggle, and then up shot her hand with a triumphant '*I* can!' An expectant stare at her from the rest, and then came forth this:

'I tried to break the glass, but couldn't. You see, I didn't break it.'

What should I do? My solution was to laugh, say 'Right you are, Elsie,' and pass on to another point. No one minded, of course, or inquired further of the matter. But I learnt more psychology from Elsie than from many hours of studying Sully. I returned to the simple grammar of my childhood for these little girls. In this style:

> *Interjections show surprise,*
> *As, Oh! how pretty, Ah! how wise.*

The hour-long lessons were a trial with the younger ones, for I hadn't learnt the technique of making the pupils do all the work. But this soundest of principles was discovered by me in the following way. The period of the week most dreaded by me was an hour and a quarter, at the close of Friday, assigned to reading. At first it was greeted by the pupils cordially, for my predecessor had allowed them to 'read round' and when once the turn of each was past she engaged in her own affairs. But I dodged them, and they had no peace. The only available Reader was more than stale, and already decorated with pipes in the mouths of the persons illustrated. 'Oh, don't let's have this one,' was the inevitable murmur whichever one I chose. Silent reading, even if there had been any books for it, would have been considered laziness on my part by the headmistress, who was a martinet. She had scolded me once up and down for having dismissed this dreadful class five minutes before time. An *hour* of horribly bad reading, with an undercurrent of insubordination, was bad enough, but it was that extra quarter of an hour that drove me to desperation. Surely heavenly inspiration is not confined to solemn matters, or else whence came my idea?

'Have you girls got any books at home?' said I.

'Yes, a lot,' was the rather indignant reply from several.

'Next Friday, then, I want each of you to bring to school any book you like, and read a bit out of it to us all.'

Questions rained on me—Did I mean it? Would poetry do? How long must it be? Must it be a school-book? May it be really *anything* we like? May it be funny? . . .

'It doesn't matter whether it's long or short, comic or tragic, poetry or prose, grown-up or childish. But there are three things you must remember. First, it must be something that will interest us. Secondly, you must practise it at home, reading it aloud to your mother or in an empty room, till you can do it really well. And lastly, you must keep it a dead secret from the rest of the class, because we all want to have a little surprise over each reading; now rehearse the three points to remember: interesting—well prepared—secret.'

It was as though a magician had waved a wand over the class. Friday afternoon became the star turn of the week. The children were seen coming to school with volumes of all sizes wrapped up in newspaper for purposes of protection and concealment, and when the turn came to read there was a solemn unveiling of a fat Shakespeare, or a wedding-present-looking Tennyson, or a tattered copy of *Alice*. I had prepared a chapter of *Uncle Remus* to read to them if the supply of matter failed. But it never did. There was such eagerness to read that I had to put names into a box and draw out by hazard. I enjoyed myself as much as they did, for they chose quite good stuff and rendered it in entirely their own fashion; and of course I was secretly glorying in the vast improvement in the reading without the slightest effort on my part. No teaching or criticism was necessary, for we agreed at the beginning that any one who couldn't hear easily, or didn't understand a word, was to put up her hand, and the reader had to repeat, or make her own explanations. The few boarders in the class were at first a difficulty, because they lacked the home for finding a strange book and a mother to practise on. So I asked the elder boarders to help them with suggestions and rehearsals, and to keep all a secret from me. I well remember one of those Friday afternoons. A rather sentimental girl rose solemnly to announce the title of her poem, 'Speak gently'.

I couldn't resist, 'Oh yes, I know the poem, a good one it is, doesn't it go like this—"Speak gently to your little boy and beat him when he sneezes"?' It was some minutes before order was restored, and our faces straight for the proper poem. I was glad to note that the reader had laughed heartily herself, and a little apology from me made her quite happy. The next contribution was also a moral poem, but with a touch of humour in it, and I learnt it by heart:

> '*Well,*' *said the duckling,* '*well,*' *as he looked at his broken shell,*
> '*If this is the world I dreamt about, it's a very great pity I ever came out.*'
> '*My dear,*' *said the duck,* '*my dear, don't think that the world is here!*
> *The world is a pond, and it lies out there; you will soon see life, so don't despair.*'
> *But the eyes of the duckling looked beyond the reeds and weeds of that muddy pond.*
> *It's certainly most atrocious luck, to be born with a soul when you're only a duck.*

§ 2

The headmistress was a martinet about her assistants, but lazy about her own work, and as the term went on I found that she was pushing ever more and more duties on me. For instance, the visiting master for Drawing was obliged to take a large class that spread over two communicating rooms. When he was in one room the discipline in the other declined. So I was asked to give up my free afternoon—usually spent in a walk with mother—in order to sit in the younger Drawing division and eye the children. I soon found that what they wanted was not eyeing but something interesting to draw. After a little furtive helping I began to supply this need, and the master was only too glad to leave me to it, and as soon as the headmistress heard of it she asked me to take on the teaching of Drawing regularly. I ought to have borne in mind Tony's dictum about servants: 'I never think much of a servant who is willing to undertake duties that she has not bargained for.'

Mother had noticed that I was getting fagged out with the ups and downs of my first term, and she had been busy devising a summer holiday. A little family reunion seemed to be indicated, for Tom was within easy reach, and Charles could very likely come from Bedford. In her varied explorations she had come across a little fishing village called Runswick Bay, that fascinated her artistic sense. She thought it would also please Charles, who had written to say that if we could get some nice, damp, inconvenient habitation that was picturesque, he would join us. It certainly filled the bill as far as being damp, inconvenient, and picturesque, but it failed on the point of habitation. Mother could find no cottage that she could fancy herself entering, let alone asking for 'rooms' in it. She climbed back to Hinderwell again, determined to try some other place along that lovely coast. There was a long wait for the next train, and she passed the time by confiding her disappointment to the stationmaster.

'Well, mum,' said he, 'why not put up here in the station?'

'Good gracious!' said mother, 'I had no idea that any one could *live* in a station.'

He thereupon showed her what he could do. There was a real sitting-room, right on the platform, most convincing, with lace curtains, and fern, and red table-cloth, and a fine view of the railway and signal-box. Tucked away behind the little Booking-office was a smaller room that would do for meals, and a tiny kitchen beyond. Along the platform was a waiting-room that could be used as an extra sitting-room if required. Over all, going the length of the platform, were three bedrooms. It was like a house in a two-dimensional land. He ended the tour of inspection by saying, 'My wife is a good cook, and you will be very comfortable.'

And so we were. Tom and his wife, and Charles and I, and

most certainly mother, were all of us children enough to be enchanted with our new mode of life, and the fun never grew stale. Four trains passed to and fro every day—two 'to' and two 'fro'. One was due to rattle in during our dinner hour, and we always had to run to the front room to see how many alighted. There was usually a half-finished picture on Charles's easel by the window, and we enjoyed watching the passengers trying to look at it without seeming inquisitive. Most of them had come for an afternoon at the sea.

Runswick Bay was enough to attract any one, when once the approach to it had been overcome. A rough stony lane led down to it from Hinderwell, and after that a path went steeply down to the sea, winding in and out among the primitive fishermen's cottages. To say that it smelt like Caliban would be merely flattery. But what matter? Once down by the sea and the place was a paradise. The insanitary old cottages took on another aspect, nestling among the rocks and verdure of the hillside; and in the foreground there were the boats and fishing-tackle on the firm white sand in a brilliant setting of sea and sky. Mother and Charles were busy sketching all day long, whilst we others read and bathed and basked. I had brought *Rudder Grange* with me, and recommended it to Charles, because it described the same kind of odd dwelling that we were in. Mother and I slept in the room next to his, and one morning we were alarmed by great bursts of laughter coming from him. We were alarmed because it was so extraordinary. Charles made others laugh but never laughed himself, and we feared that something serious was the matter—a brain attack or something. I jumped up and knocked at his door.

'What's the matter, Charles?'

'Oh,' he managed to say with fresh outbursts, 'we are like the people in *Rudder Grange*, we live in a stationary wash-tub!'

Mother and I liked to hear that laughter, for it was a sign of the new enjoyment of life that had begun for Charles. We had been troubled about him long enough. On my father's death he was a sensitive, highly-strung boy of seventeen, the only one of us ever likely to shine, and he was obliged to take the only job that offered—one that involved long hours as a clerk in a sordid factory in Kingsland. He got away from it after a few months, but not until it had half killed him, body and spirit. But now he liked his work and friends at Bedford, and had ample chance to carry on his painting.

On one of his expeditions round Hinderwell for fresh subjects Charles had come across the picturesque village of Ellerby, and on the following Sunday evening he suggested that we might all walk over there to church.

'Has it got a church?' we asked.

'Bound to have,' said Charles, 'though I didn't happen to notice one; we may as well go to find out where it is.'

It was a lovely evening, the cliffs and sea at their best, and we were half inclined to cut church and continue our walk, especially as there was no church visible, although the whole extent of the village lay stretched in front of us. But mother suddenly said, 'Look at those two girls—they have the unmistakable walk of people going to church—let's ask them where it is.' Yes, they were going, and said they would lead the way, if we would follow. Still no symptom of a church, and presently they began to climb a ladder, placed against the side of a cottage. We followed up and found ourselves in a large attic. There were plenty of people already seated, and there were more coming up behind us. The ceiling was so low that Charles, in getting up too suddenly for a hymn, hit his head against a rafter. There was a harmonium and a real clergyman, and the familiar evening prayers, but all I remember is the text of the sermon: 'There is a path that no fowl knoweth, and that the vulture's eye hath not seen.' This lovely bit of poetry harmonized with my mood, for I was imagining all the time that we were a band of early Christians, gathered together in our secret upper room, in imminent danger of a raid by our persecutors.

This was our last walk all together, because Tom and his wife had to return to Middlesbrough the next day. But Charles had another fortnight, and mother had been hunting round to find a place that would give him a greater variety of subjects for his work. At Sandsend she had found the very thing to delight him—a rickety house right against the sea-wall. It was a tiny inn, with floors aslant and narrow stairs, each one a foot high. But, as Charles pointed out, we shouldn't spend our time going up and down stairs, and the view from the sitting-room window was superb—a big stretch of sand, the changing sea, a straggling row of fishermen's cottages, and Whitby in the distance, with its abbey standing out against the sky. Moreover, we found a glorious hinterland in the Mulgrave woods, and Charles was embarrassed with his riches. Every day of his fortnight was carefully planned, almost every hour. He would do a morning's work on one picture, and an afternoon's on another, so that the lights should be right for each. He decided all his lights and 'values' at the outset, and never touched anything indoors. We both wished that mother would follow this rule, for she ruined her sketches by improving on them afterwards, and thus never getting the clean, decided effect of Charles's.

We had no sooner discovered the charm of Sandsend than mother suggested my asking Mary Wood to spend the rest of the holiday with us. She and I corresponded fairly regularly since our school-days, and she has kept several of my letters. Here is part of the one I wrote inviting her to Sandsend:

As to economy, the fare is very little. 'You must do without a pair of gloves,' as Miss Buss used to say. I believe she considered that that would raise untold sums. It used to puzzle me rather because I did go without heaps of pairs of gloves, but never received any addition to my wealth thereby. Problem leading to a simple equation: How many pairs of gloves will it take to go without to be able to go to Sandsend to see an old friend? Solution: Let $x =$ the number of pairs of gloves required. Let $a =$ the fare to Sandsend. Then $x = a$ — old friend's affection. $\therefore x = a - \infty \therefore x = 0$ Ans. 0 pairs of gloves required to be gone without to go to Sandsend to see an old friend. So you have only to come. I am afraid there is a fallacy somewhere, but that is a detail.

When she arrived we found that the inn had used up the bedroom we had designed for her, but we were told that another was to be had in the village. Mother thought it best that I should share this strange room with her, so we went forth together to find it. The village consisted of no more than the row of fishermen's cottages along the front. Outside the one mentioned to us was seated an old fisherman, very deaf. When at last we had made him understand what we had come for, he hauled himself up and climbed his narrow little stair, and then opened the door of the 'room'. It was about eight feet square, almost entirely filled by a four-poster bed. We could just squeeze along past this huge structure.

'This will never do,' said I.

'Oh yes, it will,' said Mary, 'it's the funniest room I have ever been in. But', she added after a pause, 'it doesn't smell as if it had been lived in lately.'

'Nay rather,' said I, 'as if it had been died in lately. That old man looked a bit sad, perhaps his wife has recently. . .?'

At this Mary pushed along to open the tiny window. But it was not made to open. After a lot of shaking and shifting we managed to lift it bodily from its moorings, and stood it on the floor. After this we felt better and 'took' the room. The old feather-bed was comfortable enough, but very early every morning we were awakened, positively awakened, by the smell of the vilest tobacco known to man.

'Wherever can it come from?' we puzzled. I thought I discerned a tiny hole in the ceiling, that must lead into the attic where the old man slept. But Mary had a more subtle suggestion: 'It comes through no visible hole, it's everywhere around; it comes in by osmosis.' From this it might be supposed that Mary had been going in for science. At school we had both indeed dabbled in a little chemistry in the lab., with bunsen burners and sinks and test-tubes, but our enthusiasm cooled after Bessie Davies let loose the H_2S on us one day, and little remained to us but a few choice words, which we employed, like Humpty Dumpty, to mean just what we wanted them to.

We spent our days mostly in long walks and arguments, or in watching mother or Charles at their sketching. One of these walks gave rise to our attendance at a church service as peculiar in my experience as the one at Ellerby. Mary and I had gone with Charles for a walk to Lythe, where he had planned to make a drawing of the church. He was just starting on it when out came the vicar to see what was going on. After a general chat he said:

'I hope that none of you will turn up to our service on Sunday evening.'

'Oh, why?' we all exclaimed, astonished at such an unusual request from a vicar.

'My organist is ill. The Morning Service doesn't matter so much—very few come—but in the evening all the villagers come and will feel dull and disappointed without a bit of singing, and to tell the truth I'm keeping off every one I meet.'

'Shall I help?' said Charles. 'I always play the organ in our school chapel, and if I practise a bit on your organ beforehand, I daresay it would go all right.'

'How good of you!' Then he hesitated. 'But our small boy who blows is stupid enough at the best of times, and would be paralysed at the thought of blowing for a stranger.'

'Oh, that's nothing, my sister here and her friend will blow for me. We can go and have a practice as soon as I've had an hour at this sketch, and we can put in another to-morrow.'

The vicar went off delighted, saying that he should let his people know that they were to have a distinguished organist on Sunday evening.

Charles soon showed us how to blow, and we managed to avoid jerkiness, and the following morning, when he had finished his painting, we quite astonished him with our proficiency. We took it in turns, and he couldn't decide which of us was best. Mother was specially pleased, because she had always wanted to hear Charles play the organ, and we four set off on Sunday evening in great pride. The vicar had been as good as his word, and the little church was packed. Charles had ventured on some favourite hymns and psalm-tunes, but what we long remembered was his voluntary, 'O rest in the Lord', and Handel's 'Largo' at the close.

Owing to the different dates of term beginning, Charles had to leave for Bedford two days before we had to return to Darlington. I went to the little station at Sandsend to see him off.

'Is there any chance of your coming south?' he asked, 'because I want you to meet Hughes, and he wants to meet you.'

'I shall have to go to Cambridge for my Teacher's Diploma, but not till next year, because you can't take it till you're twenty, and I shan't be that till October.'

'All right. Then we must put off the meeting till then. We will manage for you to have a week-end at Bedford just before or after, as it suits. Our headmaster and his wife know about you and will gladly put you up.'

The train came in, and to my intense surprise he gave me an affectionate kiss, the only one, so far as I remember, that he ever gave me. That little scene is impressed on my memory, for I never saw him again.

§ 3

The autumn term at Polam began much the same as before, but after a week or two the headmistress broke to us that she was leaving at Christmas. The fact itself required no 'breaking', for the only feeling anybody seemed to have for her was a faint dislike. But further implications were disclosed bit by bit. Although we did not suspect it till much later, she was leaving a sinking ship. We ought to have guessed that the finances of the Association were rocking when we heard that Polam was to be given up. Next term the school was to migrate to another house in Darlington, called West Grove. At the same time we were told that there would be a large influx of new pupils and another assistant teacher. This looked well, for mother and I were too green in the methods of school business to be aware that you can have plenty of pupils if you don't mind what they are like, and also you can have assistants if their salaries can be avoided.

The new head was still less attractive than the former one, and had not even the advantage of being a martinet. The new pupils were an unruly set, and my new colleague had no influence on them whatever. How her classes went I don't know, but her 'supervision' times were so noisy that I was requisitioned to take her place, and she could not even be trusted to take the boarders out for a walk in crocodile form. She was a good sort, and I didn't want her to lose her post, so I took her turns. But it would have been a good thing for every one if we had both lost our posts.

Evidently there was iron economy required to keep that school going at all. It was in the meals that we felt the change immediately. How well I remember our first supper under the new management. The staff hoped for something rather special after the inadequate midday school dinner. A large dish piled high with potatoes baked in their jackets was placed in front of the head, who proceeded to serve them out. I looked upon this as an original kind of hors-d'œuvre. But *nothing* followed. 'An Irish supper—a bit of a change', we said to one another afterwards. But this dish of baked potatoes came on every night, and *nothing* else at all. Our other meals we had with the boarders, and of these I think Squeers would have been ashamed. There was nothing at all but extremely thick chunks of bread, with butter scraped on them, for breakfast, tea, and the boarders' supper. The midday dinner was some-times a piece of nondescript 'meat', but more often it was a slab of fish that I believe was eel, but looked like a portion of whale. This was followed by a mass of rice cooked in water. It was no wonder that on such a diet the girls were almost impossible to manage. With my extra supervision duties I could never have kept going if I had not been able to rush round to mother's rooms. Here Miss Steele would always have ready for me some nourishing food that I could take quickly, usually a bowl of generous soup and some cake or buns to take back with me, to share with my colleague. Mother found no increase for these items in the weekly account, and protested; but Miss Steele maintained that they cost nothing, because she had all the ingredients in the house. My colleague and I used to make ourselves odd cups of cocoa with the aid of a spirit-lamp and a tin of condensed milk. Miss Steele's buns and cakes made a great addition to these feasts; but the fact remained that we were not sufficiently nourished for our work. Confusion and disorder reigned throughout the school, and my only teaching pleasure came from those few elder girls who were doing well with their Latin, and really enjoying the second book of the *Aeneid*.

I could always rely on mother for some mental stimulus, and she cared not whence she derived it. One Sunday evening she carried me off to a Salvation Army meeting, to hear Mrs. Booth, who more than fulfilled our expectation that we should have a 'peep below'. The worst of mother was that the absurdity of the affair would strike her at inappropriate moments, and I would look round to see her doubled up with ill-suppressed laughter; fortunately this had a sobering influence on me. Political meetings were safer in this way, for plenty of jokes would be forthcoming in the speeches, and then we could laugh at what we liked. Home Rule was still the burning question, and we were open to conviction in any direction, being totally ignorant of Irish affairs. At one of these meetings we were invited to sit on the platform, with David Dale in the chair, and O'Connor as the chief speaker. We owed this distinction to some Quaker acquaintances of mother's. Both she and I were strangely attracted by the Quakers and their religious ceremonies, or rather lack of them. But we could never bring ourselves to attend one of their meetings. 'I couldn't go, dear,' said mother, 'in case of fire.' By this I imagine she meant that a sudden sense of the ridiculous might seize her during the silence. It can be well understood that I didn't encourage her to risk it.

To add to my miseries at the school, I was hardly a day free from toothache, in spite of many visits to the dentist. He was a kind fellow, and no doubt understood that it was an empty stomach rather than a bad tooth that was the root of the mischief. One morning Fräulein said to me, 'You look croshed.'

'Yes, I am crushed,' said I, 'what with these senseless corrections, and endless supervision, and a raging tooth, and——'

'Ach, no! Sink of what a grade man said, "Nature, she crosh me. But I am grader zan Nature. She croshes, and knows not zat she croshes. I am croshed, but I know zat I am croshed."'

For the life of me I couldn't see what good you got by knowing that you were crushed, but I felt vaguely the pathos of such a philosophy in the mouth of an ill-fed and overworked foreigner.

A worthy soul who visited the school in some undefined capacity approached me one day from quite another angle.

'I think you would find this little book helpful. Last Lent I read a chapter every day—not exactly as a penance, but to make me realize the power of sin.'

I accepted the loan politely, but with little intention of reading it. However, the title was more attractive than her introductory remarks—*The Strange Case of Dr. Jekyll and Mr. Hyde*. When I returned it after a few days I said I thought it a capital story.

'Didn't it frighten you?'

'Not a bit.'

At that week-end mother and I were paying a visit to Middlesbrough, to see Tom's little son; the journey involved some tiresome waitings, and to beguile the way I told this story to mother. She was always the perfect audience; whether she was shown a sketch, or listened to music, or heard a tale, she managed to make it more important, more meaningful. I used to notice how the teller of an anecdote or an adventure would always tell it to *her*, and seek her eye, whatever the company. Well, this story about poor Dr. Jekyll, that had seemed to me as I read it merely a good yarn, became so terrible as I unfolded it and watched mother's increasing excitement, that I caught her terror, and there we stood on a gloomy junction platform, staring at one another and clutching each other as I reached the climax. Perhaps a weird story always *tells* better than it *reads*.

One evening in June I had skipped away from the school and its worries to have an hour with mother. She was showing me a half-finished water-colour. 'Now remember what Charles says, don't go touching it up indoors, but go to the same spot to-morrow and get the same lights.' I was just saying this when Miss Steele came in with a telegram. It was from Bedford—'your son very ill—come at once'.

'Pack your handbag, mother, while I run to the station to see when the next train goes.'

It was not till midnight, so there was time for me to go round to the school to let them know I should be late, and unfortunately time for mother and me to speculate on what the illness could be. It was a bolt from the blue, for although Charles had been delicate from his birth he had never been definitely ill. And we had had the rosiest accounts from him lately. He had spent the Easter holiday in a sketching tour in Devon and Cornwall, and since then he had begun a series of water-colours to illustrate a book he meant to write on the country-side of Bunyan.

Next day I had a telegram from mother at Bedford that was obviously vague, so I guessed things were serious, and wrote at once to Tony in Cornwall and to Dym in Plymouth, asking them to go to Bedford at once. The elder girls at school were splendidly sympathetic, saying very little and working very hard during lesson time. It was two mornings later that I was giving them Latin, in a front room, and we all saw a telegraph boy walking up to the front door. In a minute a servant came into the room and handed me a telegram. They were rare things in those days, and there was little doubt what the message was. Without opening it I thrust it into my pocket, and shall never forget the look those few girls gave me before they all bent over their conditional sentences as if nothing else in the world mattered. North-country people may be brusque and outspoken, but for a sure touch of sympathy I have seldom seen the behaviour of that class equalled.

Charles had died that morning. Mother and Tony came on together to Darlington after a few days, and I had more particulars from them. He had been taken suddenly ill, and though apparently conscious now and again, he was never able to speak. Mother, Dym, Tony, the school nurse, and one of the masters took turns to watch by his bedside. This master had been with him through the night before he died, and to him (I learnt long afterwards) Charles had made with painful effort a gesture of affection.

Mother, Dym, and Tony were full of gratitude to this master, 'a Mr. Hughes', who acted like a son in helping them to arrange Charles's few belongings and pack his many pictures. They were anxious to have him buried in the beautiful little churchyard of Elstow, but there were serious local difficulties, and it was not until they had shown his pictures of the village and its surroundings that they obtained permission.

We ought to have been equally grateful to Tony, but she was always on the spot in any trouble, and we had come to look upon her as part of the scheme of Providence. To her Charles's death was as great a blow as to mother—greater, I think, for she had understood his artistic capability from his early boyhood, and had continually urged him to devote all his energy to it. And now to lose him at the age of twenty-four, just when he had been able to sell many of his pictures, and was hoping to give up school work, have a little studio somewhere in Cornwall, and paint to his heart's delight! It is surely a nice point whether a physical mother or a spiritual mother feels bereavement more.

'That Mr. Hughes you speak of,' said I, 'is the one Charles talked to me about, and wanted me to meet this summer.'

'Yes,' said Tony, 'he seemed to know a good deal about you. And so did the headmaster and his wife. They have made all arrangements for you to come to spend a week-end when you have to go to Cambridge for your examination.'

'Oh well, that's all off now—without Charles there's no point in going to Bedford.'

'Yes, but they think you would like to see his grave in that lovely churchyard, the chapel where he played the organ for the boys, and his room and everything, and meet his friends. They sent a most pressing invitation, didn't they, Mary?'

'They couldn't have been kinder,' said mother, 'but Molly must decide for herself whether to go or not.'

When Tony and I were alone, 'You go, dear,' said she, 'Mr. Hughes is so anxious to see you, and he has been so good to us that I think you really *ought*.'

So it was arranged that I should spend the week-end (before the examination) at Bedford, towards the end of June. That examination was rather a godsend at the moment, for it took my mind off other things. I had to look up a few facts about Vittorino da Feltre, and Gerson, and Jacotot, and people like that. I could do plenty of jargon about Sensation and Perception and the Laws of Association, but did not consider the bits of psychology I had picked up while teaching to be 'examination-worthy' or that they would go down with a Cambridge examiner. Methods of teaching had become a part of me, but I had to look up the 'rules for questioning' so as to have them at my finger-tips.

As the time drew near, any nervousness about the examination was lost in my nervousness at encountering all the strangers at Bedford, and the large staff of masters.

'But the headmaster's wife is delightful, and has three dear little children, and Mr. Hughes writes to say that he will meet you at the station.'

'How shall I know him? What is he like?'

'Short and thick-set,' said mother, 'very plain, dark, a good bit older than Charles, short-sighted, and very severe-looking, not jolly a bit. He told us that Charles used to call him Diogenes, because he took such a gloomy view of life.'

'I don't care what he's like—he was good to Charles,' put in Tony.

'He has a big moustache,' went on mother ruthlessly, 'and he plays the fiddle. He tries to do water-colours, but of course is no good at it.'

I was prepared for something pretty bad, deceived as ever

by mother's trick of putting one off what she really hoped one
would like. To stave off nervousness on the journey I went
over all the bits of 'book-psychology' that I could think of.
As the train slowed down for Bedford, I took my small bag
from the rack and braced myself for the task of hunting about
the crowd for a man who presumably would be looking
vaguely expectant. What if I made a mistake, or saw no one
at all likely? We drew up, and I jumped down into the usual
platform medley. I had hardly landed when some one came
briskly up to me, shook me firmly by the hand, and said,
'There's a cab waiting. What luggage have you?' I handed
him my bag with, 'That's all. Are you Mr. Hughes?' 'Yes,
come along.' The headmaster's wife was in the cab, and
greeted me with, 'You will be just in time for tea, and they're
all expecting you. There's a big cricket match on.'

That tea on the lawn was ambrosial; it was a glorious June
afternoon, and the men in their white flannels reminded me of
my childhood when my father used to have cricketing parties;
and at this time there was a specially grand tea on account of
the Jubilee celebrations. No one mentioned Charles, but I felt
from the manner of each of the masters as he chatted to me
that he was doing his best to make my visit a jolly one—all
except Mr. Hughes, who had disappeared. As they were
dispersing again for cricket I heard his voice at my side,
'I want you to see the shadow cast by the big tree on Elstow
church. Your brother made several studies of it. In this light
it will be showing to perfection. Come along, and these roses
I have just been gathering are for you to put on his grave.'

Our walk of about a quarter of a mile lay through some
cornfields, in full view of the church and the shadow on it.
We passed the village green and the old moot-house and
threaded our way through the churchyard to the newly made
grave. As I laid the roses on it Mr. Hughes said, 'He will
wake and remember and understand.' Those were practically
the only words spoken during that walk. The evening and
the next day were made as bright as possible for me by my host
and hostess, till Sunday afternoon when I had to leave for

Cambridge. Mr. Hughes saw me off at the station, still silent, but just before the train came in he said, 'Your brother was teaching me to paint, but I'm no hand at it. I've made a little sketch of the corner of the churchyard showing his grave, where we stood together on Saturday, and perhaps you will accept it; but it is only for you, and not to be shown to any one else.' He then handed it to me and silence fell again. But just as the train was about to start he said: 'We haven't talked much, you and I, have we? But never mind, we have all the future before us.'

IX

At Hell's Mouth, 1887

O N my return I found that affairs in Darlington had been getting worse, and there was a common rumour in the town that the Association to which the school belonged was bankrupt. The tradespeople were refusing to supply what little food was ordered. The pupils stayed on with the dumb acquiescence that young people usually show. We teachers stayed on for fear of risking our salaries. But one day we were informed by the headmistress that the school could not be carried on even to the end of the current term, and that there would not be a penny of salary for any one. This left the poor Fräulein all but penniless, and if it hadn't been for Tony's help she would not have had enough to get home to Germany. Tony as usual took matters into her own hand, and insisted on carrying off mother and me at once to Cornwall. I was sorry to say good-bye to my faithful friends, those elder girls, and mother felt parting from the Steeles. Otherwise we were delighted to shake the dust of Darlington from our heels as we steamed out of Bank-top Station. Our spirits rose higher the nearer we approached the west country and heard the soft tones of the people—such a contrast to the harsher voices of the north. How we hailed the little white-washed cottages at Saltash, and when I saw Carn Brea rising out of the evening mist I felt like a crusader sighting Jerusalem.

Lack of money had prevented our going to Cornwall for several years, and I felt that my cousins and I would be almost strangers to one another. I asked Tony whether they had changed much.

'It is you who have done the changing, dear. I think they are rather dreading you as a "modern girl".'

'What a funny idea! What *is* a modern girl, Tony?'

'Well, you have been to a big modern school, and to Cambridge, and they think you know a lot, and may ride the high horse—absurd idea, of course.'

The Cornish cousins were divided into two camps. Tony ruled at the old original home of Reskadinnick, and uncle Joe had a large house in Camborne. Not a day passed without interchange between the two families, so that it mattered little at which house one was staying. It chanced on this occasion that mother and I were to be in Camborne; and immediately I felt the tonic of uncle Joe's large family of boys and girls—so entirely remote from my recent school atmosphere. A very large family at the rectory, too, had now grown up, and were continually dropping in for tennis, or sudden picnic excursions, or merely gossip.

A few days after our arrival there was a tea-party at Reskadinnick, and conversation was flowing genially when one of the rectory girls asked me what the modern young man was like. I had no idea, but was not to be behindhand with news, so I said (inventing freely):

'The last young exquisite I met was very easy to get on with, because you knew what he would say. If your tone suggested something pleasant, he would say, "How awfully jolly!" and if your tone suggested the unpleasant, he would say, "How jolly awful!"' My companion thought this funny and laughed, but then turned seriously to me with, 'They told us you were clever, but you aren't a *bit!*'

I enjoyed this compliment, and it gave me my cue. I must keep dark the fact that I was working for my degree, and my interest in books and pictures and politics. As heartily as I could I entered into the gossip about love affairs and 'the length to which some girls will go'. However, I found it convenient to cultivate the reputation for being a bit odd. Oddity didn't matter, it was only knowledge that was to be avoided. A visitor caught me one day reading *Sartor Resartus*; hanging over my shoulder for a while she at length asked, 'Do you read this for pleasure?' When I nodded, she breathed 'Oh' and said no more.

Tony had a little surprise for me one day. When she was in

Bedford she had taken a great liking to Arthur Hughes (not only out of gratitude for his kindness to Charles), and she had begged him to come down to Reskadinnick for a visit. And now she had a letter from him saying he could run down from his home in Wales for a few days—ten at most—and if convenient he would come at once. 'We must do our best to make him welcome, and show him something of the Cornwall that Charles loved so dearly. I've written to tell him to come as soon as he likes.'

As it turned out there was little left for mother and me to do in the way of making him welcome. The cousins at Reskadinnick did all. They took him on expeditions to the points of interest, and it was only in brief snatches that I had any chat with him. But I gathered that he had been impressed with Carn Brea, which had seemed to him at first a small affair; they went up its slopes, to see the huge blocks of granite, some of them upright and still showing an intended arrangement, and the remains of an ancient castle. Another of his expeditions I greatly envied him—uncle William took him down a tin mine—not a thing for a girl to do! He told me of the curious shovel used by the miners, shaped like the spade on a pack of cards, of unknown antiquity and supposed to be the identical pattern used by the early Phoenician settlers.

'Mr. Hughes admires the North cliffs,' said one of my cousins to me, 'but he is insufferable in the way he sneers at our little trout-stream, and almost patronizes Carn Brea—for ever making comparisons with Wales. So we mean to take him to the Land's End, and rub his nose in *that*.' 'A good idea,' said I, but didn't add what I felt—that I wished they would ask me to come too. But the very rarity and brevity of our talks together made them more significant. For instance, it was a day or two after the drive to the Land's End that a group of the Reskadinnick cousins and friends dropped in at uncle Joe's, and Mr. Hughes and I were together for a few moments in the garden. 'Your North cliffs are always lovely, and Perran-porth takes a lot of beating,' said he, 'but the Land's End! It turned out a grey and blustery day, and the Atlantic was coming out strong. There is surely nothing like it. I felt I could have stayed there for ever' (here some one was joining us) 'if you could be there with me.'

Mother and I were both invited to a 'musical evening' at Reskadinnick, and Mr. Hughes, who never went anywhere without his fiddle, was able to add considerably to the entertainment. A trio of Gounod's *Ave Maria*, with one cousin at the piano, another singing, and the fiddle accompanying, pleased me greatly, and at the end I asked Mr. Hughes to pass me the musical score to look at. He came over to me and handed it with the words, very much in inverted commas, "and afterward, what else?" He knew that I should recognize the quotation from *The Patriot*, and that no one else would.

Towards the end of his visit, for some unknown and blessed reason (probably due to Tony, like most good things in my life), I was asked to go for an evening drive to the Cliffs with the Reskadinnick cousins. We started after an early tea, the time of day just right for colour; the weather was at its best, heather in full bloom, sea ultramarine laced with emerald, rocks looking defiant as the great breakers tossed their foam over them. As was customary, the wagonette pulled up at Hell's Mouth, our show-piece, so that we might all get out to look down.

Knowing every inch of the ground from my childhood, I ran on ahead of the others, all eager to show our visitor the way to do it. The ritual was to run up to the edge of the cliff and then lie full length, with head over, so as to gaze in safety at the cauldron of raging sea below. Before lying down I turned to hail the others coming up. To my surprise Arthur Hughes was in front of them all, running and looking horribly scared.

'What is the matter?' I asked.

'Oh!' he gasped, 'I thought you were bound to go over— running at the edge like that! I was afraid to shout a warning —it might have startled you.' The expression on his face checked my natural impulse to laugh at his fears. As the others came straggling up he added in a matter-of-fact tone,

'If you had gone over I should have gone after you.' In the moment left to us we looked at one another in silence. We each knew that it was the key-note of our lives—where one went the other would go—to the mouth of hell or elsewhere —it didn't matter.

On the drive back it was convenient for me to be dropped at the foot of the town while the others went on to Reska-dinnick. Automatically I went up Fore Street and took the right turnings to reach uncle Joe's; sheer habit took me, for I had no idea what I was doing. It was a comfort to be among my cheerful cousins, none of whom would notice my disquiet. Amid the hilarious talk around me I tried to concentrate on *Sesame and Lilies*, but it seemed tame and unreal. I was thankful when uncle Joe asked me to have a game of chess. Here silence was respectable, and it pleased my uncle that I was taking so long over my moves. Usually he had been distressed at my impatience with his slowness, for with him chess was more like a Buddhist meditation than a game. This lasted a nice long time, for my random moves put him out of his calculations almost as effectively as any strategy—each one made him suspect a subtle attack, and each piece that I lost he regarded as a gambit. He little imagined that his king was safe enough, for instead of designs on it I had running in my head the line of Bunyan, 'Then I saw that there was a way to hell, even from the gates of heaven'. Only I was reversing it, for I saw that there was a way to heaven even at hell's mouth.

It may seem strange that I was so flabbergasted. With four brothers and their many friends, with endless love-affairs of cousins and acquaintances, and discussions and speculations about them, surely I must have imagined something of the kind coming my own way? But I hadn't. The mere fact of meeting men of so many different types and finding them capital companions, and taking them quite naturally, must have acted as a kind of barrage, enabling both them and myself to talk without self-consciousness. I remember in particular a friend of Tom's who had fallen desperately in love with one of my cousins, who would have none of him. He poured out his wretchedness to me in long letters, begging me to write about her to him and do all I could. I entered into the job with great zest, but never supposed that this kind of stuff would come my way.

Anyhow, I managed to keep my feelings to myself, and in two days' time Mr. Hughes had returned to Wales without our having a word together again, and without any one supposing that we might like it. Perhaps mother suspected something. When he called to take a formal farewell, I heard her give him a casual invitation to come to see us in London, and promise to let him know our address when it was fixed. I joined my cousins in seeing him off at the station, where his farewells to them were very warm; but no word did he address to me. I felt flat—desolate. If I had asked mother she could have told me that neglect is sometimes the warmest gesture possible; but I said nothing to her, in spite of our close intimacy and confidence; or is it simply because of the intimacy that a mother has to forgo the deepest confidences?

Well, I had plenty to distract my thoughts. A post had been offered me in Kensington, through the recommendation of Miss Buss. An ardent old North Londoner, a Miss Bennett, was starting a new school, and wanted to run it on the lines of the North London. Much to our satisfaction the post was non-resident, so that mother and I could live together. The address of the school was West Kensington, of which we had never heard. We concluded that it must be even more aristocratic than Kensington, but were soon undeceived on this point. Aunt Lizzie had been very good in finding some rooms for us close to the school. At a turn in North End Road was a large public house called 'The Cedars', and opposite this was a row of good shops. One of these, a greengrocer's, was to be our new home. We didn't have to push through the greens and potatoes, but went up to our first-floor rooms by a private entrance. Mother was perfectly contented wherever you put her down. She always maintained that it was the people you lived with that mattered, and not the place. She at once admired the spacious sitting-room, and exclaimed, 'Look at the good view we get, in two directions, and with such a lot going on.' What entertained us both, and every one who came to see us, was the wall decoration. Not the usual romantic engravings, but huge oil-paintings in heavy gilt frames. Our landlady had lived in Spain and had brought them back with her, and that seemed to account for them amply. She said they were very old masters. They were certainly obscure from dirt and age, and this was greatly to their advantage, for it lent a mellowness and respectability to scenes that were mostly bloodthirsty or crude in their morality. One was a realistic rendering of something from the story of Susannah and the Elders, and another was the figure of Judith pacing home in quiet triumph, swinging the head of Holofernes, all dripping with blood, as though she had just picked it up cheap in the market, and cared not who knew it.

The scheme of colouring in the furniture was in harmony: carpet a fierce green, tablecloth a yellower green; chairs covered with crimson velvet, and some antimacassars of vermilion; but all were faded sufficiently to provide a quiet gaiety to the room as a whole.

The new school was only at five minutes' distance. Everything in it was beautifully arranged, but for the first few weeks there were only three pupils, so my labours were light. I had time to go on with my work for a degree, and have long tramps with mother. She on her part did a good deal of exploring of the neighbourhood. When I came in to dinner on the second day she said, 'We are in the odour of sanctity here. I have discovered that Burne-Jones has his studio just at the back of us. I saw his name on the door. And our landlady tells me that his famous briar-rose is in the garden.' It was not till later on that we heard the more interesting item about his house—that it was the home of Richardson at one time, and that he wrote *Pamela* there.

As soon as we were settled mother wrote to Mr. Hughes to suggest that he should come up to spend a Sunday with us, and as October 2nd was a Sunday and our common birthday, it seemed a good excuse for a little celebration, 'especially as Molly is to be twenty-one'. He replied that he could spend the Saturday night with his old friend Bourne, living in Camberwell, and would come on to us in time for midday dinner, and added that he was to be thirty.

Mother ordered roast fowl and its appurtenances—always a sign of festivity with her. We children used to say that she said grace more fervently over roast fowl than over roast mutton. When it came to the time for starting to church she announced that she was going to sample something fresh, as the church round the corner was so unstimulating; she had a mind to try the Roman Catholic Pro-cathedral; it sounded dignified anyhow. 'You can stop at home, dear, to receive Mr. Hughes; I've been in the oven myself.' This was a reference to an old story about a girl who had disappeared; she could nowhere be found until a neighbour came in and suggested looking in the big brick oven; and there she was. When the neighbour was asked how she had guessed the hiding-place she said, 'I've been in the oven myself'.

So I was left at home alone, to await his arrival. A long time passed, and the usual Sunday-morning lethargy was pervading North End Road. I gave up looking out of the window, for the traffic was hardly more than an occasional milk cart. I tried to read, but the words made no impression on my brain. Then I began to think that he had been unable to come after all . . . or that he had found his friend Bourne too engrossing . . . or that he had changed his mind and preferred to keep away . . . or that he had met with an accident. . . . It was past twelve, and soon the landlady would be bustling in to lay the cloth for dinner, and then mother would be returning. I was just thinking that I didn't care what happened if only something would happen, when I heard a hansom draw up outside. 'It isn't at our door,' I said to myself. 'Just go on with your book.' In another minute there were steps on the stairs, the door was thrown open, and the landlady announced 'Mr. Hughes'. If she was listening at the door after closing it she must have been disappointed and no doubt surprised, for it was some time before a word was said. He stalked in, threw his hat down, took me in his arms and kissed me as if it were the natural salute.

It may be hard to believe (my three sons have difficulty in doing so), but this was the first kiss, other than fraternal, that I had ever experienced from a man of my own age. Perhaps I had missed a lot of enjoyment, but no amount of it could possibly have equalled the satisfaction of that first one. A bit unnerved, I felt that the silence must be broken somehow, and by something matter-of-fact. 'Won't you take your overcoat off?' I managed to say. No reply. Then I heard myself saying, 'Will it take off?' Even this absurdity did not strike either of us at the moment, and mother returned while we were still standing bemused.

Dinner time passed off quite gaily, for mother gallantly described her peculiar experiences at the Pro-cathedral with great gusto, and when we sat round the fire afterwards we were all talking naturally enough. We laughed over Arthur's attempts to see more of me in Cornwall. He had been so kindly entertained that he hadn't had a minute to himself, let alone a chance to walk up to Camborne. To get such a chance one day he announced that he had to send a telegram, and must go up to Camborne at once about it. Immediately a kindly cousin had offered to take it, as he was then going up to the town himself, and Arthur had been obliged to lay out a shilling on telling his mother that all was going well. Mother was merely amused at our difficulties in seeing one another. 'Those little obstacles', said she, 'merely enhance the pleasure of your meeting. One kiss behind the door is worth ten in front of it.' But, as Arthur pointed out, we hadn't managed to get even the stolen one. She was as enthusiastic about everything as we could wish, and with her unerring instinct for saying the right thing she announced firmly:

'You poor fools! You fancy yourselves in love with one another! Wait till ten years have passed, and then you will see how paltry this will seem compared to your love for one another *then*.'

That was the stuff to give us. Thus cheered, Arthur came to the main thing on his mind.

'You know, Mrs. Thomas, I'm a poor man, and my friends tell me I shall never be a rich one. I don't know why.'

'I know why,' she rejoined quickly, 'and I may tell you this, that Molly would be simply wasted on a rich man. She and I have reduced "doing without" to a science, haven't we, Molly?'

'Oh, rather! I can always make a shilling do the work of eighteenpence; and it would be flying in the face of providence for me to have to bury this talent.'

'You'll have to keep an eye on her, though,' said mother, laughing, 'for she is apt to go to the High Street to buy a pair of gloves, and come back with a new book and the old gloves.'

'That's me, too,' said Arthur, and then hurriedly plunged into his prospects. He was getting a good amount at present, but he had to help his mother, and was sparing all he could for his young brother, who was going through an expensive time in taking his medical training in Edinburgh. 'I took mathematics at Cambridge, but I'm sick of teaching it, and hate schoolmastering. I'm reading for the Bar—that's where my real interest lies, but it will be sometime before I can make a decent income at it. Will Molly wait?'

At this point I didn't stop for mother to reply, but broke in, 'Oh, I'm like Traddles's Sophie. She was willing to wait till she was sixty, or was it seventy?'

We all three laughed, and to smooth over the situation I fetched *David Copperfield* to see which age she had fixed as her limit. Dickens is the worst author in the world to find anything in, and a prolonged hunt for what didn't matter was just the thing to lead us away from an awkward topic. If we had known then that we were to wait ten years before we could be married we might not have been so light-hearted about it. But it would have made no difference, however long the wait. It was many years later that he said to me, 'If we were separated I could wait for you for a thousand years on the chance of getting you at the end.'

Before leaving that evening he left us a kind of legacy in

the shape of his friend Bourne, who (so he asserted) would enjoy coming over for a chat now and again. 'Enjoy' was hardly the right word, for Bourne surely dreaded the ordeal. I can imagine how he muttered to himself, 'A mother and daughter . . . and poor Hughes let in . . . I suppose I must do my best for him and go over to see them . . . the sooner I get it over the better.' Whatever his motive, he came very soon, and often. A man more stiff with learning I have never met, stiff in the sense of sheer amount, not stiff in the use of it, or in ability to make others enjoy it with him. He was very tall and impressive, and a little alarming to me at first. But not so to mother, who could always smell a suppressed challenge and rise to the occasion with joy. His excessive courtesy towards women concealed his complete contempt for their minds, but mother took him unawares, and his first visit had hardly lasted a few minutes before she and he were laughing and sparkling with anecdote and argument. She had won, for he was dragged into forgetting that she was a woman and letting his natural self expand. He ventured his touchstone upon us: he announced that his chief aim in life was *to make one thought grow where two thoughts grew before*. He was accustomed to get much sardonic amusement out of the usual reply to this—'Oh yes, of course, Mr. Bourne!' from people who supposed he meant the platitudinous opposite. So when mother and I burst out with a startled and delighted 'Good!' we were friends indeed.

He told us a good deal about Arthur, and his struggles to help his mother and brother, and indeed any lame dog he met, finishing with the remark, 'You know, Mrs. Thomas, I don't think Hughes will ever be even decently well off.' To this mother replied, 'True, but then, you see, he is a nobleman.' To her, indeed, he seemed all that one could desire for a son-in-law, and he always remained as dear to her as one of her own sons, and no marriage of mine, however exalted, could have satisfied her as much. My happiness was too deep for me to talk about it, but she and I understood one another without words. One can't blink the fact that healthy children are bound to neglect their parents' feelings, and be callously uncommunicative; therefore one of my most pleasing memories is the look on her face when I handed her my first love-letter, with the words, 'Would you like to read it, mother?' 'Do you really mean it?' she said in astonishment. She must have known how much it cost me to do this, and she took it as though it was a sacrament she was receiving. So it was—a kind of benison on all the restraint, absence of persuasion or interference, absence of all inquisitiveness, that she had maintained towards her only daughter. Our slight awkwardness over sharing the letter was relieved by the laughter we got from one passage in it: 'I had to tell all the men last night. Hutchinson who had gone to bed I woke up and I raved to him until he said *he* would have to love some woman.'

Unlike Arthur, I wanted to keep quiet about it; but Tony and my brothers had to be informed. Arthur had come to appreciate something of Tony's character while he was staying in Cornwall, and I had told him of her love-story. He chanced to come across some lines that seemed to him an apt description of her, and wrote them out for me. These I sent her, along with my good news.

> *Through this dim, sorry world, where some men hold*
> *We fight with shadows for a cause unknown,*
> *You move serene and confident; as gay*
> *As if Life were a festival; your ease*
> *Deferred, and others' pleasure all your care.*
>
> *Yet they that know you best call you most dear*
> *Not for your hundred charms, your mirth, your wit,*
> *But for the hidden strength which these adorn,*
> *And that unflinching temper of the soul*
> *That in the hour of darkness has not failed.*
>
> *For each of all your days, when read aright,*
> *Is like some ancient missal's flaming page,*
> *Bordered with garlands, roses, fantasies,*
> *Writ in the midst with precepts of the Law.*

Her letter in reply made no reference to these lines, but ran thus: 'Your news is no news to me, dear. I can see a church by daylight. There's no mistaking a man in love. Arthur is one of the best men in the world, and there's no hardship in having to wait.'

The reactions of my brothers were also characteristic. Dym had taken a liking to Arthur immediately, and was hearty in his congratulations. 'He's a good sort, dear—I found that out on our fishing talks at Bedford; and if he does play the fiddle, well, a man must have a fault or two.' But Tom was too astonished to be decently polite. 'Well, I'm blowed! Fancy our little Molly engaged to be married! It's impossible. Nell and I can't take it in. You say that this Arthur Hughes is a Cambridge honours man, and I have always said that if Molly ever should be married (in the remote future) it would be to a fool.'

Except for these few necessary *lettres de faire part* I hugged my happiness to myself. But mother and I had to celebrate somehow. Stationed at our corner opposite 'The Cedars' was a very old crossing-sweeper. Mother liked to watch him because he reminded her of the old man who used to sit at our corner at Canonbury and make friends with us children. As I turned out of North End Road each morning he would give an extra dash with his broom, and I would give him a smile and occasionally a penny. During the week following our great birthday Mother and I gathered together four half-crowns and wrapped them in a bit of paper. As I passed the old man on my way to the school as usual I thrust the packet into his hand with a muttered 'special occasion'. I looked back after a yard or two and saw the old chap, with his hat raised to heaven, calling down blessings on my head. Sometimes it looks as if blessings really 'took'. Mother had been watching from her window, and observed that the crossing was neglected for a while, and 'The Cedars' was one customer up, 'but', she added as she described it to me at dinner-time, 'who shall blame him?'

It chanced that on the Saturday of that same week I went to

spend the day in Camden Road with Mary Wood. As it was the first time we had met since our holiday at Sandsend, there was a great deal to tell that hadn't been fully dealt with in our letters. I made her laugh about our meals in Darlington, about my cousins' love-affairs in Cornwall, and about our rooms over the greengrocer's shop, but Arthur I never even mentioned. She had much to tell me about our old friends at school and so on. There seemed no moment when I could break in with, 'Oh, by the way, I'm engaged to be married'.

I blurted out my news in a letter immediately after my visit, and I don't think she ever quite forgave me. It was some time before we had a chance to meet again, and by then her fury had blown over, and she listened to my explanation of how hard it was to talk about a thing one felt deeply.

'Do tell me what it's like to be in love!' said she. 'I have read a lot about it in novels, but you can tell me more exactly what it's really *like*.' I laughed a denial.

'There's one thing I can tell you at once that it is *not* like. There is no adoration in it. The idea that love is blind is all nonsense—it's most clear-eyed—you know that the man is the one companion for you through life, no matter his follies or failings or crimes.' (It is only recently that I have come across a description that would have suited my book had I known it then. Love, this modern author asserts, is a single experience in life; it is the supreme acceptance of one personality by another, without any condition or approval or other consideration whatever.) As it was, I ended lamely by telling Mary that she would know all about it when it happened to her; for how was I to express to her, or to any one, that rush of experience that overcame me at Hell's Mouth?

Mary went to her shelf and took down her Ovid. 'How do you like these lines?

> *Te loquor absentem, te vox mea nominat unam,*
> *Nulla venit sine te nox mihi, nulla dies.'*

I fastened on to them at once, and printed them out (with *unam* changed to *unum*) and sent them to Arthur. Ever afterwards we used the non-committal words *nulla venit* as a secret pass-word at any time.

By some blessed Dispensation of the Law, as inscrutable as providence, Gray's Inn required Arthur to dine there twice every fortnight. He used to get off on Saturday afternoon, eat one dinner, spend the night and Sunday morning at North End Road, and eat the second dinner before returning to Bedford. In order to have as long time with him as possible, I used to meet him at St. Pancras, and we would often do a picture gallery, or the like, before joining mother at tea.

Time never hung heavy between these visits. Mother was continually discovering fresh interests in the neighbourhood, and new walks into 'almost country'. Friends and relations, mostly Cornish, were pretty frequent, and we could always have a spare room to put any one up. The mere fact of our living 'over a shop' was an attraction in itself, and Mary Wood was not the only one to be disappointed at not having to 'wade through onions to a throne', as she expressed it. One fairly constant visitor was the oddest man I have ever met. John Lloyd, the brother-in-law of my young aunt Fanny, and therefore a quasi-uncle, was small and insignificant in every way, even in dress; and yet he was very rich. His position was that of secretary to the Pacific Steam Navigation Company, and his office was somewhere in the City. He was a bachelor, and the word must have cried out for the epithet 'confirmed' from his youthful days. His life was engrossed in his three hobbies. The first was his secretarial work, and I call it a hobby because he would go to his office on every Bank holiday, Good Friday, and Christmas Day. On mother's expressing astonishment at this he said, 'You see, I can get on so much better in the quiet, with all the young clerks out of the way.' Another hobby was his knowledge of London. It was like throwing a bone to a dog to ask him how to get from one point to another. Out would come pencil and paper and there was a map of the best route before you knew where you were. This amused mother and me so much that I was guilty of thinking up fancy spots for him to connect. I had him gravelled once for a minute or two, dealing with the route for a poor old lady, who couldn't afford a cab, with an invalid brother she wished to visit; she lived in Penge, and her brother in Hornsey Rise. John Lloyd's own home, for as long as I ever heard of him, was the Euston Hotel—of course a good central position for studying the vagaries of the old town. It may well be wondered why he came out to see us in West Kensington; he always took a kindly interest in Barnholt, for whom he had found a place in his Company, and liked to have any news of him from us; but I think it was his third hobby that really drew him. He solved the acrostics in *Vanity Fair* (if I remember the paper aright). As soon as he had had a cup of tea, discussed the weather, and asked after Barnholt, he would begin, 'By the way' and draw from his pocket a cutting from a newspaper with the acrostic. I was of peculiar use to him in this direction, for my education had been superficial and I knew through my brothers a little bit of everything. Moreover, as he pointed out, ladies' minds aren't rational and logical, and that's just what one wants for an acrostic. I think he wished after he had spoken that he had refrained from stating this undeniable truth, for our mirth over it was a little too hearty.

On one of his visits we had news for him. Barnholt was coming home for a short holiday. Good luck seemed to rain on us, for a glimpse of Barnholt was quite literally a rare treat. His letters were laughably laconic. Here is one that I happen to have kept:

> *Dear mother, I hope you are all right. We are just making Iquique. Give my love to little Molly. Your loving son Barnholt.*

But his presence was another matter, for he was the prime favourite with each of us, and we all rallied round. Of course he was to stay at North End Road, but Dym met him at Plymouth to bring him on. Tom came from Middlesbrough for a few days, and Arthur put in a short visit before going to Wales for Christmas. Those whom we couldn't accommodate put up at 'The Cedars'. Barnholt was hugely tickled at the greengrocer's shop, and greatly appreciated the variety of

vegetables which our landlady served up every day as 'surprises' for us. One evening was specially gay, when Mr.
Bourne joined us and contributed his subacid wit to the conversation. The feast itself was simple, 'on a bottled beer footing', but at the close mother unveiled a bottle of special sloe-gin
that had come from Tony. Barnholt had been pouring forth
the most exciting yarns, with the straightest face, and extreme
economy of words. The sloe-gin reminded him of a man he
met in an hotel in Valparaiso, who was talking very big about
taste in wines. 'I'm glad to meet you,' said Barnholt, 'for I
happen to have in my possession three bottles of a rare liqueur,
of extremely delicate flavour, too good for ordinary people,
really crying out for a man like you to taste it. I obtained it
(don't ask me how) from the cellars of the King of Spain. If
you like I'll go up to my room and bring you a specimen to
try.' The man was interested, and proclaimed the pure water
that Barnholt brought to him in a liqueur glass to be of the
most delicate bouquet he had ever come across. He offered large
money for the three bottles, or even for one, but nothing
would induce Barnholt to part with them.

'That's right, Barney,' was Tom's comment, 'a true humor-
ist never spoils his joke by telling a man how he has been
fooled.'

Barnholt was as pleased with Arthur as the others were,
but told me that he thought it was all nonsense for me to go
on working for a degree.

'You see, Barney,' said I, 'we can't be married for some
time, and to go on working at something hard is just the best
thing for me, and really it's rather fun.'

'Right. But don't work too hard. Learn to knock off
properly when you do knock off. Some people don't know
how to be lazy. It's an art.'

X

My Second Post

IN spite of Barnholt's good advice about taking things easy I found it difficult to get any time at all for relaxation during the term. Our care-free life over the greengrocer's came to an end. Pupils poured into the school, and one or two wanted to be boarders. So a house was taken in one of the many respectable roads of West Kensington, some one was found to run it, and the two first boarders were accommodated. To make the venture pay its way mother and I were asked to live there too. Of course mother heartily consented; but how we did regret our move! The road of houses all alike, with pillared decorations of a standard pattern, was a poor exchange for our bustling corner by 'The Cedars'. The lady superintendent was all too ladylike and refined, and from her we had to endure emotional prayers every morning. The presence of herself and the boarders deprived every mealtime of its salutary merriment, so that mother and I had to confine our folly to our walks together. And these were none too many, for in addition to the increased work at school I was making fierce attempts to get through my reading for a degree. In this matter mother was my great stand-by. She read the French and English books, and discussed them. Her pleasure in the character of Falconbridge went beyond the bounds of propriety; for she liked to quote some of the more robust bits at table, shock our presiding lady, and then add very gently that it was Shakespeare. She took a lot of trouble to 'hear' me the lists of names and facts and dates from Roman History that I hung over the washing-stand, but she had a hearty contempt for my troubling to learn them. 'Why bother to know anything' she would say, 'when your neighbour is always able and even desirous to tell you?' But, as I pointed out to her, they don't encourage this method in examination-rooms.

On looking back I can't imagine how I contrived to do all the work, without proper time for it, without any tutoring, and often without even an annotated text. I was completely beaten once by a passage in a speech of Cicero's. Remembering the remark of some tough old teacher of Classics that one can construe through a brick wall, I steadily pinned down all the visible verbs, fitted cases and genders, and yet no sense would emerge. For over an hour one evening I set my teeth into it with a dogged obstinacy, but had to put it away in despair. At the next available hour of freedom I took a bus to the South Kensington Museum, where I knew there was a reference library. I asked the young man for an annotated text of the oration, retired to a desk, and hunted up the passage, saying to myself that the editor would probably have followed the example of most of his tribe by blandly shutting his eyes to a real difficulty while calling attention to some harmless little subjunctive in its neighbourhood. No, he had had the honesty to say, 'This passage is so obscure that the text is obviously incomplete'. Although I couldn't afford to buy that thrice-blessed edition, it was worth the twopenny bus-ride to be able to stake down at least one chapter that no examiner would have the heart to set.

Another thing we missed badly in our refined home was the casual dropping-in of visitors—Mr. Bourne, John Lloyd, Mary Wood, and our numerous Cornish cousins. However, I always had the fortnightly joy of seeing Arthur. Once I met him at St. Pancras in pouring rain, and wrote a description to Tony of our afternoon struggling through the streets to the National Gallery, our favourite resort. Her reply was, 'How delightful to go to meet the man you love, especially when it's raining and you've no money to spend.'

I needed these bright spots, for the work at school was robbed of its natural pleasure by the fidgets of the headmistress. The pupils were for the most part of the best type one could desire, but Miss Bennett's standard was too high. Her ideal was ladylike efficiency combined with the rigid discipline of the North London. But she had none of the awe-inspiring attributes of Miss Buss, nor the slightest sense of humour to balance the deficiency. Her working scheme was that I should be the martinet, and she the popular dispenser of smiles. Hence if anything went wrong she blamed me. Now things are bound to go wrong sometimes, however ladylike girls may be, and however elevated their home circle. If healthy, they must be noisy sometimes in their playtime, and some of them will be sure to do an unladylike thing. A bland and solemn girl of fifteen, of Spanish blood, appeared so often with a note from her mother asking leave of absence that Miss Bennett felt she ought to call and remonstrate. To her shocked surprise it turned out that the mother knew nothing of these letters, and was hardly distressed at having to admit that they must have been all written by the girl herself. Miss Bennett comforted herself with the reflection that the people were more or less 'foreign'.

Her religious principles and ideals of conduct were really exalted; and I think when this is the case the ideals themselves have the effect of works of supererogation, so that the holders of them can afford to do little acts of deception of which less exalted natures would be ashamed. For instance, Miss Bennett herself told me that in taking a French translation lesson she had spied a word coming that she didn't know. So she glanced at the clock and suddenly exclaimed to the class, 'Oh, I forgot, I have to send off a message; just go on with your work; I'll be back in a minute.' Whereupon she slipped into her study, looked up the word, and returned. This was retailed by her to me as a slick way of getting out of a hole.

Again, one day my classroom door was opened and I was requested to come outside. 'Down in the drawing-room,' began Miss Bennett hurriedly, 'there's a girl of fifteen with her mother who wants her to be prepared for matriculation. She appears to have done some Latin and Mechanics. I've tested her Latin, and it's fairly good; and now I've said that my assistant will test her Mechanics, since it's not my subject. So please go down at once and examine her in it.'

'But I'm a blank on it. I haven't touched it since I went in for matriculation myself. . . . I simply can't.'

'I am afraid I must request you to do as I say. The girl is waiting for you. I will take your class.'

I have seldom thought so hard as I did on those stairs. 'Thought' is not the right word, though, for all I could do was to try to recall something of my old school text-book— a small green one, by some one named Magnus. All I could visualize were some sentences in italics—Newton's Laws of Motion. I believed there were three, but the only one that had stuck was the first. This had remained for the simple reason that I had always doubted it—for how could Newton be sure that a thing would go on for ever if you let it alone? Then a blessed reflection came upon me, that I need only ask questions, there was no need to answer them, and sauntering into the study, I said, 'Good morning', sat down, and began benignly:

'So you have done some Mechanics, I understand?' Then in answer to her diffident 'A very little', I went on, 'Let's see how far you have gone. You can give me Newton's Laws of Motion, of course?'

She began glibly with the first, and my heart sank. What if she rattled them all off? What should I ask next? But like myself she had gone aground after the first, and while she was hunting in her mind, the blessed word 'lever' hopped into my memory.

'Never mind,' said I, 'don't worry. We'll drop that. Tell me now, what different kinds of levers are there?'

Here her confusion was still worse, and much to her relief and my own I was able to suggest that she would have to revise the subject from the beginning. I went upstairs to report my conclusion, without dwelling on my method of obtaining it. I have played the humbug in life often enough, heaven knows, but never with such abject shame as I felt that day.

Naturally, after this, our staff had to be stiffened on the mathematical side, and the new assistant, to my immense comfort, was endowed with humour as well as with mathematics. Her name was Williamson, and (as I heard in later years) the staff became at once known to the girls as 'Benny, Tommy, and Willy'. And there was another way in which Willy was a comfort to me. She shared the blame when things went wrong, and these things were sometimes so small as hardly to be visible to the naked eye. We would be hauled over the coals for not taking off a mark if a girl had omitted to put a full stop at the end of a sentence. The slightest blemish on a desk had to be notified. Every Friday afternoon there was a grand cleaning of the desks by the pupils with little bowls of water, sponges, and towels. For every stain detected after this process the culprit had to put a penny in the missionary box. This last touch was discontinued after the rebellion of one of the senior girls.

'I don't mind,' said she, 'being fined for ink-blots on my desk, but I do object to having little niggers converted with the proceeds.'

This smacked of profanity to Miss Bennett, who was deeply religious, and I think she must have been shocked at the amusement it afforded to Miss Williamson and me. For she invited us both to tea with her on the following Sunday, when conversation almost naturally turned to 'What church do you attend?' and thence to religious views. We soon found ourselves involved in 'baptismal regeneration'. While I looked profound and stared at the tablecloth, poor Willy was blurting out her disbelief in the eternal loss of a child who hadn't been sprinkled with water. The party broke up with some tenseness of feeling. On the way home:

'Do you believe all that about baptism?' asked Willy.

'Heavens! No!'

'Then why didn't you say so?'

'What on earth is the use of arguing with some one whose mind is closed?'

We then found that we had a good many more daring views in common, and were thenceforth fast friends. She was not only an alleviator of school fidgets, but also an asset to mother and me in the boarding-house, where she egged mother on to demoralize meal-times.

'Mending stockings!' exclaimed mother one day, when this

duty was being over-pressed on the boarders. 'For my part I'm like a Beau Brummell, who would never have any garment mended. "A tear or a hole," he used to say, "may be the accident of the moment; but a *mend* is premeditated poverty."' Her remarks on school affairs, however, were never made in the presence of the boarders, but were reserved for Willy and me after they had gone to bed. She thought that all the non-sense about 'interesting' pupils was overdone. 'If they don't care to work, I shouldn't begin to woo them by being amusing, but give them something really dull, like dictation. Interesting stuff ought to be the reward of good work.'

This particular talk was in connexion with the failure of a young assistant teacher who had been engaged to help with our increasing numbers. She was fresh from the Training College, and full of ideas and talk about giving 'interesting lessons'. One day she had prepared an elaborate demonstra-tion of the cause of day and night; not for the little ones but for the elder girls who already knew as much about it as she did. She lit a candle, and swung a potato from a string round it, to represent the earth's movements. It became a little com-plicated and required so much explanation that no notice was taken of our school Touchstone, who was waving her hand in the back row all the time. At last she was observed and asked what her difficulty was. 'How many times,' said she, 'must the potato go round before it gets roasted?' The poor young teacher, instead of enjoying the joke, or seeing an alluring astronomical speculation, burst into tears.

Another importation that lasted only a short while was a French mistress. Her accent, of course, was all that could be desired, but was hopelessly unintelligible to those English girls, for the glad days of the direct method were then un-known. In fact the school seemed to get on better with only Benny, Tommy, and Willy to do the teaching. If only we had been free from fidgets! I was severely reprimanded by Miss Bennett for lending *Vanity Fair* to one of the elder girls who was hopelessly incapable of the usual school subjects, and whose home reading I had discovered to be sentimental tosh. Thackeray would be 'dangerous' for her. I never could guess which episode in Becky's career would have led that great stupid pupil into the path of sin. But any least breath of the opposite sex was to be guarded against, with some rather ridiculous results. Several brothers of the pupils went to St. Paul's School, and used to meet their sisters in the road. Occasionally they fell in with somebody else's sister. Miss Bennett took alarm, and insisted on my being stationed in a first-floor window, every day before and after school, to scan the road and report to her *all* I saw. Needless to say I saw nothing, but I shall never cease to be grateful to the elder pupils who let me see how they sympathized with me in my dreadful job.

One morning after prayers the assembled school sustained a shock of joyful surprise. Miss Bennett in her most solemn tones announced that she had found a letter lying about, containing these most disturbing words: 'Darling Edwin, you are ever in my thoughts', followed by further foolish expressions of a similar nature, which she 'preferred not to read'. After a sweeping glance over the whole school, she said, 'I am afraid I must insist on knowing who this boy is. . . . *Who* is Edwin?' All eyes turned to the most daring pupil, but she was obviously as much puzzled as any one. The question was then repeated in still more impressive tones. A row of tiny juniors were right in front, and from this there was raised a little hand and a piping voice, 'It's me'. Even Miss Bennett was obliged to smile. Two little girls had played at being Edwin and Angelina and had spent spare moments in writing love letters.

For our little community such a mystery was a pleasing interlude in the work. Miss Bennett was a capital headmistress in the latitude she gave for experiments in teaching and in the warm acknowledgement of successful results. Miss Williamson and I enjoyed our struggles with the few dull pupils and the rapid advance made by a few girls of exceptional ability. It was only just now and again that Miss Bennett's passion for perfection passed the bounds of moderation. Such an occasion was the Prize Day, involving an entertainment for parents. These displays ought to be put down by law, for they foster evil thoughts in all who have to do with them. If each form were allowed to spring a surprise item on the audience, it might be fun. In our case the over-preparation killed any pleasure there might have been in the poetry recited. Some Elizabethan schoolmistress must have asked Shakespeare to write a play that would do for her prize day—to have plenty of useful history, nice long speeches, and not too much love interest. And he responded with *Richard II*. Fortunately Miss Bennett undertook the serious business of drilling the elder girls in this, while to me fell the humbler duty of getting a class of thirty to put some life into reciting *The Schooner Hesperus* in unison. One girl would insist that it *was* the schooner Hesperus. I told her that I never said it wasn't, but that had no effect on her, and the devastatingly silly poem was dinned in my ears day after day, when even arithmetic would have been more exhilarating for us all. Of course, on the day of the actual performance the children made all the mistakes they had been trained to avoid, but nobody paid the least attention to anything but clothes and prizes.

It was not only the recitations that consumed so much time. The big room had to be arranged to accommodate the parents, visitors, and pupils, with due regard to their respective importance. Miss Williamson and I had to stay on after school hours, while Miss Bennett kept changing her mind as to which end the platform should be, in what order the pupils should come up for their prizes, where the piano should be placed, and endless smaller details. Mother was greatly amused at all this, and said that Miss Bennett was like 'Old Jasper' in the *Bab Ballads*, with the 'mystic selvagee', the 'swifting in', and 'turning deadeyes up'. Indeed, the parallel was fairly close, for as Rodney was to the captain in the poem, so was Miss Buss to Miss Bennett. 'What would Miss Buss have done?' was her constant criterion, and 'How shocked Miss Buss would have been!' her most serious reproof. Another literary parallel occurred to us and we fetched out *Uncle Remus*, to read once again about Brer Rabbit in the sapling—'he feared he gwineter fall, en he feared he wer'n't gwineter fall'. That's just like Miss Bennett, we agreed; yesterday she was afraid that the number of visitors would be too few for the big room, and to-day she was afraid they would be too many. When on the following day she met us with, 'I think after all the piano had better be on the other side' we had to hide our laughter behind the piano as we shifted it for the fourth time.

For the girls the holidays began after the prize-giving, but for us there remained the Reports. Let no parent think that these are thrown off with careless ease. We had several meetings for them, in order to discuss every turn of phrase. Miss Williamson was far too straightforward in her remarks, and was therefore asked to write them in faint pencil, in case they should need toning down. Our English had to be above reproach, and the expression, 'she must try and improve her spelling' was changed to, 'she must try *to* improve her spelling'. We were warned to avoid metaphor and literary allusions. Miss Bennett told us that she had once written of a stupid girl, 'She is not possessed of all the ten talents', and the mother wrote to ask why *ten* talents were required. We racked our brains for fresh epithets to decorate the deserving, and for synonyms for 'bone lazy' and 'naturally deficient'. Our star pupils who positively never erred, such as Ethel Strudwick and Edith Calkin, gave us so much trouble to praise sufficiently without seeming fulsome, that we were positively grateful to Violet Gask, another champion, of whom we could always say that her writing needed care. When all the spaces had been filled and Miss Williamson's remarks finally adjusted and inked in, Miss Bennett signed them, while Miss Williamson stood by with blotting-paper and I addressed the envelopes. We then offered to post them on our way home, feeling safe from any alterations when once they were slipped into the box. Then at last our holidays began.

Mother and I knew all about our trains for Cornwall, but Miss Williamson lived on a more tricky railway, with all its affairs squeezed into half a page of Bradshaw. But she said that when once she reached Cumberland she knew every inch of the way to her home at Maryport. Her part of England was as remote as Cornwall, and we enjoyed comparing notes on the talk and intonation of the country people. There was a porter whose voice she loved to hear as he sang out, 'Spiátry loop oot—Spiátry loop oot', which conveyed well enough to the people of the district, 'Change here for Aspatria'. And there was an old farmer she knew who used to say of his glass of port that he liked to feel it 'splashing from rib to rib'. He was a lover of the Turf as well as of wine, and would say to any one in the dumps, 'Don't make Despair first favourite— 'edge a bit on 'Ope'.

We started off in high spirits to our wild regions, far north and far west, promising to bring back more stories from Cornwall and Cumberland. I little guessed that I was to explore a far more outlandish part of Britain than either.

XI

My New People, 1888

1

WE had been only a short time in Cornwall, enjoying ourselves as usual with riding and picnics and tennis with my brother Dym and our cousins, when there came an invitation for me to spend the rest of my holiday in Wales. Arthur had told me of his home in a remote Welsh valley, a house called Fronwen that his father had built when he was married, and where he and his three brothers had been brought up. Unfortunately his father had not realized that the actual land on which he built the house was not his, and that anything built on it belonged legally to the landlord; it was therefore a great blow to his widow to find herself, a few years after his death, turned out of her home without the slightest compensation. Indeed it was brutally sudden, for Arthur knew nothing of it when I had seen him last in Kensington. His letters told me that he had hurried to Wales as soon as his term was over, in order to find a new house for his mother and to help her move her furniture. He had settled her in Aberdovey, and everything was still in rather a muddle, but at least there was a spare room ready, and I was begged to come and help put things straight.

Mother and Tony and Dym all insisted that I should write and accept the invitation, and I needed no pressing. Although perfect from my schooldays in the counties and chief towns of Wales, I knew nothing of its intimate features except a few Welsh words my father had taught me, and his remark that 'it's always raining cats and dogs in Wales'. Being a tiny child I had pictured these animals hurtling through the air, and conceived a distaste for the country.

The Irishman's saying, 'You can't get to Armagh from here' began to seem more sensible when Dym and I tried to plan out the route from Camborne to Aberdovey. As the crow flies, easy, but as the trains went, no. Reskadinnick could produce no Bradshaw issued in historical times. 'Never mind, Dym,' said I, 'it'll be fun just to push along; I'll be sure to get there some day.' He advised starting by the night mail, so as to get into Wales by daylight on the following day, and not be involved in Welsh local lines when it was dusk or dark. The mail didn't deign to stop at Camborne, so I had to take a slow train to Redruth. Mother went with me so far, and we were full of grumbles about it, not on account of the extra trouble, but because of the age-long jealousy between the two towns. The idea that the Great Western should pass Camborne and stop at Redruth! This grievance kept our tongues busy and away from my real trouble—the dread of having to meet my new relations, especially a future mother-in-law.

'Don't you mind anything, darling,' was mother's parting injunction on Redruth platform, as the mail fussed in. 'You will be all right. Arthur's mother *must* be splendid. Mind you help her all you can, and remember the girl-guest's rule, never to stay up for a moment after your hostess has gone to bed.'

I settled down comfortably for the certainly uninterrupted run to Bristol, and was therefore annoyed to hear the cry 'all change' when we reached Plymouth. For some reason the last few coaches were to be taken off and we passengers in them had to get out and push in ahead wherever we could. Dym had advised me to travel light, in order to avoid worrying about heavy luggage at the junctions. So I had put everything into a bag that I could carry. A cheery sea-captain took this from me and made room for me in the already crowded carriage that I approached. When we had gone a little way he took out some apples, and that reminded me that I was hungry, and might as well have a bit of supper out of the basket of provisions that Tony had made up for me. Among the really bitter moments of life I reckon that one, lingering in the memory when weightier sorrows are decently forgotten. I had left my parcel on the rack in the other carriage. In my look of disappointment I must have betrayed what had happened, for that ever-blessed captain gave me an apple.

On learning at Bristol that it would be two hours before the Midland train came in, I settled down to read the only light literature I had brought—a sixpenny edition, in small print, of a highly recommended book, which I hoped would be as good as *Jane Eyre*. But a gaunt and empty waiting-room, with no refreshments to be had, round about midnight, was not the best milieu for attacking *Wuthering Heights*. Or perhaps it was, for the steady application to find out who was who, and the hope that surely the next chapter would bring some cheerful happening, helped me to pass the time until my train came in. I was instructed to change at Birmingham, and having ascertained from my fellow passengers that I was not likely to run through Birmingham without knowing it, I stilled the cravings of hunger as a dog does, by going off to sleep.

Birmingham turned out to be larger and more desolate than Bristol. For all its many platforms there was only one miserable little waiting-room open, and that very stuffy, and occupied by two sleeping women. If Mrs. Elton thought there was something direful in the sound of Birmingham, I certainly thought there was something direful in the sight of it. Walking up and down and pretending to be an explorer in Africa, I came across a genial-looking porter.

'Any chance of a cup of tea anywhere?' I asked him.

'Not till 8 o'clock, Missy, refreshment room's shut up.' Then seeing my look of distress he added, 'But if you come along of me, I'll get you a cup.'

I went 'along of him', and we reached a little shanty in a backwater of the vast station. It was like those alluring coffee stalls tucked away in odd corners of London. A man was dispensing tea to porters on their way to and from work. For a penny I was given a cup of steaming elixir, with a biscuit in the saucer. The cup was so thick that my lips could hardly get round it, and the tea slopped over and soaked the biscuit.

But it was the greatest value for money I have ever obtained. Indeed, I felt as if I ought to pour it out as a libation, as David did the cup of water.

This happy venture passed the time too, and gave me strength to walk about again and read the advertisements. It was daylight when my next train came in, and as it was nearly empty I had no fellow passengers to consult, so determined to watch for Shrewsbury all the way, in case I passed it. But I fell fast asleep, only to wake as we were gliding into another big station. Shrewsbury! Hurrah! Food was my one thought, and it was not till I had fallen upon a pork pie and hot coffee that I asked about the next train for Aberdovey. There was to be one about 10, and that was convenient, since it was then only 8. But when I found on further inquiries that it was to arrive at Aberdovey at 2, I changed my mind. To face new people is bad enough at any hour, but at 2 o'clock in the afternoon it is hideous. I pictured a lunch just cleared away, and either a dreadful attempt to warm some up for me, or else a long stretch of being polite before tea would be possible. No. Finding that the next train would not start till 2, I actually decided to spend the six hours in Shrewsbury to wait for it, little knowing that the Cambrian railway could have been relied on to be an hour late, if I had chosen the earlier train. The station people must have thought me a suspicious character, or suffering from some nervous complaint, for I kept returning to its purlieus after each little prowl round the town. My chief interest was Tom's school. But I found that the old building of his day had been turned into a public library or something equally impersonal, and that the new buildings were away on the other side of the town by the river. I went to see them and they looked all beautiful, but had no associations with my brother, so I returned to the old building, and tried to pick out which window might have been that of his old prep-room. For this had been the scene of two of his school-boy pranks that had specially delighted me as a child. One was the putting of an alarm-clock in the master's desk, arranged to go off during the deep quiet of prep-time, and the other

was the simultaneous tearing of brown paper at the third
stroke of 7 by all the boys in study.

After this I merely wandered about the town, enjoying the
little up-and-down streets with funny names (such as Wyle
Cop and Dogpole), the old timbered houses, and the country
women in their poke-bonnets and plaid shawls. Then I fell
back on the Londoner's unfailing source of amusement—looking at the shop windows. Returning to my base, the station
waiting-room, I wrote a letter to mother, and went out again
to find the post office to buy a stamp. After this I had another
determined go at *Wuthering Heights*. But the characters seemed
to have become more complicated and even less exhilarating
than the night before, so I went to the book-stall to look for
something professedly comic. But Ally Sloper proved more
depressing than Emily Brontë, and I returned to her with posi-
tive relief.

Half-past twelve at last! This was the hour I had fixed as
the earliest possible for my midday meal, and I intended that it
should consume as much time as possible. The first thing was
to capture it. This was before the days when shops offered
attractive lunches, and I was far too shy and inexperienced to
walk into an hotel. So I bought apples in one shop, buns at
another, some chocolate at another, returning with each purchase to the waiting-room, much to the amusement of the
attendant, to whom I had confided my folly in waiting so
long, and who took a kindly interest in the situation.

At 1.30 I felt it would be quite respectable to appear on the
platform and look as if I had just arrived. The train 'for the
coast' soon came along, and settling down in an empty carriage
I regarded my troubles as over. How jolly! We were actually
off! But after going a few hundred yards we stopped. Here
there were good views of the town, but I had really seen
enough of it for the time. Everything was so quiet that I
feared my carriage had been sent aside for repairs. I leaned
out and saw a man waving his arms, and guessed that we must
be only shunting. We were soon back in the station, to rest
a little before starting for the coast.

The journey was scheduled for about four hours, and, as I surmised from the many stops and general leisureliness, it would be actually longer. But I didn't care how long it was, so excited was I at my new surroundings. I had never seen mountains before, and there was the train plodding along right amongst them, now breathing hard up a steep incline and now cluttering down the other side. Every bend brought a fresh view of the great masses in all shades of grey. It was a sunny afternoon, and wispy clouds were throwing shadows on purple hill-sides, and valley after valley led away to goodness knew where. I kept hovering from one end of the carriage to the other, and lost all my fatigue in the delight of the new experience. When we went down into the Dovey valley I exclaimed some words that Arthur had taught me—'a dwfn yw tonau Dyfi' (Deep are the waters of Dovey). I surrendered then, admitting at last that Wales could produce finer scenery than Cornwall.

Light relief was afforded by the names of the stations and my attempts to pronounce them. Machynlleth beat me, but I learnt how to spell it, for the train lingered there for ages with shuntings and shoutings. Was I all right for Aberdovey, I asked, and was told that I must change at the Junction for the Coast. One more junction seemed a trifle, but I did not then know my Glandovey. The pull-up here was as decided and as seemingly final as at Euston. Not that there was any town to go to, for the junction lay in the middle of marshy flats, without even a road to connect it with any busy hum. But in itself it was certainly a busy hum, being the nerve centre between North and South Wales, just where the dividing river Dovey spread out into an estuary. The train in which I sat was bound for Aberystwyth and the south, so I gathered that Aberdovey must lie to the north. The extreme congestion on the platform was due to the fact that everybody, no matter his destination, got out. The motive appeared to be social rather than utilitarian. Little knots of farmers, commercial travellers, English holiday-makers, and so on, were chatting as if no thought of continuing their journey were troubling

them. But a number of determined-looking women, laden
with bundles of things they had bought or were going to sell
—eggs, live poultry, fruit and vegetables—were preparing to
take by storm an inferior looking train that was just appearing
round the hills to the north. Obviously it was going the wrong
way for me, and yet I saw no other. It all seemed to me like
the game of croquet in *Alice*. The only porter in sight was
too engrossed with luggage to be appealed to. Seeing a nice
young English tourist gazing at the scene with amusement, I
asked him if he had any idea where I could get the train for
Aberdovey.

'It's that one that has just come in; you see it turns back
here. Let me take your bag and I'll find you a seat, but I'm
afraid this coast train is pretty bad, even worse than our
Aberystwyth one.'

'Oh, don't let me keep you, your train may be off.'

'There's no fear of that,' he laughed, 'we have ample warning
before she starts.'

And indeed we had. 'Take your seats, take your seats,'
was shouted at intervals by the porter, in the vain hope that
he would get more room to move the luggage about. It was
evident that his request had no connexion with the starting
of the train.

My pleasant young man found me a seat at last, with apolo-
gies for 'the best he could do', amidst the market women. The
carriage astounded me, for I thought this kind of thing had
long ago been turned into tool-sheds for London suburban
gardens. It had wooden seats, minute windows, and was open
throughout.

'It won't be for long,' were his parting words, 'Aberdovey is
the next station.'

And now I was met by one of the surprises of my life.
These women, delivered from the anxieties of getting themselves and their bundles into the train, began to talk. And it
was all in a foreign language. The bits of Welsh that my father
and Arthur had taught me I had thought to be quaint survivals,
and had no idea that people talked like that all day. Meanwhile

I clutched my bag, all ready to jump out at the 'next station. On we rolled through the meadows by the side of the broadening Dovey, dotted with black cows and little white sheep. We plunged in total darkness through several tunnels where the mountains came down to the riverside. I knew that Aberdovey meant the mouth of the Dovey, so we must be very near. Still no sign of human habitation except a few isolated farms. On and on. At last, as we emerged from one of the tunnels, I saw roofs, another tunnel, then more roofs, and yes, a church tower. Here we are, thought I. Another tunnel, into the station, doubtless. No, into the open country again, and well away, with no symptom of slowing down! I was in despair, for evidently we had passed the place and were in some kind of express. I ventured to ask the woman next me, but she let loose such a flood of Welsh on me that I could only smile pleasantly and bring out one of the few Welsh expressions I knew—'diolch fawr'.

Then, with apparently no reason, the train began to slow down among the fields. I looked out and saw a wooden platform, and a board with 'Aberdovey' on it. And there, too, was Arthur looking anxiously up and down the train. With him was a large clergyman, overflowing with boisterous greetings, as I got out.

'We shall have to walk up, I fear,' said Arthur, 'there's no cab to be had.' As we left the station he pointed to a black box on wheels, drawn by an unbelievably old horse, driven by an unbelievably old man. 'That is the Aberdovey omnibus, "plying between station and town". You tell old Rushell where you want to be put down, climb in, bang the door as a sign that you are safe, and in time he starts. Luggage goes on a trolley, driven by a one-armed man who stands up in the middle. We shall see him presently on the road; it's about all the traffic we have.'

It was a goodish walk from the station, for the town straggled along between the hills and the estuary, including on its way a real port with a bright-funnelled little steamer tied up at the quay. I was amused with the walk and glad to stretch my legs after being cooped up so long. The vicar accompanied us the whole way, not from parochial duty, as I at first imagined, but (as I learned later) because he had nothing else to do, and my arrival was a bit of an event, a trifle to add to the gossip. I was amazed at the way in which both he and Arthur turned on Welsh, as though from a tap, whenever they met an acquaintance, which was about every hundred yards.

At last the vicar said good-bye. He was very stout and didn't want to do our final climb. The tiny house that Arthur had captured for his mother was at the end of a tiny row, lodged precariously on a tiny ledge of the hill-side. We could reach Brynhyfryd only by a rough and very steep path. At the open door stood Mrs. Hughes, with a 'Well, well, well, and here you are at last!' It is curious how a mere tone of voice can make you feel at home at once. A meal was all ready, and as I fell upon it heartily I was able to amuse Arthur and his mother with the story of my twenty-six-hour journey in seven trains; he, poor fellow, had been at the station since 2 o'clock, off and on.

I was pleased to find that Mrs. Hughes herself was English, and even with her long married life in Wales had picked up only enough Welsh to talk to the servant and the tradesmen. All her friends were like Arthur, bi-lingual. It had been like an earthquake for her to leave her old home among the mountains, but she was beginning to find pleasure in her little house at Aberdovey, which was high enough to give her a view of the estuary and the southern hills and the sea beyond the harbour. As she was showing me every corner and every limitation of the house on the following day, as though I were already her daughter, she confessed that she had been in some alarm about me. I was curious to know why. 'Well, you see, dear, the name "Molly" sounded so frivolous.'

The idea of my being frivolous was still funnier than my being considered modern, and Mrs. Hughes soon saw the absurdity of it when I entered with zest into all her household perplexities. Catering was the supreme problem. We could get a leg of superb Welsh mutton every Saturday, from a little lock-up shop. Superb in quality, not in size. This had to be, in some form or other, the main dish for the week. I began to understand the origin of the Friday fast, for vegetables were definitely predominating in the stew by that day. There was generally 'some ham in the house'. Butter and eggs could be obtained at uncertain intervals from a woman coming with a basket from a farm up among the hills. So uncertain were her visits that the butter had to be salted down in order to keep. There was no fruit to be had, no cake, and most astonishing to me for Wales, no cheese. There was no cool larder, and the heat was often so great that we could have frizzled bacon on the slate flags by the front door. Poultry was too dear to be considered. Bread was made at home by the servant, two vast loaves at a time, and carried down to a bake-house in the village. As it grew very stale I asked her how often she baked.

'Now *you* are here,' she said with pride, 'we bake once a week, but usually once a fortnight.'

This little servant was quite useless at cooking outside the sphere of bread and potato-peeling and mint-chopping, so I asked Mrs. Hughes if I could help a bit in this direction. The response was ready.

'Well, dear, to tell the truth, I should be really grateful if you would undertake the suppers. My sight is getting rather bad for cooking at night.'

Therein she showed great acumen. I believe it wasn't so much her poor sight as the difficulty of making a variety of pleasant meals of the lesser kind, with no resources. *Ex nihilo fiat aliquid.* For the actual cooking there was nothing but one of those open fire-places that break the heart. There was an oven, but it flatly refused to do anything *quickly*, so that any dish with pastry was ruled out. A frying-pan could be poised on the fire, and with that I managed bacon and eggs in all their combinations and permutations. Tinned things were not to be had in those days—not in Aberdovey.

The rumour of a catch of mackerel was sheer glory. Arthur would rush down to the water-side and capture half a dozen great glittering beauties for as many pence. Their colours were so beautiful that I was quite sorry to cook them. Having no experience or guidance as to how they should be 'dressed', I had to go by the light of nature, and my very first venture was a great success. I cleaned them and laid them in a tin, put flour and butter on the top, a little vinegar and water under them, made up the fire as fiercely as I could, put the tin in the oven, and awaited results. With coffee and home-made marmalade we had a meal fit for a king.

In the village of course there were shops, and I soon knew the character and contents of each. The butcher's shed was opened only on Saturday, when old Rowland would sit and flick the flies off his mutton. The draper's was a gloomy, dusty spot where a melancholy woman would do her best to supply some dire necessity of clothing; I always wondered how she made a living. These were the only two distinctive shops; all the others seemed to sell everything. The liveliest centre of trade was called 'Garibaldi's', because Mr. Jones liked to be known as an Italian warehouseman. Here we could buy oil, tea, bacon, tobacco, sweets, and on Friday the great attraction for Arthur, *The Cambrian News*. I think his name was Jones, but he was always known as 'old Garibaldi'. Sometimes a rumour would reach us that there was some cheese 'in', or some plums, and Mrs. Hughes and I would immediately go 'shopping'. 'Which shop shall we try?' was my natural question, but her routine was invariable. 'I like to patronize them all,' she would say, 'because there are little jealousies.' And how I enjoyed our morning's work to get a bit of cheese. At each shop there was a minute purchase of bacon or tea, or a reel of cotton, after a full discussion of the weather or a recent death. Finally, we would get some tobacco for Arthur at Garibaldi's and then be surprised to hear, 'Inteet there is some *cheese* to-day.'

So it was not so much the lack of money as the lack of things to buy that caused us to be underfed in the Aberdovey of the eighties.

2

One day, however, we were forcibly fed. An invitation came to spend the day at Machynlleth with some old friends of the family. When Arthur pulled a face at the idea, I naturally said, 'Then why go?' But it was almost of the type of a royal command, for they knew we had nothing to do, and any trumped-up excuse would have wounded their feelings. 'Well, let's just go to tea,' I suggested. Again Arthur shook his head, 'Mother would think that a shocking waste of railway-fare.'

A distance from door to door, that a car could comfortably manage in half an hour to-day, consumed over two hours on the railway, even when things went reasonably well. The trains were few, and not *invariably* late. An hour was the usual time for them to be behind schedule, and if this could have been relied on we could have fallen comfortably in with the plan. But sometimes they would be punctual! Now in order to be in time for lunch at Machynlleth, our feast of obligation, we had to get the 8 o'clock train from Aberdovey. This meant breakfast at 7, because Mrs. Hughes liked to start at 7.30, so as to be on the safe side. Meanwhile, Arthur stayed behind to enjoy his pipe.

Mrs. Hughes and I sat on the platform and amused ourselves as best we could, and were quite cheered to see some kind of odd train doddering in from Towyn—a goods or something. To our dismay we discovered that it was our own train, actually up to time. And of course no sign of Arthur.

'There! What have I always said? I knew he would be late, running it so close. We must go without him, that's all,' said Mrs. Hughes as she climbed into a carriage. I wanted to wait for the next train, but she said the people at Machynlleth would be at the station to meet us, and it wouldn't do to disappoint them. Reluctantly I got in too, and hoped that there would be the usual delay in departure. I hung out of the window to see if Arthur were in sight. Yes, there he was far back along the road, running hard, for he had evidently seen the train. Then the wretched thing started. All I could do

was to wave regrets to Arthur, but he was otherwise occupied.
To my alarm I saw him turn from the road, vault the fence,
run on to the line and wave his arms in front of the engine.
We stopped, and in another minute he was scrambling into
the carriage.

There was never any hurry, because there was bound to
be a long wait at the junction before the train from Aberystwyth came in. Just as we were lumbering over the river-
bridge into Glandovey Junction we went suddenly soft—
ominously soft. Arthur's head was out at once.

'By George! We've gone off the rails!'

Few things can look more helpless than a Cambrian engine
off the rails in such a remote spot. All the passengers climbed
out to walk the few yards from the bridge to the platform,
not attempting to disguise their glee at the disaster. All *we*
had to do was to board the Aberystwyth train when it came in.
But the poor station-master was at his wits' end, not having
any jack or any possible means at hand for replacing the engine.
Completely losing control of himself he tore up and down the
platform swearing in Welsh, to Arthur's rapture. This was
our last vision of him as the main-line train took us reluctantly
away from the drama.

The incident made grand conversation for our friends at
Machynlleth, which we reached about 11. Our 'early start'
and 'dangerous journey' were made the excuse for us to be
plied with fruit and cake and wine. Then a stroll round the
town, involving chats with almost every one we met, soon
brought the time for 1 o'clock dinner. This was a serious
meal of boiled mutton and vegetables, followed by apple
pudding, everything garnished with copious sauces. Help-
ings were large, in spite of protests, and I sensed that feelings
would be hurt if anything were left on the plate. Very welcome was a country walk after this, when I was able to enjoy
the colours of the hills while Arthur conversed, for the most
part in Welsh, with our host and his son. Tea-time was fixed
for 4 o'clock, because our only possible return train started
at 5, and it would never do to hurry a meal. A cup of tea

would certainly have been welcome, but behold there was a
real sit-down affair. The main dish was 'light cakes'. This
famous Welsh concoction is a kind of pancake, made with
flour and eggs and buttermilk. You eat them hot, with sugar
and butter, the very thing for a winter tea after a long tramp.
But for a summer afternoon, hard upon such a massive dinner!
The cook kept sending in fresh relays, straight from the pan,
and they were piled on our plates, with the warning, 'Remember there's a journey before you'. I could only be thankful
that the train started too early to permit a supper to follow.

Of course it was only the time-table that 'started'. The
train for England was as usual about an hour late. Arthur
was quite willing in this case to be at the station at the scheduled
time, because there was a bookstall to which he glued himself.
Mrs. Hughes was quietly triumphing in the booty she had
captured in the shops, a cake and some cheese. As soon as
the train was off Arthur said, 'I couldn't find anything decent
on that bookstall, so we must fall back on our reserves', taking
out a little volume of Montaigne which he had put in his pocket
when he started out. 'The mere feel of it in my pocket,' he said,
'helps me to bear the plethora of physical and the lack of mental
food one has to endure in Machynlleth.' We settled down to
read one of the essays together, and even the wait at Glandovey
Junction (now in normal working order again) seemed quite
short. I have never passed through that station since without
recalling some of Montaigne's advice on learning how to die.

It was not many days after this that another invitation
arrived for an outing that involved the same railway journey,
but a very different kind of entertainment. An old friend of
Arthur's boyhood wrote to ask him to bring me to see his
people in their home near Machynlleth, an old country man-
sion up among the hills and woods. He was a few years
younger than Arthur, and known to us then as 'Dick Atkin',
but he is now a Law Lord. His 'people' consisted of his
mother and grandmother—a little alarming in prospect; but
I had hardly been in the house an hour when I began to wonder
which was the more delightful, and longing for my mother

to meet them, for they seemed to be of her 'make'. The grand-mother, Mrs. Ruck, was all that one could imagine of queenly dignity combined with an engaging homeliness. She was un-disguisedly keenly interested to know the girl whom her dear friend Arthur was to marry, and in some subtle way that women always understand but can't describe, she made me feel that I was approved to the full. She showed me over the old house, talking cheerily of the deep happiness of married life, taking me into her room to see the four-poster of colossal size, on which all her children had been born. She interspersed her talk with enthusiastic praise of Arthur.

'If I don't tell you about him, nobody will,' said she. 'He has been so splendid to his mother. Although not the eldest, he has been the only one of her four sons to come to her help with time and money through that dreadful uprooting from her old home. One's own home, why it's heaven as one gets old! She looks to him for everything. And remember this, dear, a good son makes a good husband.'

I listened greedily to this and much more, and she ended with, 'I'm so glad that he is at the same Inn as Dick, and I'm sure they will both have a fine career at the Bar.'

Her daughter regaled me in another fashion. She had travelled all over the world, and had gone through amazing adventures, which she related in a matter-of-fact, off-hand style, as if it were no more than walking down the road. But the one thing I remember best about her is the rate at which she knitted while she told her stories. When I commented on this, she said she could easily make a sock in a day, but that she much preferred mending an old one. Now I could believe her marvellous adventures, but showed open rejection of this statement.

'You can't possibly *like* mending!'

'Yes, I do. Any one can make a thing all new and nice. But to make a good thing out of an abandoned one is far more creative work—a work of redemption!'

In the afternoon Dick took Arthur and me for a walk still farther up the hill-side, and I listened in silence to the talk of the two men, always an engrossing occupation for me. Presently we reached a high point whence we had an extensive view of the valley and the sweep of the river. This was a favourite show-piece of Dick's, and he was pleased at my enthusiasm. I ventured to say that my brother Dym thought that no view was perfect unless there were a river in it. This set a discussion going in true legal fashion: first whether Dym's idea was true; second, if true, what was the reason. I forget the conclusion they came to, if any, although I have long since discovered why a river is necessary to complete satisfaction. It is odd that in the dream of heaven there was to be 'no more sea', while a river was to be the main feature; into what did it run?

As for that visit, I forget about the journey there and the journey home. I forget what we had for dinner or tea. But the people, the house among the woods, the weather, the talk, the view of the river—all these remain as an abiding delight.

§ 3

A third day's outing involved the same Machynlleth opening, but in other respects was a striking contrast to the other two. Arthur wanted to show me the valley where he had spent his boyhood. No invitation was required; we were just to set out. I fancy that he had misgivings about it, for he told me afterwards that he had made up his mind never to marry any one but a girl who knew all his home people and early surroundings. And here was I, a Londoner, and a complete stranger to everything and everybody. What if I should smile at the countrified ways, or show any airs of greater intelligence! He gave me no descriptions beforehand, but plunged me into an utterly new experience.

At Machynlleth station we went down some wooden steps to the 'terminus' of a toy railway. After many social greetings with other intending passengers, we boarded one of the cars of which the train consisted, and in due time one of the engines of the Company began to agitate itself and eventually to start.

A fig for your boasted 'observation cars' in America! Without advertisements or folders, or self-consciousness, the little train rattled away (for it cheered the lonely valley with plenty of mechanical noise) along the side of a heavenly trout-stream, overhung with tall trees and surrounded by mountains. Every now and again we had fresh peeps of the winding valley, ever changing in its colour effects. Arthur saw my delight and said, 'This is the stream where we used to bathe and catch trout when we were boys.' No wonder, I thought, that you poured scorn on our little stream near Reskadinnick.

There were several stations, whose names I learnt to pronounce. In its even-handed justice Bradshaw awarded Ffridd Gate the same size print as Aberystwyth, but it surely was the smallest station in the world. The gate was there all right, leading into a field, and beside it were a couple of planks for a platform, and on this was a kind of tiny sentry-box. If by some extraordinary chance a man wanted to get in here, he would signal his idea, and the engine-driver would pull up, unlock the little box, and issue a ticket to him. At least that was the scheme. In point of fact there was very little of this ticket nonsense at all on the railway. What money the Company received came almost entirely from strangers, English tourists, and other fools. All its Welsh patrons in the valley stepped off and on as they pleased. While we were in full swing plugging up the valley there was a sudden grinding of brakes and a jerky pull-up. 'I know what's the matter,' cried Arthur, jumping out, 'there's a sheep on the line.' He returned in a few moments to report all well—he had driven the sheep out of danger.

At every station I seemed to make a new friend. Invariably the greeting at each introduction was, 'Indeed, now! Well, well, indeed!' And this can be made astonishingly warm and hearty. At Escairgailiog in breezed the doctor, who was overjoyed to see Arthur and immediately asked us to lunch with him at Corris, the metropolis of the valley. Here there was quite a crowd on the little platform, and I exclaimed at the number of travellers. Arthur laughed. 'They're not going by train; they've just come to see who has arrived, and get a bit of gossip; your appearance will be quite an item.'

I gathered from the conversation during our lunch at the doctor's that Arthur and his brothers were the main source of local interest. His eldest brother had lately become vicar of Portmadoc, and his youngest brother was about to start a medical practice in Flint. It was this youngest one, Alfred, in whom the doctor took most interest. When quite a boy he had accompanied the doctor on his rounds; for these the doctor's only carriage was the railway, and the infrequency of the trains put him in many an awkward fix. He had sometimes been obliged to give sedatives to two expectant mothers while he attended a third. Of course, young Alfred picked up endless medical lore of a natural kind, and it was said that the patients preferred his visits to those of the doctor. When I came to know him (shortly after this luncheon party) I immediately understood this preference; for Alfred was a good-looking, sunny, jolly fellow, full of good stories, and no one could help feeling better for his mere presence. I may as well say here that he had a future of absorbing devotion to his work. In later years I went to meet him once in London, where he had come up for his F.R.C.S.

'Are you funking it, Alfred?' I asked.

'No, Molly, I'm not. You just put your finger on any spot in your body, and I'll tell you *all* that lies beneath it, right away down.'

He had the reputation later still for being the best anatomist in the kingdom, and was in the middle of writing a three-volume work on *Practical Anatomy* when the Boer War put an end to his life, and it fell to Arthur (now Sir Arthur) Keith to edit and complete his book.

As soon as our lunch was over we went off again to the station. Twice a day the train made a final lap to its terminus at the extreme head of the valley at Aberllefeni. Here was the large slate quarry of which Arthur's father had been the manager. A broad-built, strong-willed man, he had been the terror of any delinquent quarryman. He carried a huge slate-whistle whose blast used to send the men scurrying to their work. Fronwen, the house that he built for his wife, lay on the hill-side between the railway and the rushing stream, and had an orchard, garden, and chicken-run. What entranced me most was the littleness, and the fewness, and the remoteness of everything. I felt that I could take it all in, and love it, and that Arthur's people were my people. At the tiny post office Annie and Bill (I never heard their surnames) received me rapturously with the very few words of English at their command. It was the same at every dwelling we entered, and I don't think we missed any.

That visit was only the first of innumerable others in later years. Meanwhile I sucked much more information about the valley from Mrs. Hughes. There had been no lack of food, although it mostly revolved round the sheep; they even had 'mutton hams'. Mutton fat was used to make candles, the only artificial light obtainable. Mrs. Hughes showed me her old mould into which she used to pour the fat for them; this and her snuffers she had kept from sheer sentiment. For the clothing of her husband and sons a travelling tailor paid annual visits. Arthur could remember seeing him sitting tailor-wise on the kitchen table, usually staying a week to complete his job. By most of the inhabitants of the valley this tailor was regarded with awe, for he could read and write. One old woman begged him to read a chapter from her Bible to the assembled family when his day's work was done. Now he had been annoyed to note that he had not been offered tea with his supper, although he had seen a pot on the hob. In those days tea was a great luxury, being ten to fifteen shillings a pound. So on the second evening he selected the latter part of Deuteronomy xxvii, and inserted a verse—'Cursed be the housewife that bringeth not forth tea to the tailor'. When the reading was over the housewife approached him with, 'Is that bit about tea really in the Bible?' 'Oh yes,' said he, pretending to look for it, and at last running his finger over a verse and repeating it slowly. Tea was brought forth for him after that, every night.

Recreation had to be provided by the valley itself, and it

seemed to have consisted mainly of mountain walking and fishing in the summer, and singing, dancing, and card-playing in the winter. The scarcity of instrumental music can be guessed from one disaster that Arthur related to me: a big dance was arranged, people came from far and near, and the band (one fiddler) from a considerable distance. When all was in trim to start dancing it was found that the fiddler had left his bow behind! I expect they made up for it by singing, for that seems to be the Welshman's supreme hobby.

I hardly wonder at a country parson's taking to drink. Often enough he is sufficiently educated to be dissatisfied with the mental capacity of his flock, but not sufficiently to content himself with books or a hobby. It was so in Corris. There the little church that serves the whole district stands in the loveliest surroundings. Thither, twice every Sunday, the whole Hughes family walked the long way from Aber-llefeni. Mr. Hughes, as a churchwarden, sat in a front pew, with his wife and boys in a solid phalanx. Arthur had a vivid recollection of Alfred's trying to play with a hassock once, and being taken out then and there and whipped in the church-yard. A little later Alfred was to figure in another scene; one Sunday morning the whole neighbourhood was duly mustered, but no parson. People began to look about them and whisper their wonder. The situation became tense. At last, by con-sultations and urgent gestures Mr. Hughes was induced to go over to the vicarage to see what was the matter (although the congregation had little doubt as to its nature). If any one could manage a difficulty, he could. Another wait, more hopeful, but still rather too long. Mrs. Hughes then took a hand (know-ing her husband). As Alfred was sitting at the end of the pew she leant over to him and told him to run to the vicarage and bring his father back, whatever. Again a long wait. I had this story from Alfred himself, and how he laughed at the recollection of that errand. As he came up to the vicarage he saw the old housekeeper standing at the door, looking very agitated.

'Come in, come in, my little boy,' she cried, obviously

relieved that somebody had appeared in her trouble, and showed Alfred into the study. There sat his father and the vicar, both comfortably drinking, but too far gone to move.

This will be credible enough to Welsh people, who know that nothing of a diplomatic nature can be done hurriedly. Mrs. Hughes told me that she once took the train into Machynlleth to have a bad tooth taken out. The dentist was distressed at the pain she was suffering, brought out sherry and chatted of livelier matters. 'Indeed, Mrs. Hughes,' said he, 'I don't think I need put you to the pain of taking out that tooth. I believe you are well enough to go home now.' And she actually returned with the tooth and feeling all right. One wonders how he made a living. But there seemed to have been very little in the way of actual money transactions, especially from a patient to a doctor. A good fat goose or a bottle of wine was a more common thank-offering.

Of crime in the valley there seemed to be none. Once only did the well-known policeman, who patrolled the whole district, appear at Mrs. Hughes's door. Some days previously a disreputable-looking tramp had come to her and begged for an old coat. She searched the house, but all she could find, that was not actually in use, was a richly embroidered waistcoat that her father had worn years ago at some civic function in Shrewsbury. Why keep things just for sentiment, thought she, and gave it to the tramp. It was an embarrassing gift, for if displayed it took away the look of poverty that was his chief asset. So he stripped and wore it next his skin until he should find a possible market for it. However, at his next casual home he was required to have a bath, and the waistcoat was discovered. 'Mrs. Hughes of Fronwen gave it to me,' he asserted. The idea of such a gift to a tramp was so ridiculous that the policeman had come all the way to have the story confirmed, but he might have guessed that no tramp in his senses would steal such an unnegotiable thing.

That first visit of mine to the valley was over forty years ago, but a recent visit has shown me little change. The quarry works are deserted at Aberllefeni, and look as melancholy as the ghosts of the Cornish tin-mines. But Corris has the same two inns, shops, and up-and-down streets surrounding the station and the beautiful churchyard. . . . At a prominent corner of the village, where you can get a sight of Cader, stands a column, a monument to Alfred. To me a more touching memorial of him is a bundle of letters from South Africa, tied up with a bit of tape, and labelled in Arthur's handwriting, 'Dear Alfred'.

XII

'A dwfn yw tonnau Dyfi'

§ 1

THOSE expeditions were of the 'private duty bound' nature. Most of our days we just wasted gloriously, doing what we liked. Our likings were strictly limited by our means. We had to look at every penny, except in the matter of newspapers and tobacco, which I had known from childhood to be the breath of life to a man. Now the railway consumed money as well as time, and there was no other means of getting about to 'see Wales' than by long walks. I have seen more of it in one day in my son's car than in all my visits to it in the last century.

There were certain special bits of the Wales that Arthur loved which simply had to be visited whatever the cost, and for these a car would have been no use. The first charge on the estate was the ascent of Cader. 'Cader Idris', I learnt, meant 'Arthur's Seat.' The mountain had dominated the valley and been the playground of Arthur and his brothers in their boyhood. They had been to the summit countless times, and more than once Arthur and Alfred had spent the night there to see the sun rise.

So one fine morning we reached the foot of Cader by way of the toy railway from Towyn to Abergynolwyn. The early slopes were easy enough, and I pranced on heartily, thinking, 'Well, if this is mountain climbing, why all the fuss about it?' I had slackened my pace a bit by the time we reached the sinister shores of Llyn Cae, and Arthur suggested a rest and an attack on the sandwiches, before the real climbing began. He pointed out to me the 'Fox's Path', away on the other side of the Lake.

'Is that the path we have to follow?' I asked.

'No,' he laughed, 'not quite so steep as that.'

I found my stick of great use during the next half-hour's climb, for it was no longer merely walking.

'There's the top, quite close!' said I in triumph.

'No, not yet by a long way. Old Cader has a way of telescoping out. Each "top" that you see turns out to be only a nice place to get a good view of the next.'

I felt a fool, and determined to plod on without offering any further encouraging remarks, although I was pretty sure several times that the coming peak was really the top.

Presently we found ourselves in a cloud, and Arthur was moving more cautiously. 'Keep close up,' he said, 'we're nearly there . . . ah, here it is. This little shed marks the top. I wish to goodness this mist would clear, or we shall get no view at all.'

We fixed half an hour as the limit that we ought to wait. It brought us no lift, but rather a thickening of the mist. So very reluctantly we began the descent. Our plan was to catch the last train from Arthog at 7.30. We scrambled down the slopes well enough, stopping now and again to enjoy the evening views all the more splendid after the mist. When we reached the road in the valley it was nearly 7, and we quickened our pace.

'How far to Arthog?' I panted to a man we were passing.

'Three miles.'

'Good gracious!' said I, 'we can't do it.'

'They always say three miles,' said Arthur, 'it's not a bit of good asking them.' And sure enough, after some ten minutes hard walking, another man told me 'three miles', for I couldn't resist asking. We laughed and took heart. When 7.30 had past Arthur threw out the comforting idea that the train was bound to be late, as it came from Dolgelly. He had hardly said this when he cried, 'There's the station', pointing to something in the middle distance.

'By George, yes, and the train is in it,' and he broke into a headlong run. Although I knew he could hold it up for me if he got there before it started, I was impelled to run too. It was now getting dark, and among the few lights of the station I distinguished the ominous red rear-lamp of the train. I kept my eye on it, as if that would prevent it's moving. When I panted on to the platform Arthur was waiting with a door open, and we flung ourselves in. That wretched train didn't start for another ten minutes! At the time I think we were more annoyed at this than if we had missed it, though what we should have done in the latter case we never cared to discuss. But those who happen to know the kind of walk it is from Arthog to simply anywhere will guess what Arthur was worrying about as he ran.

A still worse predicament threatened us another time. One hot day we determined to try to reach our old friend Glandovey by water. While Arthur went down to the shore to see whether he could bargain for a boat, I cut sandwiches, hard-boiled two eggs, and put some tea in a bottle (wrapped in a rug to keep it hot).

'Let's start at once,' said Arthur on his return. 'I've captured a boat. The tide will be high about 4, and if we can reach Glandovey by 3 we can have our tea there and come back on the ebb. Now have you got plenty to eat in that basket?'

'Yes. I've put in enough for lunch on the way, and for tea when we get there. And I'm taking our sketching things too, as we shan't have to carry them.'

'And I got a bottle of beer from the inn. So off we go.'

However happy one's life has been, there are few days to which one can point and say, 'I would like to live that over again, exactly as it was'. But every bit of that day had either its fun or its thrill, both at the time and in retrospect. Mrs. Hughes saw us off with some misgiving and urgent warnings not to be out late on the river. She was always full of warnings and misgivings, but she knew no more than we did of the difficulties in front of us. The Dovey estuary looks broad and beautiful and inviting, as if butter wouldn't melt in her mouth, but she is a lady of moods and asks for navigation, not just rowing up and down. She has sandbanks always shifting, and we had to follow the channels that seemed best. When we came to a fine stretch of deep water, up would go our sail, and if there was the least puff of breeze how lordly we felt floating along for awhile without effort. But soon would come a dead calm and sagging of the sail, or a sandbank and a struggle with the oars again. It was hungry work, requiring the sandwiches and beer.

As the river broadened out towards Glandovey the sailing was easier, and we laughed at the train puffing heavily along, while we were gliding serenely, coming into the almost lake-like expanse of water near Glandovey. Here a tongue of wooded land stretched out into the estuary, and as we spied a convenient post for mooring our boat we disembarked, having a good hour in hand before the tide would turn. First of all we reconnoitred round for a good subject to sketch. Not that there was any lack of subject in all directions, but we had to find something we could manage. We had to avoid trees, and confine our attempts to the hills and marshlands of Ynyslas. We dashed the cobalt about recklessly and jeered at each other's results.

While Arthur was enjoying his after-tea pipe, I went down to the water's edge to see whether the tide had turned. Yes, it was an inch below the mark we had put, so I proposed our starting at once. Then came the best of the day, the tide and a gentle breeze both with us, and the perfection of Welsh scenery. A sandbank now and again would persuade us quite feelingly that we had better not linger, but a shove with an oar soon got us into a channel again. The tiller was hardly any use, for the wide stretch of water looked equally deep and our first notice of a sandbank was the actual sensation of the keel grinding into it. These banks soon became more frequent, and we ran on them so quickly with the breeze, that Arthur thought it safer to take the sail down—not so picturesque or so lordly, but safer.

A spectacular sunset was thrown in for us, and we disguised our rhapsodies over it by discussing the colours that ought to be used for it. I was all for a 'touch of rose-madder', but Arthur scorned this as theatrical. He maintained that you can do everything in nature with light-red, cobalt, and yellow-ochre. 'What about that bit of emerald green marsh-land over there?' said I, and he gave in.

'Sunset! By Jabers!' he suddenly cried. 'We must be getting on.'

He was always late for everything, or only in time because 'the party of the second part' was late. I soon came to know his three oaths, varying according to the seriousness of the situation. 'By George' was so common that I took no notice of it. 'By Jabers' was more cause for anxiety and set me rushing for a man's four last things—hat, stick, bag, and baccy. But when I heard 'By the piper that played before Moses' I stood back, knowing that the pressing need was a clear field for a rush. In fact there was never time for the reference to Moses, and I only found out about his share in the oath when I asked Arthur one day (in tranquillity) who the piper was.

Well, after the sun had disappeared we got on, but not very fast, and it was definitely evening when we slithered on to a rather obstinate bank. The more we got our oars to work and the more desperately we pushed, the more the keel snuggled comfortably into the sand.

'By the piper!' cried Arthur, and leapt into the water. And me too. Upon the word 'piper' I plunged in. But the old boat was not much lighter for our having relieved it, and there we were, one on each side, tugging with no effect. It was no occasion for being mealy-mouthed, and with a stronger expression than 'the piper' Arthur said,

'We're only making things worse. We must push her back instead of forward.'

The tide had driven us on a bank we couldn't cross, and now we had to go quickly into reverse and undo the little we had already done. For some time our pushing had no effect, for the tide was ebbing pretty fast. Then we agreed on a mighty effort—one, two, three—*go*. She moved. We hurried to another effort before the tide could get busy on us again, and then another and another, till at last she was free and in a channel again. We jumped in, but went along with the utmost caution, continually sounding. It was now getting dusk, but we could see a light or two in the distance from the scattered houses of Aberdovey, and the channels grew broader and safer.

We could now afford to laugh. I hadn't dared to when we were pushing, because Arthur looked so fierce about it. I had not worried about the troubles attendant on our sticking on that sandbank; I could only see the funny side of our having to push our own vehicle.

'Won't mother be in a taking!' was our main thought as we climbed our steep path. And indeed she was. She had placed the big lamp in the highest window, to guide us. She had put kettles of water on the kitchen fire, as a kind of general preparation for recovering people from drowning. She had looked out her reserve of brandy, and was pacing up and down the flags of our little Brynhyfryd Terrace. We hailed her cheerily, and came in very wet, dirty, and hungry, but not bad enough for brandy.

§ 2

Those sandbanks showed another of their ugly tricks a few days later. It was the bounden duty of Arthur's brothers to come to see their future sister. The first to come was Alfred, the doctor. He was so charming that I was quite unaware of being inspected, and only felt that I had now collected another splendid brother. He was full of energy, and as he looked out over the estuary he had a shrewd notion that there would be cockles in all that sand. He was fond of singing 'Molly Malone', and perhaps that put it into his head that it would be jolly to go 'cockling with Molly'. We consulted the old Aberdovey salts, who waved their hands towards the Borth shore, and told us that there were plenty of cockles to be had over there at low tide.

'How do you catch cockles?' said I, having no notion of what they even looked like.

'Oh, quite easy,' said Alfred, 'you just pick them up and stow them in a bag or a pail, but they jump about like anything.'

So while the boys went to hire a boat Mrs. Hughes looked out a kitchen pail, a canvas bag, and a fishing-basket, and as soon as the tide was about right we started across to the farther side of the river, stranded the boat, and strayed apart from one another with our receptacles in the grand pursuit of trying to get the biggest amount. The cockles certainly jumped astounding distances, by what internal mechanism I couldn't make out. I was examining one intently to see how he did it, when I heard a shout from Alfred, a shout of that peculiar quality that suggests terror. Arthur and I, both far away absorbed in cockling, rushed towards him.

'Keep away! For God's sake keep away!' he shouted. 'If you come near you'll make it worse. Get a rope.'

But Arthur had already seen what was the matter, and had turned and rushed to the boat to fetch the rope. Meanwhile I was horrified to see Alfred dragging his feet with the utmost difficulty out of the sucking sand. He managed to get the better of it just as Arthur came up, but he told us that he had quite thought he was in for a ghastly death, till the mere sight of the rope gave him zip enough to keep calm and cease struggling and floundering wildly, which is fatal.

This incident dashed our enthusiasm for cockles, but we took back our spoils to Mrs. Hughes, not telling her of the risks of the chase. She was quite equal to cooking them, although she had never faced them before. Only give me the food, was her slogan, and I'll cook it. Seeing the quantities we had brought, she unearthed her largest cauldron, which might have come straight out of a fairy tale. Our little servant flew about making up the fire and pouring forth her excitement in Welsh. When the water came to the boil, in went all the cockles. How long should they have? Arthur and Alfred held a medico-legal consultation, and up and down they had it until Arthur stared into the cauldron and gave his considered opinion that the cockles were no longer fighting against fate. So they were decanted on to our plates, and by the time we had got them out of their shells our appetites were not critical, and we ate rather freely. But what with one thing and another we didn't care if we never heard the word cockle again.

'I'll take you for a day's real fishing.' Thus Arthur to me a day or two later when we were alone again. As there was no stream near Aberdovey, the scene of the festival was to be Tal-y-llyn, another playground of his boyhood. Like my brother Dym, when he was 'in trout' all other interests went under. He buried himself for hours in preparations, testing his rod about the room, hunting out his other fishing-tackle, putting his extra-strong eyeglasses where he wouldn't forget them, and going through his fly-book. This selection of flies amazed me. They all looked pretty much the same, and I had no idea that trout were so picksome about their food. It seemed that they would eagerly jump at some delicacy with a long Welsh name, meaning the red devil. I went to bed leaving Arthur buried in these intricacies. We were to be off by the first train in the morning, but there was no fear in this case of Arthur's missing it. Throughout life I found that only two things would get him out of bed spontaneously—a day's fishing or a case in Court.

We started like two explorers, with everything needful slung about us, but no sandwiches this time, as we were to have lunch at the inn. To ordinary tourists a boat for the day at Tal-y-llyn is expensive, but we had one for nothing. Arthur was well known to the people at the inn who let the boats out. They received us as honoured guests, offered us any boat we liked to choose, and wouldn't take a farthing for the good lunch they gave us. The inter-relationship of these people was the most extraordinary I have ever come across. A widow with two children had married a widower with two children; two more children were born and were now grown up, and the parents were dead. These six lived together and carried on the inn, and their names and relationship to one another were an amusing puzzle to visitors, and a kind of extra attraction.

One thing I did thoroughly know about fly-fishing; my brother Dym had taught me that trout don't like petticoats. So I made it my business, while Arthur stood up in the flat-bottomed boat and flung his line, to say nothing and keep myself as small as possible. For this purpose I had secreted the little Greek text at which I was slaving for my next examination, and I calculated that during that stern afternoon I made out two (or three at most) sentences for every trout that Arthur caught.

This was not so dull for me as it sounds. It was my first experience of being not only neglected by Arthur, but completely forgotten in the absorbing pursuit of his hobby. As time went on I caught myself hugging little neglects of all kinds, as great compliments. Evidently he trusted me not to mind, and not to be looking for trifling attentions and consideration. No doubt I had my brothers to thank for having early schooled me in the idea that a man has his own life to lead and there are times when he is like the trout in a distaste for 'petticoats about'. But I had no one but our two selves to thank for discovering that such neglect over trifles is compatible with the deepest passion. It was a great pleasure to me, too, when Arthur would break out excitedly in the middle of one of our discussions with 'But, my dear Sir!'

Such arguments on every kind of topic we carried on usually during our tramps over the hills in sunshine, wind or rain. And yet not quite every topic; at least there were some things that we didn't probe too deeply, tacitly assuming one another's ideas and feelings about them, or preferring to leave closer discussions for the future. I regret now the many things I left unasked and unsaid. But on the whole perhaps the best rule for married life is the one that is imposed on Arctic explorers, who are forbidden to discourse to one another too freely on their private concerns and innermost thoughts. Arthur and I felt the amplitude of the life before us, and did not strive to express ourselves fully. Against our background of matter-of-fact talk an occasional break-out of deeper feeling took on a special emphasis. For instance, Arthur said to me once as he was stuffing the tobacco into his pipe, and apropos of nothing, 'If we had met in such circumstances that we couldn't be married we could never have been friends, could we?'

In fact, we never did attempt to put our love for one another into words—until the end. After twenty years of married life, Arthur was run over at the foot of Chancery Lane and taken into Barts to die. I reached him in time for half an hour of life, which he spent entirely in pouring out all the pent-up expressions of love that he had strength to utter, in which the word 'glorious' was incessantly repeated. In my own anguish I hadn't the sense to reply in the same language, but could only keep on imploring him to fight for life. 'No, Molly, I'm done for,' he said, and began again on his chant of triumph.

§ 3

Setting aside the few 'expeditions' of those holidays, our main amusements were sketching, walking, and bathing. When the tide was up the long stretch of shore beyond the bar was grand for Arthur's bathing, but at low tide he said he had to walk half-way to Ireland to get a swim. Mixed bathing had never even been thought of. Women had to bathe in a secluded nook up the estuary, and only at stated times (varying according to the tide). The town crier walked up and down the front, proclaiming, first in Welsh and then in English:

'Ladies to be bathed. . . . At Penhelig. . . . From 11 to 1.' The changes that fifty years have brought about can be illustrated in another odd way. There was a retired sea-captain living on our hill-side whose wife was regarded as little short of an abandoned woman; the only foundation for this opinion that we could discover was that some one passing her window had seen her behind the curtain, *smoking!*

Our evening occupations after supper followed a fairly regular routine, as we gathered round the one big oil lamp. Mrs. Hughes generally knitted, Arthur read Law, and I struggled with a bit of Greek. We always broke the evening's work with one game of chess. At this I was only a little better than Charles, whose main idea of strategy was to move his king now and again 'because that puts them out'. By keeping on the defensive, and occasionally making an attack that surprised myself as much as Arthur, I sometimes won a game, and was always strong enough to keep him from slacking. I also chastened him by inventing the rule that the winner must put away the pieces—a job he detested. On the few occasions when he saw his king hopelessly cornered he would exclaim, 'Now you can put the men away'.

Last thing every evening we plotted some scheme for the
next day—how we could get the most for the least money. The
ordinary 'tourist places' didn't tempt us, but when Arthur's
parson brother, Llewelyn, came to visit us he insisted that
'Molly ought to see' this and that. So to please him we agreed
to let him take us to the Torrent Walk. This was a regular
guide-book affair, and didn't make much impression on me,
and might have slipped my memory entirely had it not been
for a curious incident on the way. Llewelyn, acting as host
and guide, stood us a lunch at the inn nearest to the Walk. As
we were starting off he asked the landlord which was the
shortest road to take, for the short cuts were rather intricate.

'Take the dog with you, Sir. He's quite used to showing
tourists the way. . . . Here, Prince! Take these visitors to the
Torrent Walk.'

Off we started, with the dog a yard or two ahead.

'Be sure you don't speak Welsh,' shouted the landlord after
us, or he won't take you. He thinks Welshmen ought to know
the way.'

'All right, we'll remember,' answered Llewelyn, laughing,
for we naturally thought this was one of those 'dog-stories'.
All went well for some way, the dog duly trotting ahead, till
one of those showers so common in Wales caught us suddenly.
Spying a cowshed we went into it for shelter, dog and all.
Presently a farm labourer came in for shelter too. Llewelyn,
parson-like, began to chat with him about the weather and
what not, in Welsh of course; and Arthur joined in.

'Look there!' I cried, and pointed to the dog, who was fast
disappearing along the road to the inn. We put it down to his
impatience at the delay, but the labourer said that every one
knew the dog, and that it was true that nothing would induce
him to show Welsh people the way.

This incident made me ashamed of my own lack of enter-
prise. Even the dog was bilingual. The smallest children in
the street would be shouting at one another in Welsh, and be
able to turn on good English whenever required; and there
was I, only able to say a few phrases in Welsh that Arthur had

taught me, such as 'Ydwyf yn dy garu di'. However, I was hoping to surprise him by picking up a little quite quietly from our servant. Her English was so simple, so free from the trammels of gender, number, and case, that I concluded her Welsh would be equally uncomplicated. Her invariable reference to her mistress as 'he' showed me how easily we could discard gender from our pronouns as we have from our adjectives. So, like Gonzalo, I had great comfort from this fellow, and finding an odd hour when Arthur was out of the way, I begged her to teach me some Welsh. She was all willing and proud. Now I knew the numbers from 1 to 7 from 'The Bells of Aberdovey', so I asked her to begin by teaching me some further numbers. In order to fix her mind definitely on the problem, I pointed to the old grandfather clock, and extracted the numbers in Welsh up to 12. Flushed with victory, I said,

'Now can you tell me what "five minutes past twelve" would be?'

Yes, she could, and steadily we went on to 'ten-past', 'fifteen-past' . . . up to 'five-to'. I then approached a more delicate problem.

'How would you say "twenty-three minutes past seven"'? She shook her head and denied that there was such a thing.

'But suppose your train starts at seven-twenty-three, and you want to catch it?'

'Well,' she replied with finality in her tone, 'you must just go early.'

My most valuable lesson from this was that if you want to pick up a language you must pick it up, and not try to extract it forcibly. However, there was one word that I did learn carefully from Arthur, in all its strange mutation of consonants—'cariad', 'gariad', 'f'nghariad i'. In later years I once received a telegram in London from Arthur in Scotland: 'carried, carried'. I wondered what the postmistress thought as to the meaning of the message—either that some one had been anxious for the success of a resolution at a meeting, or that it was a secret code, as of course it was. My favourite context for the word

was a line from Dafydd ap Gwilym, inscribed by Arthur in a
book he gave me:

> *Hanodd ym bron, hon a hyllt,*
> *Had o gariad.*

(In my heart, this stormy heart, she sowed the seed of love.)

§ 4

The life on Sundays at Aberdovey in '88 was more restricted
than any I had known before—if life it could be called. It made
me think of the Pharisee who thought the best way to avoid
breaking the Sabbath was to remain in bed all day. Neither
work nor play of any kind was permissible. Boating, sketching,
bathing, chess, law-reading, Greek translation, knitting, novel-
reading—all had to be forsworn. However, Arthur managed
to play his fiddle *ad lib* by wisely beginning with 'Adeste
Fideles', and leaving Mrs. Hughes to assume that all the rest
were hymn tunes. Presumably this insistence on Sabbath-
keeping arose from the conviction that boredom would send
people to church. No one but the definitely disreputable had
any idea of staying away from a morning service of some kind.
So each Sunday morning, after a late breakfast, Mrs. Hughes
and Arthur and I dressed ourselves as grandly as we could,
found our gloves and prayer-books, and walked sedately to
the accompaniment of the wretched little tinkle called the
church bell. This was always a source of annoyance to me,
because one of my excitements in visiting Aberdovey was the
chance of hearing the 'Bells of Aberdovey'.

Services as a rule were in Welsh, but there was an extra one,
in English, on Sunday morning for the sake of the English resi-
dents and the few summer visitors. As we went in we met the
Welsh congregation coming out from their previous service.
Arthur would much have preferred to attend this, but his mother
couldn't follow it easily. However, he always used a Welsh
prayer-book, and all his life sang the Psalms in Welsh wherever
he happened to be. In Aberdovey he had to read them instead
of singing, but nothing made much difference to the miserable

mutter of alternate verses that was customary. Only the
Gloria was sung, and that I was soon able to sing in Welsh
with Arthur; it sounds much more impressive in Welsh than in
English. Sermons were dull, but I got some recreation out of
them by noticing how the parson worked out his scheme. This,
Arthur said, consisted in taking some word, such as 'courage',
looking up all the places in Cruden where it occurs, and talking
a bit about each. One Sunday I was pleased to see a young
visiting curate mount the pulpit. His English was clearly
limited, and his Welsh accent very strong. I was all ears.
Giving out his text several times in different directions, he proceeded to tell us all that the sacred writer had omitted (much to
the sacred writer's credit, I thought).

'Does he say that Enoch was honest? No. Only this,
"Enoch walked with God".' (He pronounced it 'wokkt with
Godd'). 'Does he tell us that he was generous? No. Only
"Enoch walked with God". Are we told that he was kind-
hearted? No. Only that "Enoch walked with God". These
four words "Enoch walked with God" sum up all that we
know of his life—just this—"Enoch walked with God". What
more do we want to know than this, "Enoch walked with
God"?' And so on.

Some English public-school boys on holiday were sitting
in the pew in front of us, and I saw them bending as if in
prayer or meditation. Mrs. Hughes was eyeing them with dis-
pleasure. I was biting the inside of my cheeks, and trying to
think of a funeral, in frantic effort to keep back one of my egg-
laying displays. I thanked goodness for the only consoling
feature in the situation, that Arthur as usual in the sermon was
quietly asleep. Stealing a glance at him sideways to make sure
of this, I heard him mutter,

'If he says it again I shan't believe it.'

This finished me. Resorting to my last line of defence I
dropped my handkerchief, and under cover of picking it up
I stuffed it into my mouth and shook as noiselessly as Tony
Weller. As I rose I heard to my relief of the demise of Enoch:
'He wass not, for Godd took him.'

Fortunately my behaviour had not been noticed by Mrs. Hughes, whose whole attention had been devoted to 'those ill-mannered English boys who were laughing all through the sermon'. I had better luck in this way than a well-known scientist (I think it was Huxley) whose friend took him to a Welsh church when they were on holiday. As distinguished visitors they were shown into a front pew. In full career of his sermon the preacher suddenly stopped and pointed at them.

'Ye come to the house of God, and ye *smile*,' said he, and then added menacingly, 'but there'll be no smiling in Hell.'

I wish I could reproduce in writing the fervent accents of another sermon, which was described to me by one of Arthur's Welsh friends. The preacher took for his theme the morals that could be drawn from the characteristics of certain animals. Of these my informant could remember only two, the elephant and the peacock, which went like this :

'The elephant, my brethren, has but one bone in the *whole* of his boddy. This bone, my brethren, is situated in the smaal of his back. Now the pekkuliaritee of the elephant, my brethren, is this, that if the poor animal sits down, without help he cannot get up again. Once there was a poor elephant who sat down. There, my brethren, he sat. Presently there came by a kind gentleman. Now that kind gentleman, my brethren, helped that poor elephant to his feet. Ever afterwards, wherever that kind gentleman went, that elephant followed him! *So*, my brethren, we may see the Power and the Effects of LOV.'

The moral of the peacock ran thus : 'The pekkuliaritee in the flesh of the peacock is this, my brethren, that the longer you boil him the rawer he gets. *So*, my brethren, it is with the hypocrite.' No further explanation followed, and the connexion between hypocrisy and being underdone remained impressively mysterious.

Such intellectual refinements were mainly confined to the established Church. The nonconformists of Wales as well as Cornwall were simpler in their addresses, which were frequently given by 'local preachers' in the country districts. These were earnest working-men who knew their Bible and the needs of the congregation. Arthur told me that when he was a boy he used to go to hear them for the sake of trying to discover what the trade of the preacher was, by watching his gestures. A carpenter would saw the air, a blacksmith would thump down hammer-strokes on the pulpit, a cobbler would draw out his arms slowly sideways as though striving with the leather. This seemed to me a pleasing thing, as if the man had developed his ideas as he went about his daily routine, and I wondered whether St. Paul borrowed a gesture from his tent-making, or St. Peter from his fishing.

Wales differed from Cornwall considerably on the Church and Chapel question. Since the days of Wesley the Cornish, so I gathered from my mother, were quite tolerant in the matter, many of them attending church in the morning from ancient habit, and chapel in the evening to get a little religious excitement. No enmity existed between the two persuasions, the fundamental reason being, I fancy, that Cornwall has always been pagan at heart.

In Wales it was far otherwise. Ill-feeling, often virulent, seemed to exist between Church and Chapel, as though they were entirely different religions. The latter was not simply Wesleyanism, but had many shades of belief or behaviour, and suffered from internecine warfare. Wherever two or three cottages were gathered together there would spring up almost as many chapels—Methodist, Primitive Methodist, Calvinistic Methodist—all of them too ugly to be borne. And the congregations were united only in their dislike of the Church. The chief battle-ground was the village school. Chapel people had to send their children to the Church school because there was no other, and vented their spleen by pin-prick persecutions, such as complaints of inefficient teaching, lack of equipment, and so on. The young schoolmaster at Aberdovey lived next to us, and told us how miserable they made his life and how they hindered his work, which he had to carry on without any assistant.

Although Arthur raged against this kind of thing and against nonconformists in general, he was greatly attached to a few individuals among them, who had been friends of his boyhood. Among these was John Owen, who had now become a widely respected minister in Mold. It chanced that he was invited to preach one Sunday at Towyn, and as a matter of course came to spend all his spare time with us at Aberdovey. He was a cultivated, keen-brained man, and I am sure that he found Arthur a stimulating companion. I went with them on their walks and can still recall some of the arguments. Accustomed to speaking Welsh almost entirely John pronounced English with the elegant precision of a foreigner, and it charmed me to listen to their heated discussions on religion and politics, on no single point of which did they agree. Home Rule was the burning topic of the day. Arthur was a rabid Unionist, and John thought it best for a country to govern itself, even if it made the wildest mistakes in the process. Good government, like all other good things, he maintained, was no good if imposed upon you, for all real education must come from within. On this point Arthur was inclined to admit that he might be right, but on questions of religion John was badly worsted, and I was sure that he would like to have conceded far more points than he dared. Now and again he would invite me to give an opinion, and after a while he went the length of complimenting Arthur on his choice of a wife.

'Oh, she's all right,' said Arthur, 'she's got some common sense.'

At this John told us of the old Welsh farmer who used to say to his son, 'My boy, when you are thinking of getting married, there are three things to be desired in a girl: money, the grace of God, and common sense. As for money, never mind—it may come; as for the grace of God, never mind—it may come; but if she hasn't got common sense, don't marry her, for it'll never come.'

Then John added that there was another point that he himself would consider an essential, and I was afraid that he was going to elaborate something akin to the grace of God, in which I knew myself to be deficient. But no; to our great satisfaction his idea of the *sine qua non* for married life was a sense of humour. This he held to be a kind of 'fourth dimension', and unless both husband and wife lived in it they could not be married in the fullest meaning of the term.

On the Saturday evening when the lamp was lit and the curtains drawn after supper, Arthur settled down to further argument, and John drew forth a pipe.

'Hullo!' said I. 'I didn't know you smoked; all the time we were out you never once lit up.'

Then the dreadful truth came out that he did not dare to be seen smoking, and until the curtain was drawn he was afraid that a passer-by might let some member of his flock know of his sinfulness; for his particular brand of religion disapproved of *any* fleshly indulgence in their minister. We were too profoundly sorry for him to make any remark on this. He was obviously cheered by Arthur's promising to go over to Towyn to hear him preach on the Sunday evening. One good listener made all the difference to a preacher, he said.

Mrs. Hughes would not have been seen in a chapel at any price, but I had no such scruples and went off happily with Arthur and John to Towyn.

'You may find it rather tiresome to sit through the whole thing in Welsh,' said John as we paced along, 'but I'll do what I always do when I know there is an English stranger in the congregation, I'll put in one prayer in English.'

'How jolly it must be,' said I, 'to be able to turn from one language to another like that. Very effective sometimes, surely?'

John laughed and told me the story of the Welsh preacher in an English country church who said in the middle of his sermon, 'How far more impressive is this passage in the original Hebrew. Listen.' He then rolled out in his richest Welsh tones, 'If there is a Welshman present will he kindly keep it to himself that I am talking Welsh and not Hebrew.' In such a way, John admitted, a second language could be very impressive.

This anecdote put an idea into my head. We reached the ugly little chapel up a side street of Towyn, and it was already fairly crowded when Arthur and I took our seats, and John disappeared behind somewhere. When he began to preach my idea took shape. His face was a fine one, inspiring in itself. His voice, rising and falling as he warmed to his theme, had a magnetic influence on his congregation. Since I had no notion what he was talking about my idea of imagining it to be the Sermon on the Mount was easy to carry out. I pictured its first delivery in Aramaic, to the eager people on the hill-side. When the congregation sat up a little in their interested attention, or one gave a sympathetic groan, I imagined that they had just been startled by the injunction to hit a man back good and hard by offering the other cheek.

Instead of being bored I was sorry when the sermon came to an end. Then some prayers 'from the bosom' followed, and right in the midst of them fell on my entranced ears my favourite collect 'Lighten our darkness'. Although I had heard these words countless times, with what a fresh beauty they struck me in those strange surroundings, and my heart warmed to John for his kindness. Then came a hymn sung to the tune *Hyfrydol*. Any one who has not heard a Welsh non-conformist gathering sing a hymn has really no idea what a hymn should be. All the world's sorrows and all the triumphs of religion are in it, and you feel ready to face anything.

XIII

Under Roseberry Topping

§ 1

THE following winter brought a holiday that was a contrast to the Welsh one. Mother and I were invited to go north again, to spend the Christmas with Tom. We were glad to get away for a week or two, not only to escape from the decorum of the boarding-house, but also from London itself. For a cloud had been hanging over the town—a mental one in addition to the customary fogs. After the lapse of over forty years Jack the Ripper has become as legendary as Dick Turpin, and to many he is almost a joke. No one can now believe how terrified and unbalanced we all were by his murders. A thriller in a book is quite different from a thriller round the corner. It seemed to be round the corner, although it all happened in the East End, and we were in the West; but even so, I was afraid to go out after dark, if only to post a letter. Just as dusk came on we used to hear down our quiet and ultra-respectable Edith Road the cries of newspaper-boys, in tones made as alarming as they could: 'Another 'orrible murder!... Whitechapel!... Murder!... Disgustin' details.... Murder!' One can only dimly imagine what the terror must have been in those acres of narrow streets, where the inhabitants knew the murderer to be lurking. John Tenniel departed from his usual political subjects for *Punch* in order to stir public opinion by blood-curdling cartoons of 'murder stalking the slums', and by jeers at the inefficiency of the police. From all the suburban districts police were hurried to the East End, and yet we would read of a murder committed within a few moments of the passing by of a policeman. Naturally, I suppose, the murderer knew the time of the policeman's beat, and waited till he had passed. Some sensible fellow thought of making the police more stealthy by putting india-rubber on their heels; and it was this that started the widespread use of rubber-heels by the public at large. Another strange by-product of the crimes was the disuse of black-bags for the ordinary professional or business man. A suspect had been described as 'carrying a black bag', and no one cared to be seen with one, not from fear of arrest, but simply from the ugly association—a curious instance of the whimsical way in which trade can suffer from a sudden drop in demand. The press was full of theories about the murderer. One idea was that he must be a sailor, because he could join his ship and get away quickly; another was that he must be a madman, because he hid so cunningly (though why this ability should be a sign of mental derangement I could never see); another strong suspicion was that he must be a doctor, because of the skill and rapidity with which the mutilations were performed, and also because of the uncanny disappearance of the man in a few seconds after the deed, for a doctor carrying a black bag of instruments was a familiar figure anywhere at all hours, and might easily masquerade as a passer-by and natural first-aider. Horrible though the murders themselves were, I think it was more the mysterious disappearances that affected people's minds, giving a quality of the supernatural to the work—declared, of course, by some to be a judgement on vice. The murders stopped completely after one of surpassing savagery, looking as if an avenger had been seeking a special victim and had found her at last.

§ 2

We found Tom in far pleasanter conditions than when we were in Darlington. He had moved out of Middlesbrough, a short train-run to the lovely little village of Ayton. Here he had bought a small house with a chicken-run and a quarter of an acre of garden. As he explained to me, any fraction of an acre always sounds 'landed'. In addition to the baby we had first seen in our few visits from Darlington, he had now a second son, not quite a year old. They had moved into the new home in time for him to be 'born at the foot of Roseberry

Topping'—the hall-mark of a true Yorkshireman. Following the approved custom of babies he arrived at what an old servant of ours used to call an 'ill-convenient' time—when they were so lately settled into the house that they hardly knew where anything was, in the middle of the night, with neither doctor nor nurse at hand. Tom was quite unperturbed, and became, as he described it, the sole officiating priest.

The elder boy was at the ravishing age of two and a bit, able to talk in his own fashion in a most companionable way. We had hardly arrived before he managed to ask me where I got my eggs. 'From a shop in Kensington,' I said. '*Ours*,' he solemnly confided, 'are *laid*.' What he lusted after was to be among those present at every doing, preferably in kitchen or garden, and especially to hang about mother, whom he called 'Gamble', the nearest he could get to 'Grannie'. She liked this name, and it stuck to her. He found 'Molly' easy to pronounce, and gave me no respectful prefix. I was his willing slave through most of his waking hours, which began far too soon for my liking. He slept in a cot in my room, and every morning about 6.30 he would wake, creep into my bed and demand a story. I would pretend to be sound asleep. He would then say 'Molly way *cup*' in ever louder tones, varied with 'Once a pinny time' (a kind of imitative magic). At last in despair he would wail forth 'Molly goes to sleep *all* day long'. At this I could never help laughing, and then had to surrender and produce some kind of story till 8.

Tom was amused at my devotion, and said I was practising for the future, adding cheerfully, 'It'll be a long time before you have a child as big as that, though'. He said I must be sure to have a little girl, for there were boys enough in the family already. I didn't tell him that my great ambition was to have a son. Secretly I went farther and hoped for three sons and one daughter—which turned out to be exactly what came to me.

It was a mild and open winter, so that we were able to do gardening, walking, and sketching nearly every day. One superb morning Tom asked me if I were game for a walk with him round the Topping. I was eager enough, for a walk alone with one of my brothers was always one of the special pleasures of life. The mere invitation was a pleasure, for it was certain they would not ask me if they didn't want me. And with a brother there is always the understood and unexpressed background, the old family life and jokes and relations and friends that need but the slightest allusion to come in and enrich the conversation. In fact it was the conversation on that walk that sticks in my memory rather than the details of that Yorkshire landscape which acted as a kind of *obbligato*. On a walk, too, you can be far less reticent than in a room, for you do not eye one another, and the least object of the wayside can be used to interrupt any too-deep train of thought.

Tom and I had a great deal in common now, and I got indirectly from him better hints on teaching that I had ever met with in a book. His ideal of discipline would certainly never enter any treatise on education, and yet I am sure it is sound: 'Be a devil in class, and a good fellow outside it.' 'Is that really the whole of it?' I asked. 'Pretty well,' he said. 'You see, boys like to be ruled, and to be made to do the very stiffest work they can. These modern ideas of luring them to work are rotten. It's quite interesting enough in itself, without all the fuss of "leading up" and "drawing forth". Our Geography man told me that one day an inspector essayed to "take the boys for a bit", and began genially with some "interesting" questions. The boys' guesses flummoxed him, for he didn't know enough geography to say whether they were right or wrong—and looked pretty ridiculous.'

'Did he come into your class, Tom?'

'No, I only saw him passing through the hall. A month or two later I met a man in a train and discovered in chatting to him that he was a school-inspector, so I naturally regaled him with our Geography incident, as an example of the merriment that some inspectors provide. But he saw nothing funny in it at all, and got out at the next station; and then I realized that it was the identical man!'

'I suppose the moral of that is—don't talk in railway carriages?'

'Not at all. It's always a good thing to have a chat with a stranger, for even the smallest boy or the biggest duffer will be sure to provide you with a new idea or something funny.'

'You are always on the look-out for the funny side of things, Tom. Are you by any chance ever low-spirited?'

He laughed. 'Odd that you should have asked me that now, for it was on this very road that I really was miserable once, and not long ago. We had a Middlesbrough man to stay the week-end with us, to show him our new house. The Saturday was ghastly weather—murky, damp, depressing fog, and we could settle to nothing. So Nell, to get us out of the way, suggested that we should go for a "nice long walk". So we set our teeth and started along this road, with a distant inn for lunch in our mind's eye. The fog grew a little less, and we were warmed with our walk and pleasantly hungry when we reached the inn. We sat in the little parlour for some time before any one appeared. At last the barman came in with a "Cold ham, Sir? Yes, Sir," and a jerky attempt to arrange plates and glasses. We had barely put in a mouthful when he said to me in a confidential undertone, "You'll excuse us being a bit upset-like, Sir, the landlord has just died upstairs."'

'And then you went home to have a good laugh, and find everything jolly by comparison?'

'Yes, and so you can blow away most troubles.' After we had paced along in silence for a bit my mind went back to school life and I asked Tom whether his boys were as a rule responsive.

'Fairly well,' said he, and then added: 'When I look round at the boys in my class, some lazy, some blockheads, a few promising—just all sorts—I sometimes picture to myself the old scribe who was in charge of the synagogue school at Nazareth. I can see the dozen or so small boys squatted at his feet, spelling out their rolls, or more likely having to learn by heart the passages he declaimed to them—long bits of Isaiah and perhaps a psalm now and again as a treat. I expect there were blockheads and lazy boys there too, and one dreamy little chap who would ask tiresome questions that the old fellow couldn't answer. "Wait till you are old enough to go up to Jerusalem, my boy, they will be able to tell you everything up there." '

'And he found when he did get there,' said I, 'that he didn't get half so much as he got from the queer and disreputable people he met casually—"in the train" as you would say.'

'That's just what I say,' said Tom, 'we fools feed the mighty ones . . . there's no waste.'

§ 3

That walk and talk were the more memorable because Tom was seldom to be caught in a serious mood; no doubt it was the rarity of our being alone together that induced it. General conversation is quite another matter; at that he was always felicitous. The family took special delight in his power of repartee, and we treasured many an instance of an enemy discomfited by it. But, family-like, we treasured still more the occasions when he failed. Once he was worsted by a very small newspaper-boy; it was the evening after a disappointing cricket match at Castleton, and a late edition of the local gazette was thrust towards him with 'Paper, Sir? Cricket results, Sir.' 'No,' said Tom a little testily as he turned away. 'Ah!' shouted the urchin after him, 'I sees tha got a doock.'

It was a sore point, for Tom was a leader in the cricket world, and on another occasion was quite ready with his reply to impudence. A bouncing captain of a visiting team was irritating every one by laying down the law, and exclaimed to Tom who disagreed on some point, 'Why, any novice knows that!' 'But, thank heaven,' replied Tom, 'we are not *all* novices.'

His wife was by no means slow-witted, but she had a capacity for inconsequence that amounted to a talent; and sometimes this oddity was awkward. At the end of a short excursion to see us in Kensington, Tom arranged to meet her for their journey north by the midnight train. 'Mind, Nell, King's Cross main departure platform, under the clock.' This clock was Tom's favourite trysting-place, and she knew it well. He arrived in good time, but there was no sign of her. Expecting to see her rushing up he stood waiting till the train started, and then wandered about in search of her, to find her pacing up and down among the cabs outside. She explained by saying that she thought she would make *sure* of his coming in time by going to meet him. The result was that they had to sacrifice their cheap tickets and pay full fare for the next train. We used to wonder how Tom could be so patient with her. But he was not patient. By some blessed alchemy he turned even her blunders into amusement, and sucked quite the money's worth of the ticket out of the situation. He used to say that the world would be a much duller place without Nell. She was a jolly, companionable soul, never heavy-going, and as her boys grew older they encouraged and treasured her absurdities. The younger one had been out for a long walk by himself one day and made her anxious. 'Where have you been all this time, you naughty boy?' was her greeting. 'Only for a walk, mother.' 'Then it's the last walk you take in this world, my boy.' Her anxiety was genuine, although it took such a curious mode of expression. Once she said to me, 'I can't think what I should do, Molly, if Tom were to die, or do something ugly of that kind.' Occasionally she took a leaf out of Tom's book and made a little drama out of a contretemps. One day during our holiday Tom had to go into Middlesbrough, and was not to return till supper-time. So Nelly and Gamble and I arranged to put off our midday dinner, and turn it into a hot supper for him to share on his return. We plotted roast veal and the usual accompaniments. Unfortunately the butcher didn't come, and when we went round to his little shop in the village we found it closed, and indeed all the other shops, because there was a funeral. Nelly fretted a great deal at the lack of a joint, so that Gamble and I were relieved when a telegram came to say that Tom was staying to supper with a friend and would be late. We had eggs and went to bed. All was serene. But the next morning Nell could not cease talking of her annoyance at Tom's absence from supper, of the trouble we had all been at, in order to make it a really grand supper, of our disappointment that he should miss it, and so on. Gamble and I were laughing, but she grew more and more eloquent till at last Tom said:

'Well, let's hear what this wonderful supper actually was.'

'As it actually turned out, dear, there wasn't any supper at all, because the butcher was shut, and being buried.'

Tom was quite capable of trying return tricks on her, and one morning he alarmed us all by coming into the kitchen where we were busy over dinner preparations, to announce, 'I've got the plague!' Holding himself as though in agony, he added, 'I've got a pain in the groin, and that's one of the early symptoms.' The word 'groin' made us laugh, and the joke was over when he explained that he had been reading the *Journal of the Plague*. But he told me later on that it was not entirely a joke, for Defoe's writing was so vivid that it really did start an imaginary pain. He thought that most illnesses were spread by the pleasure people take in describing their symptoms.

'You have never been ill in your life, have you?'

'Never. Not even toothache. Nor Nell. We choke one another off if we see any likelihood of giving way. I'll show you this evening.'

At supper, accordingly, Tom breezed in with 'Feeling a bit tired, Nell?'

'Yes, dear, I've got a little headache, but it's nothing to speak of.'

'Then,' said Tom, 'why speak of it?'

Nell laughed happily, and I thanked heaven I was not in a home where a kind and thoughtful husband would have prescribed lying down, fetched eau-de-Cologne and petted his wife into a real headache.

Supper was usually the jolliest meal of the day. The little boys were safe in bed, and could get into no more danger or mischief, so Nell was at peace. Gamble and I were flushed with our triumphs in getting them there. While I dealt faithfully with Viv, Gamble was allowed to bath baby Llew. Gamble was sketchy in everything she did, and I believe Nell was in tortures of anxiety as she watched the casual way in which her baby was handled. Once (when Nell was out of the room) Llew was dropped on the floor. I was aghast, but Gamble said it would do him good rather than harm; and indeed he seemed none the worse and was picked up smiling.

After supper I seized on Tom every evening to give me some help with my Greek. I have never come across such a teacher as he was. He enjoyed smoothing down all the troublesome little passages, and showing them to be examples of some general principle that would be useful for future difficulties. He agreed with me that most annotated texts evaded real troubles, or explained them in some fantastic way. He assured me that he had come across this explanation of a subjunctive: 'The fact was so certain that the Indicative was too feeble for it, so the Subjunctive was used as a gesture.'

Fortunately for me one of my set-books was the part of the *Odyssey* that describes the return of Ulysses, and Tom made me enjoy its humour and pathos. The droves of cattle and pigs going to stock poor Penelope's larder, to pacify her detested suitors . . . the contented death of old Argos, after pricking up his ears in recognition of his master . . . the excitement of the shooting with the great bow. I got so worked up about it that I burst out:

'There's nothing in Latin that can come near this.'

'Wait a bit,' said Tom. 'Greek is far finer, I admit, but Latin can do something that Greek can't.' Then he showed me how concise and terse Latin can be, delighting me with Tacitus' summing up of Galba in one sentence without even a main verb. 'And look here,' said he, 'see whether you can express in only three Latin words these fifteen words of English: "as soon as the soldiers appeared upon the scene the insurrection was at an end". Lots of my boys have enjoyed having a try at that.' After a few moments' contemplation of it I declared it to be impossible. 'Here you are then,' said Tom, '*viso milite quies.*'

While we were carrying on with this kind of stuff Gamble

and Nelly were reading or sewing. Nelly's complete ignorance
of anything remotely learned was a source of open amusement
to us and even herself. But one evening while we were deep
in some Greek, Tom looked up and muttered, 'By the way,
who *was* the father of Calypso?'

'Why Atlas, of course, Tom dear,' came from Nelly without
looking up from her knitting.

'Oh yes, that's right,' said Tom, and then exclaimed in
sudden amazement, 'but how on earth did you come to know
that?'

'Why, of course, we were taught mythology at school.'

So far as we could judge that was the only subject she had
seriously studied. She had probably used a text-book like
one I found in the book-case at Reskadinnick—a fascinating
little volume some four inches by three, with copious illustrations and lively details of the gods and goddesses. Nelly
had been born and brought up in Brighton, and her school
must have been one of those finishing academies against which
Miss Buss fought so hard. Her ignorance of Nature and the
ordinary affairs of life was almost past belief. Little Viv ran
in one day calling out excitedly, 'Moon! Moon! Come see,
moon,' for I had just pointed it out to him.

'Nonsense, dear,' said his mother without stirring, 'it can't
be the moon in the daytime; the moon shines only at night.'

Nelly never opened a newspaper, and when Tom was
reading us an account of a burglary and the shooting of a man
by the burglars, she broke in with, 'Well, I never! I had no
notion that burglars were allowed to carry firearms.' Another
day apropos of some trouble at sea that was recorded, she
mediatated aloud on the difficulties of a sailor's life, and wondered how people found their way about on the ocean.

'It's fairly easy,' said Tom, 'there are regular lines that they
follow.'

'How funny,' replied Nelly, 'to think of the number of
times I've been out on the sea at Brighton, and I never noticed
them!'

In early days Tom had been optimistic enough to get her

to try some good books, and hoped for the best with his own favourite *Vanity Fair*. But she put it aside as 'not quite nice'. Wondering what she could have comprehended so rapidly, he asked her to explain.

'Thackeray uses such bad language.'

More mystified still Tom asked to be shown the passage, and she replied that every time a regiment was mentioned it had '—th' in front of it.

Novels of a simpler kind, however, made a great appeal to her, and she always had one on hand, though it was a matter of speculation to us what she got from it. Like most mothers she was continually interrupted by some one at the door, a cry from one of the children, or the need to look in the oven. Stuffing her handkerchief into her novel to keep the place, she would slip out. Tom's delight was to shift the handkerchief some distance forwards or backwards and wait for Nelly's reaction to it on her return. If the shift had been forwards it made no difference at all, and she would placidly go on from the fresh place; but if the shift had been backwards she would occasionally complain, 'How this man does repeat himself!'

News came one day that there was a theatrical company in Middlesbrough, and that *Hamlet* was to be played. There were no second thoughts about it—we must go. There was no great expense; as well as I remember the fares on the little railway branch line came to as much as our four stalls. Scenery and properties were of the crudest—pillars waving in the breeze, the ghost grotesquely attired, the by-play all folding of arms and strutting about. But—it was *Hamlet*, and what more does man require? A little before the end Tom passed the word along that we must go or we should lose the last train home. We had plenty to discuss on the way, not about the production so much as the rapt attention of the audience and the eternal pull of the play itself. Tom said how amazed he had always been by Shakespeare's knowledge of madness— the real in Lear, the assumed in Hamlet and Edgar, the peculiar mental twists of a young and innocent girl in Ophelia—all seeming to point to intimate medical lore. While Gamble and Tom and I were going at these points Nelly wore a peevish air.

'What's the matter, Nell?' said Tom at last.

'It's too bad,' said she, 'to have come away like this before the end. I did so want to know which won that fencing match.'

That was the only large-scale outing we had. Our regular dissipation of an evening after 9 o'clock was a game of tiddly-winks. We four sat round the table with a small wooden cup in the middle; into this we flipped coloured counters in turn, and the one who flipped all his counters in first took the cupful. The counters were a penny the dozen, and one or other of us would sometimes go to bed the richer by as much as eight-pence. It was absurd, but we developed quite a technique, and Gamble got as excited as anybody, especially if one of us in our zeal played out of turn. She said to me she had seldom enjoyed a holiday more, or had such a brainless one.

This remark was made when we were back again in Kensing-ton. And my reply was that it seemed a pity that a man of Tom's mental capacity should spend hours in such a game as tiddly-winks.

'Well, there was a time when I should have felt the same. What ambitions I had for him! From his very birth. I remem-ber how his father and I were almost alarmed at the responsi-bility of being trusted with the care of an immortal soul. And as he grew strong and clever we imagined a great future for him. But I have come to see that greatness is all nonsense. Just ask yourself—what better thing could he be doing than making a happy home for his own family, and putting manly ideas into the heads of all those Middlesbrough boys in the school? Even if he had become a headmaster, as we so often hoped, he would have done no better work—probably much less. And as for tiddly-winks—a game is a game. A solemn game of chess looks well, but doesn't create the uproarious fun and relaxation we had together over our ridiculous coloured counters. I used to say to myself as I watched Tom's fervour in grabbing them, 'A great mind engaged in trifles is like the sun when setting; it pleases more while it dazzles less.'

'Mother!' said I, 'where did you get such an elegant sentiment? Don't say you made it up!'

'No dear; when I was a little girl at school in Falmouth, where they taught very little indeed, they made a great point of Penmanship, and I had to copy this sentence out with such frequency, such pains, such flourishes, that I could never forget it.'

XIV

Easter at Elstow, 1890

§ 1

THE last of the eighties was a patchwork of bright-coloured streaks on a drab background. No doubt the jolly times were all the jollier in contrast with that cramping boarding-house existence. But mother and I were always plotting a get-away. I worked harder than ever at my books for the B.A., expecting with any luck to get my degree in '90. With this I could look out for a better post, and we two would be able to live together, no matter where. I had great hopes of doing some work in the training of teachers, for even while I was in Darlington Miss Hughes had written to say that she intended to have me eventually as her vice-principal at Cambridge. So with this rosy prospect we put off our escape from the boarding-house. Mother suffered far more from it than I did, for she could only get away by long walks, while I was thoroughly enjoying the work at school. Few teachers can have had such a fine set of pupils as fell to my lot just then. Among them were the three sisters who had been the nucleus of the school when it started. Their mother had been kind enough to call on us in our 'greengrocer days', and the whole family gradually became our close and life-long friends. The visits of Mrs. Sergeant to mother therefore became one of our chief assets. She had two sons at St. Paul's, her husband was a leading journalist, and the whole household was ultra-intellectual, with literary people of the day continually dropping in on them. Mr. Sergeant I liked best of all, chiefly because he and Arthur got on so well, smoking together over their politics or chess. At the latter I was rejoiced to see Arthur badly beaten. He said that his defeat was owing to Mr. Sergeant's large board, but that excuse hardly held good for long. Mr. Sergeant had to be careful, but his eldest son, Philip (now a well-known authority on the game), could beat Arthur without being even careful. Mrs. Sergeant reviewed the novels for her husband's paper, and always had one in hand. This seemed to me delightful, but on my eager inquiries she could never say what it was about. 'They are all about the same,' she burst out one day, 'and the very sight of a novel makes me feel queer.'

Arthur and I managed to get a good deal of common life by reading worth-while books, noting passages and comparing these notes during his fortnightly visits. A few of these I recall were *Amiel's Journal*, *The Egoist*, *Plain Tales from the Hills* (Mrs. Sergeant had recommended Kipling to us as a promising young writer), and above all others the *Letters of Dorothy Osborne*. Browning we had somehow discarded, but we were never tired of Keats, whose *Eve of St. Agnes* we knew almost by heart, haunted by the mysterious fulfilment in the lines :

> *And they are gone; ay, ages long ago,*
> *These lovers fled away into the storm.*

Books we never could resist buying, but we made a solemn agreement never to waste our hard-earned money on mere 'presents' to each other. However, I felt that it would be within the rules if a present were *made*, and in this mother backed me up. Arthur's cover for his cherished violin was a disgracefully old and shabby black silk handkerchief, that had belonged to his father (and probably his grandfather!). It was dropping to pieces. So I conceived the idea of making him a new one. If he had but known it, I could give no greater proof of my devotion than to face a needle for his sake. The hours of consultation that mother and I spent on that cover during our walks and 'between times'! At last we agreed on silk and fine wool for material and old rose for colour. All by myself, but with mother abetting, I contrived to join the silk to its lining and to work an initial *A* in one corner. Arthur was full of admiration on receiving it. But the next time his fiddle appeared, lo! the same old black handkerchief. I forbore any comment, thinking horribly of Dora Copperfield's activities. I also reflected on the superiority of a brother to a lover, as a critic. Each one of my four brothers would have said to such a present—'Coosh'.

An ever-welcome visitor in any circumstances of joy or sorrow, dullness or excitement, was Mary Wood. She certainly typified the 'modern girl' of that time, tame though it must seem to one of to-day. She had been long before this one of the first women to ride a bicycle, to go on the top of a bus, and to indulge in mixed bathing. But her companions in these excesses were always of the kind that would be called to-day 'highbrow'. As the boarding-house atmosphere was no fun, she and I used an occasional lecture or an educational meeting as an excuse for an evening together. This was definitely for fun, with no alloy of desire for mental improvement. What we liked best was the acrimony with which the followers of Pestalozzi and Froebel would attack one another, each maintaining that his particular idol was the real originator of some world-shaking method of teaching. Wherever we happened to be there was sure to be found one particular man, a well-known educational enthusiast. He was a secretary of some Guild or Circle that met in Gower Street and wore the worried look of one whose main objects are good attendances, 'fruitful' discussions, and subscriptions paid up. But these were not quite all his objects, as it turned out. He would sit by Mary and me, and urge us by word and look to keep the discussion going. This we did light-heartedly, being happily ignorant of the subject, and totally indifferent as to the issue. One night he astonished me by asking if he might see me home. Me! an old Londoner! to be seen home! 'Thank you,' said I, 'but I can get a bus all the way from Gower Street to Kensington, and there are no real dangers on the route.' But no protests would keep him off, and there stood Mary suppressing her laughter. Too enraged to laugh or be even decently polite, I gave the curtest answers to all his queries during that bus-ride about 'your friend, Miss Wood'. How mother laughed when I regaled her with this incident on my return.

'Why, he's in love with Mary of course.'

'Nonsense, mother, if so, why didn't he see *her* home?'

'My dear, you don't understand the oddities of a man's adoration. Mary was too unapproachable, and you were the next best thing. "Je ne suis pas la rose, mais j'ai vécu auprès d'elle".'

'What a silly! Anyhow, I could have told him that he hasn't the ghost of a chance.'

Mother and I were both correct. He was foolish enough to propose to Mary by letter, and got the reply such a poor-spirited approach deserves.

A gay interlude for mother and me was a visit from Tom. Whatever the occasion he managed to spread gaiety about, even in the present case, which does not sound cheerful. He came up for his M.A. London degree, a matter in those days not of a thesis merely but of a stiff examination. He made it the excuse for a jolly little dinner or theatre every evening for mother and me, to keep his brain fresh, as he argued. I was awe-struck by his papers. In one of the Latin ones he said he had done all except one piece of translation.

'Why did you leave that out?' I asked.

'Couldn't do it.'

'Nonsense, Tom, it looks quite possible. Why even I can make out the general hang of it.'

'Yes, so could I . . . all but one word that beat me.'

'But you could have put a blank.'

'No. Blanks aren't done. They are like mother's idea about a darn—confessed poverty. But to leave out a whole passage suggests an accident, that you misread the instructions or something, and that you could do it as perfectly as your first bit if necessary. No sensible examiner is going to reject a good man for that, but imperfect work in Latin is disgusting. So I pulled my ready-loaded pipe out of my pocket and sauntered out of the examination room an hour before the time, to the pitying astonishment of the other fellows.'

'If you are so sensitive about bad Latin,' said I, 'you must suffer a good deal over your boys' mistakes.'

'Not a bit. The boys have got to do perfect work. It's just as easy to be absolutely correct in Latin as in mathematics,

You don't say about some problem in algebra that bits of an equation are quite nicely done—the thing is either right or wrong.'

'But surely your boys make pardonable mistakes?'

'Oh yes, careless ones, but they get no mark for a sentence unless it is absolutely perfect, order and all, without alterations.'

'Don't they grumble, when it is a tiny slip in a long sentence, and they have corrected it tidily?'

'No, because I get them used to this rule from the very first, and it makes them jolly careful, and able to hold a sentence in their head before they start to write it. Of course, I allow any variety of renderings, if good.'

Fired by this, I began the plan at once with my group of stalwart pupils. I explained the idea, and they leapt to it with enthusiasm. A by-product of the new régime was an improvement in Violet Gask's handwriting, for if a word were illegible the sentence had no mark.

I told Tom that I wished I could see him at work with his Sixth Form. He admitted that they had a good time, and were a sort of star turn for any visitor to the school. One day he was taking them in Livy when the door was flung wide, and there stood the headmaster heralding the approach of none other than the Archbishop of York, who had dropped in to have a look at one of the leading schools in his diocese, and expressed himself specially interested in what was being done in Classics.

'Ah, Livy, I see. I should like to take the boys for a little,' said he, all geniality and condescension.

To the horror of the headmaster, who was standing behind in a lather of inferiority, Tom replied as he handed the book:

'Oh, certainly, but I think your Grace may find it a bit beyond you.'

The book was taken with a touch of surprise and hauteur, and a boy was put on to translate. All went swimmingly for a sentence or two, and then the boy stuck, for it was Livy in one of his tougher moods. With a hearty laugh the Archbishop returned the book to Tom:

'Carry on, Mr. Thomas. You were quite right. It's beyond me. My Latin is not what it was.'

As he retreated he asked Tom to come and have lunch with him at his hotel, only too pleased, no doubt, to find some one who didn't toady to him. It was an enjoyable lunch, with exchange of yarns on old public-school ways, and Tom told us how he had amused his host with descriptions of the sermons he had sat under at Ayton. One had been devoted to the doctrine of the Trinity; the vicar described at some length his visit to Switzerland, 'and there before me, at the end of the valley, stood those lovely mountains, Jungfrau, Mönch, and Eiger—to my mind, a proof of the Trinity!'

'If he had shifted a little farther along he could have proved a fourth. That is nearly as foolish as a "proof" of the Trinity offered to his congregation by one of my young vicars. He placed on the edge of his pulpit (so I am credibly informed) three tumblers of water, and explained quite fully that the water was the same although the vessels were different. I hope, Mr. Thomas, that you follow the reasoning? This proved that it was the same God in three different persons.'

'Our man at Ayton,' said Tom, 'could beat him at vivid presentation. In his view one Sunday we were all too apathetic and lukewarm—Laodiceans. In his mind's eye he saw a long train of carriages standing motionless on the railway, because the engine had become uncoupled. He saw the people sitting quite unconcerned, some eating, some playing cards, some chatting, and some (alas) even laughing. But they could not move! "Now to my mind," he added, "that engine is God."'

'How do you manage to keep from laughing?'

'Oh, well, I suffer fools gladly; and even such queer history as a reference to David's worshipping in the Temple of his fathers adds a bit to one's gaiety, but when he said that Jerusalem was destroyed in 68 I nearly got up in my pew and protested. After all, ideas about extending the Trinity may differ, but dates are sacred things, aren't they, Sir?'

This little episode, and many another in which Tom showed himself quite unperturbed by 'important' people, aroused the jealousy of the headmaster; and this was greatly increased when Tom took his M.A., for the headmaster was only a B.A. However, his M.A. was one great advantage to Tom, for thenceforth his work was almost entirely confined to Classics. In earlier years he had been obliged to teach uncongenial subjects, simply because there was no one else in Middlesbrough who could do them at all. The following is taken from a letter to me in '87:

> *I am working very hard this term. The headmaster said the other day, 'Oh! Mr. Thomas, you'll coach those boys in the higher parts of Trigonometry, De Moivre's Theorem and so on, won't you? You're fresher at it than I am.' Oh, yes, of course, I am indeed fresher at it. But what man has done man can do. And if De Moivre can imagine $\sqrt{-1}$, I can bring myself to treat it in the familiar spirit required by the Journal of Education. My conic sections man, too, is becoming a burden; he has got on to the parabola. He generally has a week's illness after a violent leap upward like that, so I have time to read up ahead.*

Good old Tom! He taught in that school for over forty years, and when the age for retirement came, he told me that he hated giving up the job, and knew that he was far more capable of a good day's work than the younger fellows.

§ 2

In the summer we naturally fled to Cornwall as soon as my school-term was over. My uncle Joe invited Arthur down, too, and Dym came from Plymouth for a week or two, so it was a jolly holiday. My cousins used to say that they liked 'Aunt Mary' to be staying with them, because she added to the fun and didn't reprove them for their follies. While she indulged her passion for sketching, Dym and Arthur had as many days' fishing as they could manage, and the rest of us either accompanied them in the background or went off for tramps along the cliffs. Long expeditions were now beyond our means, but I had always been anxious to see Falmouth, which had held a glamour for me since childhood. So Arthur and I plotted to go by train and have a long day there. We took my cousin Alice with us, a girl of about fifteen, and for all three it was a red-letter day, spent in exploring the defences of the harbour, the shipping, the tempting old curiosity shops (in one of which I had some trouble to restrain Arthur from buying a ravishing tea-service 'for when we are married') and in eating strange meals as cheaply as we could.

I mention this day's outing, not on account of anything special that happened, but because of Alice's happy face throughout. I am certain that never for one moment did she feel herself an awkward 'third'. Arthur and I hated being obviously left alone together, and behaved so little like the traditional engaged couple that no one bothered about us. I think it was only Tony and mother and Dym who understood us in this way, and realized how much we managed to communicate in the midst of the crowded and jolly family life. It was not till long years afterwards that I came across some lines of Blake's that sum up for me the whole of my life with Arthur:

> He who bends to himself a joy
> Doth the wingèd life destroy;
> But he who kisses the joy as it flies
> Lives in Eternity's sunrise.

When mother and I got back to Kensington we sucked a good deal of amusement from the remarks that had been made in Cornwall about the engagement. 'A very tame affair.' 'They are not at all suited to one another—Arthur so grave and Molly so light-hearted.' 'Of course, it will never come to anything.' 'Reading for the Bar indeed! It will be years before he can marry, and Molly will soon be tired of waiting.' Mother had met all such remarks with variations of 'Quite, indeed, yes, how true, but after all they must use their own judgements, mustn't they? You and I are not called upon to marry Arthur, are we?'

A more direct attack was made upon me. A distant cousin, a Mrs. Tyack, had been very faithful with me and seriously advised me to 'break it off'.

'Yes,' said I, 'and then what would happen? What would be my next move?'

'You might see some one else you liked to marry.'

'But I can't imagine ever wanting to marry anybody else, however desperate the circumstances.'

'Still, it would be a good thing to break it off . . . just to stir him up a little.'

'How does one do it?' I asked, trying to appear anxious to pick up a wrinkle.

'You say something appropriate about not seeing your way to wait any longer, and return the ring.'

'Oh, that's no good at all,' I replied. 'I tried that last summer in Wales. My ring came off in some soapy water by mistake, for I never take it off, and I thought it would be a good joke to pretend to return it. So I screwed up my face, found Arthur sitting reading the paper, laid the ring by his side with the remark that I wished to end our engagement. His response, without turning from the paper, was, 'I say, look here, what Parnell has been saying.' Naturally I found Parnell's latest effort more interesting than my little joke, so I slipped the ring on my finger again.'

At this Mrs. Tyack tossed her head and exclaimed that I had no sense of my own dignity, took nothing seriously, and might expect a miserable future with a man of that type.

'What did she mean, mother, by all that notion of breaking off an engagement?' I asked.

'It's just one of the tricks women play on men. I could point out lots of instances even among our own acquaintance that would astonish you.'

'What do they do?'

'It's generally the mothers rather than the girls who do the mischief. What do they do? They seize on anything—say a man dances with a girl more than twice, or sits out with her for a talk, or takes her to a theatre. Her mother will "ask his intentions".'

'Well, if he has none, that's easy.'

Mother laughed. 'Not so easy as it sounds. I had a dreadful

business once in getting Dym out of a hole of that kind. It was too ridiculous. A girl whom you know quite well had been snubbed and ill-treated, Dym found her weeping and sympathized, kissed her no doubt—you know how soft-hearted dear old Dym always is—that was really all that had happened, and if you please he was expected to marry her! I could tell you of others who have been caught by such methods, and unfortunately not rescued.'

'Yes, but when they are actually engaged, what's the sense of breaking it off, as Mrs. Tyack suggested to me?'

'Why, that's to hurry on the marriage, for fear the man should come to his senses and wriggle out of it.' Here she instanced several cases from our own circle, where the husband would certainly have backed out if he had had time.

These were real eye-openers to me. Looking back on those days I see that mother made several attempts to enlighten me on many other points. Remarks and anecdotes of hers, vivid in my memory, passed over me at the time like water from a duck's back. Mother must have hoped that I would inquire further about these incidents, but I was amazingly lacking in curiosity. As for her views on a *happy* married life, on these she was quite explicit, and she shot them at me bit by bit.

'You must be ready to go anywhere in the world with your husband, from the Arctic to the Tropics.'

'Oh, rather,' said I, 'that would be fun.'

'It doesn't matter what sort of a house, or even hovel you live in, so long as you are happy together inside.' That seemed to me too obvious to require assent.

'One of the pleasantest things in married life is that you have no money of your own, but have to come to your husband for every sixpence.' Here mother and I saw precisely eye to eye, for we both hated money calculations.

'Some husbands and wives agree to go their own ways— each not minding what the other does. There may be points about this, but it's far better to discuss things, and come to some common plan . . . especially about anything to do with the children.'

'Oh yes, far better,' I agreed with an appreciative smile.

I have found throughout life that the easiest way to say anything extremely difficult is to call it over the stairs or across the garden in a casual tone. This gives the recipient time, for he can always pretend he didn't hear and ask for a repetition. It also gives him a chance to hide a tell-tale countenance. Perhaps it was some such idea of avoiding hateful 'tactfulness' that led mother to say casually one day, apropos of nothing, while she was writing a letter and I was busy over some Latin, 'I suppose you realize that you will have to sleep with Arthur?'

'Oh yes,' I replied, with the same appreciative smile that I had given to all her other remarks on a happy married life. I think now that she must have been puzzled as to how much or how little I knew. But she probed no further, and I think her restraint was wise. In all our talks, however, there were two injunctions reiterated so often that it was impossible for me to forget them. It was not until later years that I discovered the darker parts of her life that had given rise to these injunctions, which she had learnt 'with her blood'. One was 'be deliberate', sounding far more obvious and easy than it really is. The other was 'be sure you are never capricious with Arthur'. Obviously in her scheme of things men were the important people. Well, they are. And I shall never cease to be grateful to her for training me from childhood to appreciate this point.

Material considerations never troubled her. As for the possible date of our wedding, and all the ways and means and prospects of the future, she never referred to them. Nor did I, even mentally, for I knew it must be a long time ahead. There were some lines I came across and learnt by heart that fitted my present case exactly, and I used to say them to myself as I pounded off to school. They may not be correctly remembered, but they began like this:

> *Most sweet it is, with unuplifted eyes,*
> *   To pace the ground, if path there be or none,*
> *While a fair region round the traveller lies,*
> *   Which he forbears again to look upon.*

§ 3

Where does a decade end? This is a story of the eighties, and perhaps should end with the winter of 1889. But a compromise will suit me best, for the early part of 1890 brought such a change in my work and life that a full stop seems natural. As soon as the autumn term was over mother and I put out for Cornwall. We were so anxious to arrive at Paddington in time that we started absurdly early, only to find that the winter time-table was different from the summer one, and that we had an hour and a half to wait. But mother thought there were few things more amusing than a railway station when oneself was calm and other people were not. But one can be too calm. Dym met us as usual at Plymouth, and took us off for a cup of tea in Mill Bay station, where the refreshment-room was away from the platforms. We had heaps to talk and laugh about, and Dym assured us that there was no hurry, for refreshment-room clocks are kept fast, but when we thought it was about time we were taking our seats again, we found an empty plat-form and the red lights of the last train to Cornwall just dis-appearing. There was nothing to do but laugh, incriminate one another, send a telegram to uncle Joe, and go to an hotel. Now it is just possible that mother's bed was damp—one seizes on any explanation, but ever after that holiday she was subject every now and again to mysterious pains. She would be per-fectly well for a week or two, and able to take her long walks, and go sketching when it was fine; so that we hoped the trouble was passing off. When Easter was close at hand Arthur and I planned a special little holiday for her. I suppose we owe it to Moses, or perhaps some ancient moon-worshipper, that schools break up at different times in the spring. It chanced in '90 that my school was dispersed a full week before the one at Bedford; so Arthur suggested that mother and I should take rooms for that week at the Swan Inn at Elstow, where he could come over to see us every day; and he hoped to get his friend Bourne for a day or two.

In those days the town had not encroached on Elstow, and

the little village was one of those lovely spots of beauty that
people are now beginning to value and try to 'preserve'. In
addition to the usual beauties of old timbered cottages and
thatched barns, great trees and a vivid, velvety 'green', it had
an ancient moot-house, and a church with the curiosity of a
tower separate from the main building. The association with
Bunyan was another great attraction, and I liked to picture
the jolly tinker drinking in the bar of the 'Swan' in his unre-
generate days. Mother and I were entranced with the old
inn itself, its rickety stairs and uneven floors, the homeliness
of the innkeeper and his wife, the generous meals, and the one
decoration on the wall of our sitting-room—a faded sepia print
of biblical history from Adam and Eve to Revelation. I caught
mother and Arthur laughing quietly together one day over an
episode in this print, which had been depicted with more
vigour than delicacy, and I heard her say, 'Believe me, it's
always the woman who does the tempting'. I was rather
shocked at the time, but have since come to pretty much the
same conclusion.

Everything combined to make that a happy week for mother.
She was in surroundings that recalled her boy Charles continually; she had recently had a letter from Barnholt who was
expecting to come home in the summer; we had daily visits
from Arthur and his fellow masters; and the weather was
April at its best. What was not so pleasant she managed to
keep to herself, as the following letter will show. It was written
on our return to London, and came to my hand for the first
time only a few days ago:

*West Kensington. April 17th '90. Here we are again, Tony
darling—returned on Tuesday night, and dreadfully sorry were we
to leave the sunny, quiet old village, beloved Elstow. How kind and
thoughtful Arthur was I cannot possibly express. Our little spree
cost us more money than we counted on, but never was money better
spent in the procuring of happiness; it was altogether lovely and with
much of a certain romance about it. Molly made a little sketch of
the church, from our window, for you, but was so dissatisfied with its*

finish that she tore it up, thereby making both Arthur and me angry.
I did two or three sketches, which you will see when you come up.
I do not feel much better and am altogether disheartened about myself.
I am sure you have no idea how far from well I am; but as Molly says
'it's a poor heart that never rejoices'.

The sacred resting-place of our boy was looking lovely and Molly
put some fresh flowers there every day—azaleas, lilies of the valley,
and some sweet polyanthus and daisies.

Mr. Hutchinson came to call twice, and took tea with us in
Arthur's room. Arthur said I was setting my cap at him. Mr.
Bourne came on Tuesday to spend a day and night with Arthur; of
course, he was brought to our rooms immediately; he's a delightful
man as I am sure you will say if you ever see him. He and Arthur
and Molly and I walked down to the station together; it was quite
jolly tramping along in the dark. Had a letter from Dym this morn-
ing, or Molly had, same thing; he is fishing on Dartmoor. Please tell
me how you are, you pearl of Antoninas, and when you are coming
up. With dearest love

Mary.

I find that quite by chance I began this story with a letter
from mother, and am now closing it with the last she ever
wrote. For about a week after our return from Elstow she
seemed in splendid health and spirits, and we were full of
plans for the future as well as getting ready for Tony's long-
promised visit. We had just been to a good shop near South
Kensington Station, to buy her a new paint-brush, when her
mysterious pains became suddenly worse. In spite of her protests I called in a doctor, with the result that she was ordered
to a nursing-home and operated on. She lived for a few
days so cheerfully that I hoped all was well; but there was
a sudden relapse, and with a last thought for Tony she died
on May Day.

The nurses kindly led me away into an empty room, and
I looked out on one of those suburban streets that seem to
wipe out of life every vestige of dignity and grace. At that
desolate moment I would have welcomed a dense fog, a

downpour of rain, or a thunderstorm; but it was a brilliant sunny day, and a barrel-organ must needs burst into a merry tune. It struck me like a dreadful mockery, but as I look back on it now it seems a fitting requiem for one who had braved her full share of tragedy, and yet had always managed to suck merriment from the least cheerful surroundings.

OXFORD

OXFORD PAPERBACKS

A complete list, including The World's Classics, Twentieth-Century Classics, OPUS, Past Masters, Oxford Authors, Oxford Shakespeare, and Oxford Paperback Reference, is available in the UK from the General Publicity Department, Oxford University Press, Walton Street, Oxford OX2 6DP.

In the USA, complete lists are available from the Paperbacks Marketing Manager, Oxford University Press, 200 Madison Avenue, New York, NY 10016.

A LONDON HOME IN THE 1890s

M. V. Hughes

Now a confident, literary-minded young woman, Molly Hughes becomes one of the first lecturers in a teacher training department at Bedford College, travels extensively, and is married in the year of Queen Victoria's Diamond Jubilee. She describes both light-hearted and serious domestic details, including her shopping expeditions in the Portobello Road, the birth and tragic death of her daughter, and the election campaign in which her husband stands against Lloyd George for the constituency of Barnet.

A LONDON CHILD OF THE 1870s

M V Hughes

Molly Hughes's humorous and gentle account of growing up in London in the 1870s gives a classic description of life in Victorian England. It is the first section of the trilogy *A London Family 1870–1900.*

'Whether this is a work of art or simplicity, it is a book at once entertaining and deeply moving.' *Times Literary Supplement*

'A book for us all; open it and you will not easily put it down.' *Observer*